The Women Who Walk Through Fire

The Women Who Walk Through Fire

Women's Fantasy & Science Fiction
Vol. 2

edited by
Susanna J. Sturgis

The Crossing Press
Freedom, California 95019

To Ann C., and all of us
who daily spin straw into gold,
and gold into straw when straw is called for,
this book is gratefully dedicated.

We are grateful to the following authors and journals for permission to reprint previously published stories:

"Shark-Killer," by Carol Severance, was first published in *Dragon* magazine, February 1988 (XII:9).

"A Ceremony of Discontent," by Eleanor Arnason, was first published in *Room of One's Own*, vol. 6, nos. 1 & 2 (1981), edited by Susan Wood.

"The Forbidden Words of Margaret A.," by L. Timmel Duchamp, is scheduled to appear in *Pulphouse* 8 (1990).

"My Lady Tongue," by Lucy Sussex, was published in Australia in *Mathilda at the Speed of Light*, ed. by Damien Broderick, Sussex's collection *My Lady Tongue and Other Tales* (Heinemann Australia, 1990).

A slightly different version of "Mamugrandae — The Second Tale," by Merril Mushroom, was published in *Common Lives/Lesbian Lives*.

"The Girl Who Went to the Rich Neighborhood," by Rachel Pollack, was previously published in Great Britain in the anthology *Beyond Lands of Never* (Unwin Paperbacks, 1984).

Cover art by Beth Avery
Cover design by Elise Huffman
Typesetting by Archetype Publishing and Design

Printed in the U.S.A.

ISBN 0-89594-419-7 Paper
ISBN 0-89594-420-0 Cloth

CONTENTS

1   **Introduction**/Susanna J. Sturgis

12   **Earth and Sky Words**/Cathy Hinga Haustein

23   **The Inkblot Test**/Rosalind A. Warren

27   **New Age Baby**/Deborah H. Fruin

34   **Night of the Short Knives**/Phyllis Ann Karr

53   **The Forbidden Words of Margaret A.**
                /L. Timmel Duchamp

76   **Road Runner**/G. K. Sprinkle

85   **Picnic Days**/Cleo Kocol

93   **Net Songs**/Elaine Bergstrom

111   **Shark-Killer**/Carol Severance

132   **Firebird**/J. L. Comeau

162   **A Ceremony of Discontent**/Eleanor Arnason

173   **Mamugrandae — The Second Tale**
                /Merrill Mushroom

182   **The Girl Who Went to the Rich Neighborhood**
                /Rachel Pollack

194   **Sahrel Short Swords**/Ginger Simpson Curry

208   **My Lady Tongue**/Lucy Sussex

256   **Hills of Blue, an Orange Moon**/Ruth Shigezawa

268   **Contributors' Notes**

THE WOMEN WHO WALK THROUGH FIRE:
A Vindication of Heras and Heraism

Susanna J. Sturgis

Why fire?

Fire is passion, fire is sexuality, fire is will. By fire we see our way in the dark. By fire we cook our food. By fire we warm our bodies. For three winters now, fire in the wood stove has been my primary source of heat. Fire transforms wood into ash, which is in spring returned to the garden, the soil.

The first winter, fear of fire came over me at unexpected moments, fear of the fire throbbing at the heart of my little house, fear of fire raging out of control in the chimney, fear of cast iron glowing red in the night. Now, most of the time, fear yields to profound respect, and no small sense of wonder. In winter I serve the goddess of fire. I call her Sharra, goddess of the forge-folk on Darkover.

Why fire? The women of these stories invoke thoughts of fire, from the chemist-narrator of "Earth and Sky Words" who studies phosphorescence, to the flash of light that introduces flutist Serena Jackson to "Hills of Blue, an Orange Moon."

To walk through fire is to be tested. Tests and quests

are staples of science fiction and fantasy. Sacred literature is full of journeys, from the descent of Inanna to the exodus from Egypt to the search for the grail. Those who seek are utterly transformed by their seeking; death and rebirth are their story.

Take Morgaine, hero of C. J. Cherryh's *Gate of Ivrel, Well of Shiuan, Fires of Azeroth,* and *Exile's Gate,* pursuing her appointed quest across worlds and time. Her story examines both the importance of heroism and its appalling cost; she embodies both the courage of the traditional hero and the heroine's self-sacrifice. Her name links her clearly to The Morrigan, Celtic goddess of life, death, and rebirth, and her descendants — including Morgan le Fay. And Morgaine's complex, poignant relationship with her sworn man Vanye turns convention on its head.

I know she's out there, riding her big gray stallion Siptah as I work, sleep, run errands — closing the world-gates, unable to return home, without a home to return to. Like Sharra, she is part of my pantheon.

Truth to tell, I feel unnerved by these women who walk through fire.

Funny, I thought I wasn't looking for heroes at all. I thought I knew what I didn't want: sword- or laser-wielding women who displayed the courage, intelligence, and physical prowess of male heroes but either were condemned to solitude or turned out to be princesses in disguise who married the king they put on the throne. I wasn't looking for women who thrived on conquest or wielding power over others.

When I started editing women's fantasy and science fiction, I expected to be reading dozens of nonsexist utopias, Whileaways and Wandergrounds and Mattapoisetts.† But there have been few among the hundreds

---

†The references are, respectively, to Joanna Russ's *The Female Man,* Sally Gearhart's *The Wanderground,* and Marge Piercy's *Woman on the Edge of Time.*

of stories received so far. Shirley Hartwell's novel *Daughters of Gelasia*, excerpted in *Memories and Visions*, was one. "My Lady Tongue," in this volume, is another, a vital and witty extrapolation from contemporary lesbian-community mores. But "My Lady Tongue" also incorporates a quest and a hero's struggle for the hand of her lady love, and *Daughters of Gelasia* is also—like Joan Slonczewski's *A Door into Ocean*—a story of heroic resistance.

I did not expect such insistent *individuals*. I came to feminism in the 1970s; the organizations I worked in were collectives, our aspirations were egalitarian. The women's newsjournal *off our backs* still puts an author's byline at the end, a legacy of that decade's attempt to emphasize the content of the piece rather than the name of the writer; my eye skips involuntarily to the end before I start reading. Hierarchies arose in virtually every group I knew.

I'm not ready to consign female heroes—or heras, as I've come to call them—to the dung heap of history, wherever it is we dump things too bourgeois, western, patriarchal, and politically incorrect to be recycled.

What I'm ready for is an expanded definition of heraism. In their stories and poems, their critical studies, and/or their own lives, women writers are actively pushing the boundaries of traditional heroism in all directions.

Feminist and radical political theory—perhaps reacting against the individualism idealized in U.S. culture—tends to emphasize the acts of institutions. When I consider the individual's role and responsibilities, I find myself almost immediately tumbling in rocky terrain, midst inward cries of "you're blaming the victim" and the knowledge that in the past I have been held responsible for events beyond my control.

But even my rational, nonswashbuckling self has been skeptical of theories that lay all evil at the (barred and double-locked) doors of institutions. I can't blame "the U.S. government" without holding myself accountable for obediently paying my taxes every year.

In the anti–Vietnam War movement, we likened ourselves to moving parts within a gigantic bulldozer. If we refused to play our assigned roles, the machine would grind to a halt. As a secretary, I continually fantasized the day that all of us clericals took off for lunch and never came back.

What inspires me to act, or simply to stick with it, is less often a theory than a woman who walks through fire. And the women who walk through fire rarely do so without the support of other women (men too, sometimes). I owe my creative persistence in large part to the women who staff feminist bookstores, publications, and presses, day in, day out. I acknowledge at the same time the essential importance of choices I have made, risks I have taken. Let us honor ourselves as feminist heras.

So what is feminist heraism? Not the solitary success that generally wins a hero a crown and the hand of the princess. Take "Sahrel Short Swords." Here a highborn young person is tested before she can assume the throne—not an uncommon theme. But for Sahrel, success does not depend on a one-shot test, like pulling a sword from a stone or galloping up a glass mountain. Success or failure is secondary; what matters most is what she learns. To learn she must risk her safety, her life.

Laurell K. Hamilton's "A Token for Celandine," in *Memories and Visions*, described a vivid but not atypical fantasy journey. Asked to explain why it felt *feminist*, I would have pointed to the class-complicated connection between the two protagonists, a noble-born healer and the (female) mercenary hired as her bodyguard, and to the theme that Joanna Russ identified as "the rescue of the female child."

But the image that has lingered longest in my mind is of Bevhinn the mercenary—herself an outsider among the people who hired her—making a blood oath with the ensorcelled, enslaved demon Krakus, discovering herself now demon-kin without knowing fully what that means. Now *that* speaks powerfully to my feminist experience: of venturing through strange and possibly hostile territory, finding myself dependent on a strong and possibly dangerous Other, of necessity making alliance with that Other —and realizing that we are both changed, that I am part of Other and Other part of me.

But demons and exotic settings are not required; these tests come up in the course of ordinary mortal existence, and often the prize is simply the right to live another day. Often the tests are rigged but have to be endured and passed anyway. The horrific "Night of the Short Knives" reminds me of city streets and big corporations. What Tiryn fights for, in addition to her life, is the right to have children. Strange?

Feminists, and particularly perhaps those of us who have chosen not to bear children, are understandably leery of whatever supports the convention of self-sacrificing motherhood. In fact and in fiction, motherhood has been organized in a way that disqualifies a woman for heroic adventures, even basic self-determination. Not so long ago the women in science fiction were home minding the kids and didn't go adventuring at all.

Then—again, understandably—the pendulum swung; women were writing fantasy and sf in larger and larger numbers, and the female heroes they created often didn't have kids. The ones they did have were more often sons than daughters. The tale might end conveniently before the child was out of infancy, or with the child being raised by a foster parent or clan—a popular convention in fantasy societies.

As the pendulum swings back again, women who are mothers speak of their adventures; both "motherhood" and "adventure" are being redefined. In Argentina, by standing up in the *plaza de mayo*, *las madres* confronted a brutal dictatorship that was kidnapping, torturing, and killing their children. In the U.S. women have gone to jail to protect their daughters from sexual abuse. Those of us who struggle for the right to *not* have children are reminded that many women don't have the right to give birth. The unheralded heraism of mothering is being recognized and explored.

When Jacqui Brannon ("Road Runner") rejects her husband's bullying, she loses her economic privileges and is pushed toward heroic action in order to keep custody of her children. The narrator of "Picnic Days" risks as much to maintain a relationship with her eldest daughter, Radonna, in what is a bleak, murderous world for all but the most privileged.

The heraism in "ordinary" women's lives has been more often recognized in feminist poetry, from Judy Grahn and Pat Parker to Irena Klepfisz and Hattie Gossett, than in fantasy and science fiction.

From the outside Kathleen O'Neal's *An Abyss of Light* (1990) looks like just another intergalactic space opera. But woven through the story of a people fighting against external oppressors and internal dissension to preserve its culture, is the struggle for survival of *a resistance leader and her eight-year-old daughter*. This extraordinary angle isn't even mentioned in the cover hype or in the advance publicity.

Real-life feminist heras often become visible by passing some kind of test. They are elected to public office, organize unions, excel in a sport; their novels become best-sellers. Feminist fantasy and science fiction approaches tests and quests from new perspectives and asks irreverent questions, like "Who's running the show?" and "Who takes the test?" and "What happens to the losers?" and "How can you tell if you've won?"

Worker 168's only chance to get what she wants is to play along with "The Inkblot Test." "New Age Baby" has The Right Stuff, but this isn't her story. The journalist narrator of "The Forbidden Words of Margaret A." has trained toward one goal with the single-minded perseverance of an Olympic athlete; she wins the gold, but that's only where the story begins.

A hera may find that as a result of her travels, inner and outer, she no longer fits in, or wants to. She perceives what others cannot or will not. Allison in "Net Songs" knows too much about the epidemiology of the killer plague, IV-4; her life is sorely threatened, not by illness but by those who manipulate large numbers of people with the threat of disease. Karen Silkwood comes to mind.

Iuti "Shark-Killer" has paid a terrible price for the chance to rest; the struggle catches up with her anyway. Is safety an illusion, and does it cost too much? In feminist terms, are there any individual solutions?

Serena Jackson, the traveler in "Hills of Blue, an Orange Moon," seems well situated enough in her contemporary society, yet for her something is clearly missing. In her story, readers may recall James Tiptree Jr.'s classic "The Women Men Don't See."

Consciousness complicates matters considerably. The ability to perceive and understand through other eyes as well as one's own creates more facets for an already challenging reality—and is an essential task for those who embrace feminism. One commentator, Kathleen Cioffi, has suggested that feminist f/sf concerns itself with the female hero's attempt to "reintegrate" herself back into her community, whereas the male hero's story can end with the triumphant conclusion of the quest; no one expects his journey will alienate him from his society.

We are outsiders; we know too much.

The contemporary feminist movement has developed a rich language to describe being, in Adrienne Rich's phrase, "split at the root." Feminist philosopher Marilyn Frye urged us toward "binocular vision," the capacity to see from both outside and in, from two (or more) angles at once. *This Bridge Called My Back*, edited by Cherríe Moraga and Gloria Anzaldúa, embodied the experience of women of color called upon to translate between races, cultures, genders. Gloria Anzaldúa wrote of living on "*la frontera*," the borderlands.

F/sf commentator Nancy Vedder-Schults, of the University of Wisconsin at Madison, points out that women have traditionally been ambassadors. Marriage took a woman from her father's house, castle, clan, or country to that of her husband; her lifelong task was to develop the connection between the two. The heraism of such a project, the courage and skills required, is obscured because the task was *expected*, and expected of *women*. Emissaries and ambassadors and, certainly, those who establish first contact with other beings are far more readily recognized as heroes; not coincidentally, they are also likely to be men. (In f/sf, I should add, the situation seems to be changing faster than it is in "real" life.)

"The Girl Who Went to the Rich Neighborhood" is an emissary on a classic quest, complete with magical helpers. But what the   ᵈ Rose learns and chooses to do about it are not common developments in heroic fantasy, where poor neighborhoods and neighbors often don't exist at all, and rarely at center stage.

Favored are they who find companions for the journey, and even more so those — like Rose, Mamugrandae, Sahrel, and Raffy of "My Lady Tongue" — who have a home to return to.

The more I read, the more eclectic grows my definition of feminist f/sf. I am less likely than ever to sort stories into feminist, non-, and anti-, by character, style, or plot. I do, however, continue to set aside those male hero, female supporter stories no matter how well written they are—most of the time.

I review dozens of women-authored f/sf titles a year for *Feminist Bookstore News*. Occasionally I mention works by male authors: John Varley, Samuel R. Delany, David Belden. With due qualification, I even suggest works with mostly male protagonists, like R. M. Meluch's *Jerusalem Fire* (1985), which undermines heroism with breathtaking finality, and even more, refuses to replace it with the obvious, and probably tempting, opposite: villainy.

At a reading and discussion of *The Wanderground*, a

woman of color told author Sally Gearhart how much it meant to her that many of the hill women were dark-skinned. I am sustained by such visions of nonsexist, nonracist worlds, where no one is persecuted for her gender, race, age, appearance, or any other of the differences that so bedevil our society. They enable me to make a crucial leap of imagination, into a world where these distinctions may enrich the society, but they don't set one up to be hated.

At the same time, such visions do risk "depoliticizing" the question of difference, acting as if it's simply a matter of skin color, or reproductive organs, or the gender of one's partner. Is one course more feminist than the other? I think not. We are challenged and healed both by works that consciously explore issues of difference and by those that take them for granted. Feminist literature needs both.

Feminist f/sf might even include works that make many a feminist reader queasy. Marion Zimmer Bradley's *Darkover Landfall* (1972) provoked a major debate in feminist "fanzines" of the 1970s, notably *The Witch and the Chameleon*. In *Darkover Landfall*, a ship carrying Terran colonists crash-lands on an unknown planet. To ensure the survival of the impromptu settlement, the men deny the women—by persuasion and by force—any semblance of reproductive freedom.

Joanna Russ's novel, *We Who Are About To . . .* (1977), explored another route, taken by a woman in a similar situation when her male colleagues want her to perpetuate the race. Is suicide a more feminist solution in such a situation than involuntary pregnancy? It should be noted that in Russ's novel, unlike *Darkover Landfall*, there were too few colonists to keep a settlement going for many generations without hyper-inbreeding and probable genetic collapse.

But Marion Zimmer Bradley was not endorsing forced pregnancy; she was offering a plausible explanation for the patriarchal evolution of Darkover. Why did

Darkover spring from the writer's imagination with men so in the ascendant? Good question—but not one to be answered with a glib one-liner. *My* imagination is as familiar as my kitchen, as strange as uncharted space, and not subject to laws of cause and effect.

The f/sf I consider feminist, or recommend to feminist readers, often makes me queasy. The imagination often isn't politically correct. In R. M. Meluch's *Sovereign* (1979), a Terran woman is pregnant by a man whose people possesses a strong racial memory. The woman plans an abortion; the fetus cries out to her father for protection. Translated entire into late-twentieth-century terms, this sounds like anti-choice propaganda. For me it provided a startling perspective on the issue: For a people who bond across generations, who can communicate from the womb, is abortion an ethical—an even conceivable— alternative?

Susan Schwartz's *Heritage of Flight* (1989) posed an even more disturbing dilemma: I found myself understanding and sympathizing with humans who advocated genocide. Human refugees from interplanetary wars crash-land on a habitable world and are awestruck by the beautiful, sentient, winged Cynthians. Then they encounter the slug-like "eaters," who prey voraciously on humans. The humans set out to exterminate the eaters, then learn that slugs and Cynthians are alternate generations of the same species. To kill one is to doom the other.

These books trouble my thoughts long after I've read them. I am grateful and relieved not to be a human who must act based on that information. But I can't duck the questions, any more than I can avoid the issues raised by feminism that don't seem to apply to me personally at the moment.

To walk through fire is to face the questions, to risk being singed, to be changed, to be changed utterly.

Acknowledgments

I'm blessed to be working at the intersection of two well-organized independent press networks: one devoted to feminist writing, the other to f/sf. Without them, my calls for manuscripts would never have reached so far, nor generated so many hundreds of stories. I thank especially *Scavenger's Newsletter*, edited by Janet Fox (519 Ellinwood, Osage City, KS 66523); the Small Press Writers and Artists Organization (SPWAO) (contact *Scavenger's Newsletter* for current address); *Feminist Bookstore News*, edited by Carol Seajay, P.O. Box 882554, San Francisco, CA 94188; and the *Index/Directory of Women's Media*, long edited by Martha Leslie Allen, and now published by the National Council for Research on Women, 47–49 E. 65th St., New York, NY 10021.

While completing work on this book, I had the great good fortune to attend Wiscon, where both feminism and science fiction are spoken fluently, eloquently, and with irrepressible exuberance. Anyone interested in an opportunity to wallow in my favorite subjects for 48 hours can contact the convention organizers at P.O. Box 1624, Madison, WI 53701.

Finally, I thank everyone I thanked last time around, especially Irene Zahava and Elaine Gill of The Crossing Press, and Maggie MacCarty, arch-Trekkie, for listening to endless one-sided conversations on all of the above subjects, and more.

EARTH AND SKY WORDS

Cathy Hinga Haustein

Spring in the Heartland

One Saturday morning the air smells like manure and I suspect my neighbor, Mrs. Vander Hou, an eightyish woman, a retired farmer, stocky with legs like tree trunks and a wide flat face.

"You've heard about the burglaries, I imagine," she says, leaning her large bosom over the chain link fence that separates our yards, the fence that was constructed to keep my toddler, Anna Kay, out of the street. The fence that Anna Kay learned to scale within two weeks.

"They break down your door," says Mrs. Vander Hou. Although we've been neighbors for three years, I don't know her first name. She never uses it to introduce herself or signs it to Christmas cards. Her husband's name, Ed, is still in the phone book although he died of a heart attack while fishing almost ten years ago.

Her news adds to my feelings of uneasiness. Feelings that I shouldn't have since I live in a picture perfect small town in the middle of wholesome Iowa. I stop hanging up my laundry to answer her. "It must be someone from Des Moines preying on us innocent small towners," I say, sniffing. "Hey, are you fertilizing with manure this year?"

"Yes, Lola and Chuck say that natural farming's the way of the future so they brought over a pickup load of horse crap and threw it on my garden. It doesn't make sense when I still got a big bag of FertAll in the garage." She shakes her head and picks up a large canister and begins spraying her garden.

"You're a scientist. Ever hear of this 2,4–D stuff?" she asks.

"It was in Agent Orange. I think it's banned now because it might be contaminated with dioxin, stuff that gives guinea pigs cancer."

"Well, I got a tank left over from the farm. Maybe I'll get cancer in twenty years," she laughs.

"Anna Kay, stop climbing over the fence!" I reply, pulling my daughter upwind. I am a chemist and know of Agent Orange. Mrs. Vander Hou, being an old farmer, has it in her blood. I take down my laundry, rewash it, and put it in the dryer. I think to myself, "Here's the famous scientist, re-doing her wash." But I'm not a famous scientist, just one that's barely hanging on, like laundry on the line in a stiff prairie wind.

In the evenings and early mornings I hear screams which make me think of death and I suspect Delmer Pothoven. A fortyish man, thin with a greasy strip of yellow hair, he drives a hog truck for a living and every Saturday tinkers with his eight go-carts in the garage. He races them at the Knoxville Speedway on Sundays in the summer. Sometimes his daughter Tami will tell me, "Dad got hurt at the races," and I'll see Delmer limping to his load of hogs. He always recovers, fixes his go-cart, and races again in a week or two.

One early morning, awakened by the hog screams and unable to sleep, I go for a drive on the country roads in my unairconditioned car that I bought when I worked for Xerox in Webster, New York, where it gets cold but not too hot. When I worked for Xerox I drove through forests on my way to work and I wore a badge to permit my entrance into the lab and I had a Princeton Applied Research potentiostat with coulombmeter—very costly. I wore a suit and nylons every day and had three layers of middle management over me. I couldn't take it. I moved back to Iowa where the land is dry and flat. At my small-town grocery store, there are only three check-out lanes, not thirteen, and the only traffic jam is after church. I turn this way and that along the country roads laid out like squares. The wind through the open car window is my hairdresser parting my hair just above the ear. The air is thick with water, pollen, and insect pheromones. Balloon-ists love it here. They are high before they even leave the ground.

Only Paper

On the walls, above the computer in my study, are pieces of paper—diplomas from various graduate programs. I have a PhD an MFA an MS a BS. I should be happy and accomplished but pieces of paper mean nothing to me and I am going to rip all those papers down someday if my manuscript is not accepted. Life will mean nothing if I am not heard.

A Letter to Dr. Wabbles

I have spent nine years researching the room temperature phosphorescence of indicans, a little-known subject. I have sent the manuscript outlining my discoveries to Professor R. L. Wabbles and am waiting for a reply and publication in *The Analyst*. If only I could find the Silent Unity prayer request form, I would write on it that I must receive Dr. Wabbles' reply immediately. My soul is crying for recognition. Then I will feel my world turning, over-coming inertia, and throwing off dust like the old centri-fuge in the basement of the Vermeer Science Center, where I work. Then I will truly be a scientist.

Dear Dr. Wabbles: Do you still exist, although I don't hear from you?

Once upon a Time

In September there are apples and I climb our tree and toss them down into a basket. I cut them up for pies and applesauce, cutting out the worms that thrive because I don't use pesticides, although far away in Delaware, Bill makes such stuff for DuPont Corporation, "Uncle Dupy" to chemists. I think of Bill and I know that he's just gotten divorced but he is behind me now. Bill and I both studied analytical chemistry in graduate school and both had a 3.876 GPA and one night when we were in lab working and cooling beers in the ice machine I leaned back in his arms and cried, "Ack help me, this science is eating me up!" He leaned his chin on my head and put his arms around me but I was a spectroscopist and he a chromatographer and diffusion separated us. I married someone else.

Midlife Crisis at a Tupperware Party

My frustrations come to a head at Lola Klompenberg's house in the north part of town. She lives in one of those new places made to look older with a big porch, a turret, and barnboard siding. Hers is the type of house with scented soap in the bathroom and old-fashioned prints from Yield House in the den. There's no radon in her basement and her dishes are always done. Mine sit in my sinks, my kitchen sink and my lab sink. My hands are always chapped while hers are smooth with red nails. Lola works as an investment counselor at First National Bank so she always wears tailored clothing and looks like she knows what's going on. I feel obligated to go to her party since she is Mrs. Vander Hou's daughter-in-law, and I am feeling guilty because recently I pretended to cough as my neighbor sprayed more pesticides. Also, I want some cups with no-spill lids for Anna Kay.

We sit in Lola's picked-up living room, her husband is out doing boring manly stuff like watching junior high football practice. Donna Quist, one of the bank's five vice-presidents, sits beside me. In a rush of sudden kinship, after all we are both professional women, I cry out, "How are things at the bank, Donna?" and she replies, "I'm at home full-time now."

"Good for you," gushes Carol Van Sittert, who has four children and isn't worried about overpopulation because hers are "quality children" and she'll never let them eat Jumbo Burgers that come in ozone-destroying containers that last 400 years in landfills. I always wonder who is richer, me with my four degrees or Carol with her four kids. I decide that Anna Kay tips the balance.

I don't want Carol or anyone else to have anything over me. My competitiveness has gotten me where I am today. I recall an article about baboons in *Science 86* which emphasized how competitive female baboons are and how they hold each other's babies and drop them on their heads and step on them, perhaps to ensure the survival of their own offspring in a land of limited resources. Then Lola has us all introduce ourselves and say a little something about our lives. Everyone just mentions her husband's name and how many children she has. When Carol mentions that number five is on the way, no one rushes to congratulate her and I chalk it up to the new ecological movement, of which I approve. I also recall that female baboons thrash those in heat on the rump and the stress reduces their fertility.

When it's my turn to introduce myself, I look at Donna, newly freed from prestigious employment, and I don't reveal that I'm a scientist and I feel modest with only one small daughter and when I get home I rush to her, warm and sleepy in her bed, and I cry into her hair, "I'm sorry, I'm sorry." About what I'm not exactly sure.

At the Grant-Writing Workshop

At the grant-writing workshop at prestigious Marx Bible College, I listen to Rebecca Sandberg, once a marine biologist, now grants coordinator at the University of

Iowa, give a lively talk on the Art of Grantsmanship. I speak to her at coffee break: "Why aren't you a marine biologist anymore?"

"I met my husband. That's the downfall of all women scientists, isn't it?"

"Do you miss it?" I ask, nervously sipping my coffee.

"I live through my three kids and my husband. I don't have a great resume, but I'm happy. And my kids won't have to go through any of what I went through. Will they?"

"I have a husband and daughter and a good resume, except for this one paper that I can't seem to get right. It's on the room temperature phosphorescence of . . ."

Rebecca Sandberg is gazing out the window now. She says, "Once I found myself standing in front of the aquarium at Cozy World Pet Shop giving a lecture on marine invertebrates to passers-by."

I take my seat and as I dream of getting a grant for a new spectrophotofluorimeter with a solid sample holder, I suddenly feel tears coursing down my cheeks. I feel all of the woman flowing out of me and soaking away on the grey linoleum beneath my wooden chair. Another baby with a warm head will be left behind as I run the scientific race. And I don't really think that the National Science Foundation or even the Sara Lee Foundation will be interested in my dilemma. It seems that there is no place for a simple scientist interested in raising a family and learning the truth about glow-in-the-dark molecules.

Curse the day I became a scientist! Curse that first microscope and the paramecium in pond water. Damn the spectroscopic determination of manganese in steel. Better to live in quiet ignorance.

The organic chemist from Marx Bible College looks at me with disdain; after all, his college has a new nuclear magnetic resonance spectrometer worth over half a million dollars. So I pass him a note that reads, "I've just experienced the loss of a family member."

During my lunch hour I walk to the Marx Bible

College bookstore and buy a postcard of their science center and I scratch a note to Bill.

"I'm wondering if I'm really the scientist I wanted to be. I wonder if I'm really a scientist at all. Should I give up?"

Just a Sandwich

Sometimes I think the chemicals are getting to me. In the lab. In Delmer's exhaust. In Mrs. Vander Hou's garden. In my husband's smoke. They are reaching for me and pulling me down into oblivion. I think this as I'm outside raking leaves one Saturday in October. I have to shout to Mrs. Vander Hou over the noise of Delmer's go-carts, "Don't put on Weed and Feed in the fall, it just leaches into the groundwater." But she only smiles and says, "Oh, come in and have a sandwich." When I get into her small neat kitchen with pictures of Jesus and her children on the walls, I say, "You know, I think I should quit my job. Anna Kay needs me and I need her. I want to have another baby and rock it for hours. It's just too hard being a research scientist with my head in the clouds. I want to be like most women who have gone before me, a wife and a mother. Besides, I'd still be a scientist, like I always have wanted to be. I'd just be in well, remission. If someone like Donna can quit . . ."

Mrs. Vander Hou should be sympathetic since she has five children of her own, but she frowns. "Those kind of things you got to decide for yourself. Forget what Donna did, or anybody else for that matter." She butters the bread so slowly while Delmer's carts are vroom vrooming and rattling my temples.

"Why doesn't that fool just give up?" I moan.

Vroom vroooomm, bang!

"Here," my neighbor says at last, awarding me the sandwich.

"Mmm, what's in this?" I ask.

"Head cheese."

Pills and Prayers

Every day I go past Second Reformed Church on my way to work. I tell myself that someday I'll fling myself on its steps and beg God to take me and my burdens. But I hustle on to work and the doctor gives me antidepressants instead. They make me realize that the world of Room Temperature Phosphorescence will trudge on without me—but could I remain behind, a nonluminous pebble in the gravel? So few molecules glow in the dark!

Postcard from Bill

I am doing well in pesticides. I put mixtures into an HPLC; the components come out one at a time. I do this every day. I remember our days together when we were doing research and searching for the truth. What a laugh! Fondly, Bill

November First: An Indistinct Sound

A crunching sound awakens me to darkness and the cries of a storm. Winds, ice hitting the windows, branches of the old ash tree scraping glass, and an indistinct sound, rhythmic pounding not regular enough to be mechanical. I look out of the window and into the storm. A huge tree has fallen, taking power lines with it. Anna Kay and Alex, father and daughter, sleep and breathe in stereo. Small quick breaths, deep noisy breaths, and in the background, the rhythmical knocking coming from somewhere in the swirling whiteness outside my window. I see him at last; a large figure in a hunting jacket is at Mrs. Vander Hou's door, chopping at it with what looks like an axe. It is Sunday night, 11 o'clock or so. I think of her alone, sleeping, or perhaps lying still, afraid. I pick up the phone but it is silent. I glide out of the room and down the stairs, my hand touching the familiar banister in the dark.

I am downstairs now. But why? My chemist's reflexes move me to act in the face of an emergency. Benzene fires and mercury spills I can handle, but a dangerous stranger—what can I do? I glide to the dining room, to a window that looks out on Mrs. Vander Hou's door. The stranger is smashing at the door harder now. She must be deaf to not hear it. What could he want? Surely she couldn't be rich, an old farmer living alone in town. I open a window and am a little glad that we haven't put in the storm windows yet.

"I've called the police. They're on their way," I yell through the screen in my deepest voice.

"What?" says the prowler.

"I've called the police," I yell and then I close the window farther and duck down.

"Well, I've almost got the ice off now. This old door is froze up but I got an axe from the garage," the prowler replies. "But thanks for being such a good neighbor."

I peek over the sill at the prowler who suddenly becomes Mrs. Vander Hou in a camouflage coat. I feel puzzled and shaky.

"I thought you were . . . well, umm, good night," I stammer.

She shuffles closer to the window. "Wait a minute, wait a minute, I've got something I've been meaning to tell you."

I open the window a crack, but it is freezing and I don't want to try to explain that in the dark, she looks like a strange man.

"It's hard to walk in this old coat of Chuck's. It got so cold so sudden, I had to borrow it," she says, stumbling up to the window. She looks from side to side, as if someone would be out eavesdropping on a night like this. Thrusting her mouth in the open crack, she whispers, "Donna didn't quit. She was fired. Money was missing from the bank, if you know what I mean. But don't let it get around. You know how we like to do things quietly in our town. Donna has lots of relatives that might hold a grudge. But it seemed to be bothering you. So I thought I'd tell you, since you're such a good neighbor and all."

"Thank you," I say, "Thank you, Mrs., ummm, I don't

even know your name."

"Grace. Grace. It's an old-fashioned name, really."

"Oh no, it isn't. It isn't. It's coming back into style."

She winks, "Where are the police anyway?"

Earth and Sky Words

"Mommy!" Anna Kay's voice is small and frightened in the dark.

"I'm coming," I call as I climb up the familiar stairs. I take her into my arms. Although she's three she still has that warm baby smell and wispy hair.

"Read me a book!" she cries. "That will make me better."

"Honey, the lights are out. A tree fell on the power lines . . . but I could get a flashlight from the kitchen."

I do that and we snuggle on the couch to read her choice, *500 Words to Grow On.* Anna Kay soon grows sleepy as I point to the pictures and read, "'Earth and Sky Words': balloon, airplane, cloud, rainbow."

"Those are the sky words," she says as her head droops onto my arm. "But doesn't a rainbow touch the ground, Mommy?"

"No, it never touches the ground."

"Well, it tries and that's what makes it so pretty."

"Hmm . . . tree, barn, house, daisies. These must be the earth words, don't you think?"

"Those earth things reach for the sky," she remarks with certainty before popping her thumb into her mouth. I remember that a few months ago on a July night she stretched out her arms, ran through wet grass, and laughed as she tried to catch the moon. Her legs, I'd noticed, were becoming long and hinted of womanhood.

I watch the snow falling outside for a while, then I say, "I'm a scientist, you know, but I love you."

"I know, do you love Daddy too?"

"Yes. I do."

Once she is breathing deeply, I slip away and check

the mail for the letter from Dr. Wabbles just once more. The box is empty. I sit on the porch steps in the snow with my head bowed, then I begin to laugh, my burdens moving upward into the street lights. I pad out onto my porch and dance a little, my slippers leaving hollows in the dust of snow. A police car goes by slowly and I wave as I skip into the house, and after tucking Anna Kay into bed, I throw all of my orange and blue nonphosphorescing imipramine tablets into the toilet, while I think, "The potentially famous scientist manages to hang on for a little longer."

"I'm better now," I tell snoring Alex and I tickle his bare back with my hair. In his sleep, he reaches a hand out and I take it, completing a bridge from Earth to Sky.

THE INKBLOT TEST

Rosalind A. Warren

"Regard this inkblot," the Psych says to Worker 168. "What do you see?"

Worker 168, a thin young woman clad in overalls, peers at the inkblot. "I see a beautiful summer day," she says. "A young woman, wearing a lovely soft garment, sits beside a stream. She is writing a poem. This vision gives me pleasure."

A murmur sweeps through the viewing audience. The correct answer has appeared on the video monitor over their heads. They know the young worker is dead wrong.

The correct answer reads: IT IS A PRODUCTIVE DAY IN THE MISSILE FACTORY. A YOUNG WORKER, CLAD IN OVERALLS, IS STANDING BY HER POST. SHE IS WORKING ON THE DELICATE MECHANISM THAT WILL GUIDE THE MISSILES TO THEIR TARGETS, SMASHING THE ENEMY. THIS VISION GIVES HER MUCH PLEASURE.

Worker 168 can tell by the audience response that she is off. She knows that members of Society who are incapable of formulating reasonable career goals are considered useless and are quickly disposed of. She puts on her most serious face and looks earnestly back at the inkblot.

23

"Wait a minute!" she says. "It appears to be changing. Now . . . it looks like . . . "

"Factory!" hisses a member of the viewing audience. He is promptly smacked on the head by his neighbors. The Psych stifles a yawn.

"It looks like a factory!" says Worker 168. "A clean, loyal, well-run factory," she elaborates. The audience is silent.

Worker 168 realizes that this isn't enough. She looks back at the inkblot. She looks at the Psych. The Psych gazes back at her.

"A poetry factory?" suggests Worker 168. Muffled snorts and giggles from the audience.

"I guess not," says the Worker. "But there is a young woman."

"Yes," says the Psych. "A young woman. Like you," he prompts.

"A worker!" says Worker 168. "Just like me. Wearing comfy old overalls. At her post. Working diligently. Happy. Satisfied. Thrilled."

"Don't overdo it," says the Psych. "You're almost there. A factory and a worker. Now, why does this vision give you pleasure?"

"It doesn't," says Worker 168. "It makes me want to puke. I don't want to be a worker. I hate being a worker. I want to be a poet."

The audience stirs. "Why can't I be a poet?" asks Worker 168.

The audience leans forward in order to hear the Psych's answer.

"We don't need any more poets," the Psych says. "We've got at least five poets already. That's plenty of poets."

"More poets!" screams the viewing audience. "Poets! We want poets!"

SHUT UP, reads the video monitor over the audience's heads. IF YOU DON'T SHUT UP, YOU WILL BE DEMOTED FROM YOUR POSITIONS AS AUDIENCE

24

MEMBERS & MADE INTO ELECTRICIANS.

The audience is suddenly silent.

"Now look," says the Psych to Worker 168. "Let's be reasonable. Let's not goof around here. This is a very important moment in your life. Your personal response to this inkblot will determine your future role in our Society. It should be obvious to you that you can't be a poet. We don't need poets right now. You know that we really need workers right now."

Worker 168 nods. This is true.

"And you know what kind of workers we need, right?" continues the Psych. "You watch your home video. You know about the war. You're patriotic. What kind of factory would a patriotic worker like you want to work in?"

"Munitions," says Worker 168. "Missiles." The correct answer was obviously munitions. "But . . . "

The audience is cheering wildly. There is pandemonium. Worker 168 has psychologically determined her own future!

MAKE LOTS OF NOISE, instructs the video monitor. JUMP UP AND DOWN. HUG EACH OTHER.

Under cover of the noise, Worker 168 leans over and speaks quietly to the Psych.

"This game is rigged," she says.

"Of course," says the Psych. "I rigged it myself. But I was doing you a favor. You're a great poet. We don't need great poetry. We need mediocre ideological rhyming bullshit designed to acquaint the masses with Society's goals. You would have hated the job. You might even have tried to rebel. Then, we would have killed you. This way you can make the bombs Society so urgently needs, and still write great poetry on the side."

"Thanks a lot," says Worker 168. "This planet sucks. I want to go to the moon."

"You mean you want to be a space explorer, despite the awesome risks?" asks the Psych. "Why didn't you say so?"

"I always wondered how they found the clowns who

were stupid enough to take that job," says Worker 168.

"Now you know," says the Psych. He motions to a technician.

SHUT UP, says the video monitor to the cheering audience. BE QUIET. PIPE DOWN. The audience re-addresses its attention to Worker 168.

"Wait a minute . . . " Worker 168 is saying. "The ink-blot is changing again . . . I see the surface of a planet. There is a young woman wearing a spacesuit . . . "

IN THE BACKGROUND HANGS THE PLANET EARTH, agrees the video monitor.

NEW AGE BABY

Deborah H. Fruin

Often in the evenings I come into her room, lie back on the bed, stare at the stars and try to name all the planets on the view-of-the-Earth-from-space mural her dad and I painted ourselves: an orderly progression of planets, generously littered with moons, meteors, a dusty, distant quasar or two, Earth rising blue on the wall beside the bookshelf. We're not artists, but we didn't do such a bad job, even if our Halley's Comet does look a little like gone-to-seed milkweed. We only wanted to do the best for our baby. No pink, blue, buttercup-yellow baby ghetto for Crystal. Honest to god, we spent the months of her gestation wracking our brains for the right thing. Now I gaze at the navy blue ceiling twinkling with gilt stars and wonder why we didn't paint sea serpents or snow-capped mountains or circus clowns or Puss and Boots, anything but this map of infinity with Saturn orbiting forever over the bathroom door.

We had postponed bringing a child into this world until we believed ourselves experts on everything earthly. I was 40, Jerry, 43, having waited until our baby could have a whole new millennium to explore. Our only regret was that the year 2000, that distant place where the Jetsons lived, was not so different, neither more outlandish nor enlightened, than the world Jerry and I had been born to. We joked about it as we filled in the nursery ceiling with #2 Cobalt Blue Lacquer, bemoaning the fact that the future had arrived and there was nothing futuristic about it. "My car can't fly," I said with dismay as I began painting in the planets, using as my guide a book of photographs taken by robots in space.

I can't help sometimes thinking that if Crystal had taken us by surprise, the outcome of a passionate double bill at the drive-in, or during a roll on the rug when we were newlyweds waiting for the couch fund to mature, we would have her still, for she, too, would be 20 or so years older, and would have grown up in more tranquil times, before life as Jerry and I knew it changed so irrevocably. I think of her short time with us as a downpour of stardust, a momentary miracle. But we did not make our plans with anything so transitory in mind: We were building a baby to last, assembling a complex but perfectible organism, one molecule at a time.

I had to be one-hundred-percent natural, pure-as-a-mountain-stream, as neutral and nourishing as agar on the bottom of a petri dish. I started to detoxify two years before we began trying to conceive, which gave Jerry and me plenty of time to wrangle with the baby's lifestyle. We subscribed to every popular parenting magazine and a few obscure pediatric journals that we thumbed through and discussed in bed, blithely vetoing baby gyms in favor of mellow infant swims; ix-nay to flash-card tutorials, ok to read-aloud story time; yes to nonsexist, educational toys, no way to bride dolls and nurse kits. Halloween? No. Easter Bunny? Maybe. Even Santa Claus fell under our parental scrutiny because make-believe fosters false hope, doesn't it? That's what the McCracken Study published in *Pediatric Symposium* claimed. Thusly the fairy-tale monarchy—Cinderella, Snow White, even sad little Sleeping Beauty—was banished from Crystal's tiny republic long before she arrived on the scene.

I read Julian Lewis, Ph.D., Harvard, on "The Socio-

Psychological Implications of the Given-Name Phenomena in America," in which he stated, "An ill-thought first name can be a noose around a child's neck, strangling potential . . . ," and I began research to find first names that would imply the right stuff. We named her Crystal because we wanted her to grow up as strong and brilliant as the rainbow's source. Her middle name is Christopher, a worldly name, to give her clout if the gender implications of Crystal became a burden. We did not know, could not foresee, would not have believed that the Bambis, Mimis, and Angels of Crystal's generation would run international banking and corporate boardrooms. It was only one of the lightning-like changes that seared our 20th century sensibilities to the root ends. You see, all the while we fretted about sex discrimination and overpopulation, dwindling resources and lowered expectations, as though our daughter were a late-blooming baby boomer faced with the same concerns as her mom and pop, the world was busy making a different future for her. One that we could not have dreamed up.

Not unlike other infants, I suppose, Crystal's world view was very touchy-feely at first. If it shined, fluttered, bounced, twirled, she wanted it. Soft was good and bright was not bad either. I thought that might mean she had an artistic bent until my next-door neighbor's mother, a child psychoanalyst, said that an overactive interest in such things was a sign that Crystal was a materialistic super-consumer in the making. And I took full responsibility for keeping Crystal from throwing her life away on Weeboks and Baby Guess! Of course, had I left well enough alone, she might have spent her fifteenth year cruising through malls, and could right now be found on the undersea ultraglide for a bout of shopping in Shanghai or Sweden, or shuttling to a weekend on the moon with a husband she chose for his net worth. But Crystal's mommy studied hard so that nothing so prosaic would happen to her only child. I learned that the brain has right and left hemispheres which dictate our proclivities toward art and criticism, form and function; therefore I encouraged Crystal's duality. My motto was "Spirituality tempered by hard truths," not "Shop 'til you drop."

While I lie here in the starlight, I believe I can hear her still. Listen! She's murmuring. Speaking to the trees. In her infancy we played a recording of a breeze through ancient sycamores. It was similar to, but not the same as the tunes I played for her while she was in me: songs of the dolphin, the slithering of eels, the whisper of a spider spinning her web, and, of course, the sea crashing against cliffs, etc. I had attended a Pre-Conception Pregnancy-Preparation Seminar where a strong case was made for these tapes. Nature's song, I was informed, helped soothe baby and made her more receptive to her own internal rhythms. I bragged to my bewildered mother that I could not imagine what parents had done before environmental soundtracks came out. Mom mentioned lullabies, but I was certain it was my choice of mood music that made Crystal's emergence from her cozy innership so easy. She arrived with a gurgle, not a cry, and a cherry-drop smile, seeming to feel immediately at home.

I know it sounds as though Jerry and I were slaves to the fashionable infant experts and child developers, but everyone was doing it, and doing worse, promoting their talented, gifted, exceptional offspring as tiny Einsteins. We deserve some credit for holding back as much as we did. Even when we realized that Crystal could more than hold her own with the whiz kids, Jerry and I were determined to instill not instruct. Jerry read to her, but from e. e. cummings, not Kafka. Crystal would coo in her crib, dandelion-fuzz head resting on pudge arms, a happy, pretty, butterscotch baby, listening to daddy's sure voice, mild as milk, "plant Magic dust/expect wonder hope doubt . . ." I stood nearby painting the moons of Jupiter or a shooting star, and felt sure we were raising our baby right. To us she was not just another striver for the top, but despite our very best intentions, at age two our clever toddler was reading e. e. cummings to herself by the light of her personal silvery moon.

Later, I began to worry that she was too bookish or that her serenity might be a form of baby melancholia. I had heard the subject guardedly discussed at a First Years Workshop: Parturition to Pre-School, but didn't believe such a thing could happen to us. She would drag her blanket to the window seat, where she watched snow fall or leaves blow, and slip into a daydream, eyes closed, head cocked as though she were just able to hear the far-off music of the spheres. So quiet, not at all what I'd been told to expect during the terrible twos, but then with Crystal things were never ordinary. It wasn't until years later they told us that during those spells she was meditating, mastering her alpha waves, a technique she had begun practicing in the womb inspired by the Dolphins' Greatest Hits I played for her. And that wasn't the half of what they had to say, although much of it made Jerry and me blink with incomprehension. We were always so sure of ourselves before, but no pediatric journal, child psychologist, sociological survey, workshop, or seminar had ever hinted at the kind of thing that had happened to Crystal. Ma & Pa Kettle Face the Future. I don't think Jane and George Jetson would like it here.

By the time her cornflower eyes turned #2 Cobalt Blue, she had lost her baby fat and her coo. Her dad and I, believing we had been lenient long enough, began our work in earnest. It was sufficient, we felt, to bubble as a baby, but we did not want her to end up a half-wit, a left-brain dreamer with right-brain flab. We tutored her in geometry, calculus, Esperanto. We encouraged her to volleyball and polo as well as high diving and aikido. She would go to Harvard, or commute to Oxford; either way we wanted her ready to play on the "old boys'" team. When we met with the scientists who tested her for Project Morpheus, they shook our hands and congratulated us for the myriad, everyday things we had done to make our daughter such a perfect pioneer. "She has the hand-eye coordination of a trapeze artist," they marveled. "The heart of a marathon runner," they raved. "The nerve of a burglar," they said, "and a lovely, lofty IQ. She is the ideal candidate for the mission! How did you do it?" I wondered if Mr. and Mrs. Magellan had felt the way Jerry and I did that day, more lost and lonelier than their son ever was circumnavigating the globe?

◆◆◆◆◆◆

Knowing what I know now, if I could snatch back time, turn back the calendar to before she was born, I would swallow a tiny transmitter and blast her with rock and roll, reggae, polkas. I would drink martinis through my ninth month and eat hot dogs and smoke pack upon pack of cigarettes. Burn my library card. I would hold her and never let her go.

Jerry never joins me under our Milky Way mural. He is divided in his feelings about Crystal, between exaltation over what she has done and self-chastisement at his part in making her turn out that way, but in either case, he can't stand to look at stars. She went to him first when she was recruited. I watched them, sitting together in a pool of amber lamp light, he was distracted, reading the paper, and she leaned toward him holding her hands to her heart, wheedling, I thought, until at last he put the paper down and heard her.

I was not alarmed watching the performance because at 16 she beseeched about everything from a short-term loan to an extended curfew. But her father grew very still as she continued talking, and I had never seen him look so afraid. After a while, she could not meet his eyes, so like her own, and she gripped the edge of the coffee table as though it were the last solid thing holding her to Earth. I watched from the safety of the kitchen, relieved that she had gone to her father with today's teen tragedy since it was obvious he was about to nix whatever she proposed, and I didn't enjoy the dirty work. Only when he reached out to touch her bright hair, the true burnished auburn of autumn leaves, and pulled her into his arms, did I know I would not be spared. She left us ten days later, and the first night she was gone I came into this room to look at the night sky and thought, if only we had given the moon a wink and a smile, this might never have happened, but we had been perfect parents, not given to whimsy in child rearing.

She was twenty when she graduated from Project Morpheus and departed on the first crewed expedition to the cutting edge of our solar system. In doing so she will begin a new age unlike any her father and I will ever know, for we will most likely be gone from this life when she reaches her goal. She now dangles between sleep and death somewhere two-and-three-quarters years out there and very, very far to go. She is one for the history books, our little first citizen of the second millennium, but I will never think of her as astronaut or galaxy traveler or even second lieutenant, which is her rank, but always as my Sleeping Beauty whose dreams I hope are sweet. They are called heroes, she and her fellows, by those of us who track their progress as best we can from Earth and moon and Mars. She is a seeker, my weightless darling, sailing past Saturn in a trance. If only I knew that she could hear my voice the way she once heard an ancient wind rustling sycamores, so that, at last, my love could reach her and fill her sleeping heart.

NIGHT OF THE SHORT KNIVES

Phyllis Ann Karr

Tiryn O'Dunhew uv Shipwafa had had one stroke of good
luck and bad luck together. When she met Jorj Vastik uv
Oaklair, who could smatter her any time, he had already
made his kill and been on his way to the nearest EXIT.
But the head he carried for his passport had been that of
Mathy Hanss, whom Tiryn could have killed and glad to
do it.

A bit earlier, she had met Cobbin Parker uv Bloom,
poor little Cobbin who should have been an easy one, just
lying there in the old Bigstore, pitiful with the Sickness,
glowing to be killed. But at the last minute . . . she couldn't
do it, no, not even in mercy.

A bit later, at one of the never-again staircases,
someone jumped out at her, and they grappled and slid
around at close quarters in the shadows for what felt like
a long time before she saw it was Steevie Garder. She had
him down, too. She should have sliced into his neck one-
two-three, and by now she would have been safe outside,
ready to begin her grown-up life and bear her children,
birth-withered right arm and all. But—Great God Jaycey!
again she couldn't do it! She let Steevie throw her off, and
maybe when she ran away, he thought it was because she
got spooked.

Okay, it hardly mattered anymore. Looked as if all she'd been born for was to make somebody else's passport out. Should have been Steevie's.

Mathy Hanss, now, she was sure she could have sliced him up clean as stew. Still fit enough to swing himself round the sidehorse three minutes at a stretch, for all he was glowing green with the Sickness, and meaner than sin even when he'd been healthy. Fifty-five years old, too, and who would ever want to live much longer than that? Unless it was Granny Dubs or old Sainie Hopin who taught the advanced classes in Sacred Red Tape.

But Jorj Vastik had beat her to Mathy, and now she doubted there was anyone else left in the Game whom she could kill. Oh, she might have liked to do it to Moggie Hojboom. He was almost as mean as Mathy Hanss. Problem was, she wouldn't stand a snowball's chance against Moggie. And she'd rather dodge him than make his passport.

She wanted to flop down for a while, rest and think. About the safest place in the building was the old dry-fountain area beneath the Holy Round Clock that had stopped forever at the Hour, 4:13. After three centuries, nobody could say for sure if it had been AM or PM, not even Sainie Hopin, but they always started the Pre-Game Ceremony at 4:13 the afternoon of March 20 every other year, snow or warm. Nobody ever said there was anything in the Red Tape to prohibit fighting beneath the Clock, but experienced gamesters passed the word to first-timers that it was usually bad luck. So after the last salute before sunset, almost nobody poked around here except passport carriers going right on through to the EXIT around the next turn.

Tiryn found a corner where two high old planters met, and huddled there being private. She had just decided she would look for Steevie to let him take her head—if he was still alive and needing somebody's—when she heard a low, whishing sound down on the sunken floor. Slinking to the end of the right-hand planter, she peeked out.

Two people in funny clothes, and a dog. Strangers. Snoffs?

There hadn't been a Snoff raid around here since Granny Dubs was a preteen, but Tiryn O'Dunhew guessed she was seeing Snoffs now. Nobody else would crash the Game. Even if they wanted to, nobody else could get through the cordon outside, but these high-and-mighty Snoffs from the South Side—Argenteen and Afriky and thereabouts—they still had blasters and nukeys and lift-off airboats and all the rest of that fancy Before the Bombs stuff.

One of the Snoffs wore what looked like a real sword, right out in plain sight, and Jaycey only knew what kind of power weapons tucked away out of sight. Tiryn had to act fast.

✦✦✦✦✦✦

Looking around, Frostflower stifled the impulse to attempt flattening Dathru's Circle between her palms. Thorn was cursing, Dowl wagging his tail in trustful bewilderment.

"I'm sorry, Thorn," the sorceress apologized wearily. "I thought that at last I had solved the riddle."

"Probably not your fault. That demon's sneeze Dathru must've knotted it up with some kind of hellbog trickery to keep it from working right for anyone else."

They stood in a curious twilight shed by green-glowing things—stones? bones?—cased in crystal globes of water. The building around them seemed to exude an atmosphere of age and immensity. Most of the building materials were unfamiliar to Frostflower, but she saw they were cracking and crumbling.

"Well, don't worry, Frost," her warrior friend went on, giving her a grin. "You'll figure it out sooner or—"

Dowl yelped.

36

Frostflower looked left, and a shove sent her sprawling to the floor, her newly fashioned shoulderbag with Dathru's book of sorcery thumping hard on her hip. There was shouting and barking, and after a few heartbeats she understood that Thorn had delivered the shove.

She twisted around. The attack had come from the other direction, and Thorn must have glimpsed it in time to knock her friend clear, but not in time to dodge the blow herself. The sorceress gasped to see blood staining the warrior's tunic at left shoulder and collarbone.

The attacker was a thin young woman clad only in a sleeveless, knee-length tunic of animal skins. Her hair was cropped even shorter than Thorn's, her eyes glittered, and her lips were set in a fierce line. Her left hand clutched a dripping dagger. Her right arm hung heavy, looking as if it had never quite developed in her mother's womb.

"Damn Southern rich-better-than-anyones!" she accused them, holding her stance a stride beyond the reach of Thorn's sword Slicer. Frostflower had worked out enough of the dead Dathru's magic that she and her friend could speak and understand the languages of each new world they wandered into.

"Look, bogbait," said Thorn, speaking through pain, "we hadn't planned on hurting anybody. But now you've started it, my Slicer here is three times the length of that little stewpick of yours."

"Why don't you rich-better-than-anyones just leave us alone?" The stranger started circling.

Frostflower moved back, searching the air for anything she might interpose. Occasionally even an indoors atmosphere would be humid enough that she could condense a small mist out of it, but her powers did not always work in these strange worlds exactly as they worked at home.

Thorn lunged forward, aiming—Frostflower guessed—to knock the weapon from her opponent's hand. The stranger leaped back, then darted in under Thorn's guard. After a brief struggle, the warrior threw her off and retreated a few paces, trying to draw her own dagger.

The air inside this echoing building was very dry, but charged with something . . . not the lightning-power of storms and spark-snaps (though some of that was present as well) . . . but something that prickled Frostflower's trained weather sensitivity with faint, almost pleasantly painful tingles.

Thorn fumbled her dagger from its sheath, dropped it, and cursed. Her left hand was shiny with the blood that flowed down her arm—Frostflower hoped no nerves had been severed.

The stranger sucked in her breath and leaped again. Thorn sidestepped, swinging at her thighs. The woman eluded her sword with a whirl like a dance step, to land facing her from the middle of a short flight of stairs.

Frostflower forced all her concentration into gathering a ball-lightning sphere of the unknown tingles. Almost at once it appeared, hovering chesthigh in the air before her: a pulsing lump of prickles that glowed with the same green cast as the lights in the crystal globes above them. Dowl whined and shrank down behind her skirt.

Clearly weak from loss of blood, Thorn was drawing back as if for a desperate slice at the midsection. Her opponent was tensing as if to spring down on her neck. Frostflower struck the spiky green lump with a mental directive that sent it hurtling to a point between the combatants.

Both jumped back from it, Thorn with another curse, the stranger with a scream. The stranger slipped and fell on the stairs. Thorn ducked beneath Frostflower's missive and was on the fallen woman, attempting to throttle her with a wet and weakened left hand. Instead of striking back, the woman tried to scrabble away backwards from the hovering lump.

Thrusting Dathru's Circle into her shoulderbag, the sorceress hurried forward. "Now call truce, both of you! It is senseless to fight!"

"Tell that to this bogbrain!" Thorn panted. Nevertheless, she cautiously relaxed her grip.

Still staring up, the other woman cringed a little farther from Frostflower's green lump. "Is that . . . ," she whispered, "is that a . . . a *bom*?"

"It may be," Frostflower replied. For all she knew, it was, and if the idea kept this fierce creature quiet . . . "I made it with my sorcery," she added, wondering if that word would be as incomprehensible in the wild woman's language as "bom" was in her own Tanglelands speech. "Now lie still."

✦✦✦✦✦✦

Tiryn lay still, keeping one eye on the maybe-bomb. The oftener she glanced up at it, the surer she felt that it was more maybe than bomb. Granny Dubs, Sainie Hopin, the Teach, and old Prof Jornsin all agreed that bombs came in metal cases, smooth and shiny. But if this thing didn't look like any Big Boom Bomb or Just Kills People bomb, it did look like the Great Grandaddy of all Sickness Bugs in person, and she sure as the devil didn't want it brushing her hair!

Meanwhile, the science-witch from the South was pressing her fingers to the swordfighter's shoulder wound, trying to stop the bleeding.

"Just close it up, Frost," said the swordfighter, sounding as if she'd rather be swearing. "Your powers seem to work all right in this world."

"The weather power, perhaps. I have not yet tested the time power. But in any case, you do not want edges of cloth healed up into your flesh?"

"Hellbog and Azkor's claws! I can't stop and strip with this demon's belch waiting to knife us." The swordfighter dug her knee into Tiryn's middle a little deeper.

That woke Tiryn's anger up again. Besides, if she was good as dead anyway, what difference did it make how? "You can't stay here anyway, you Snoffs," she told them. "Twenty-eight of us came into this Center tonight, so you can bet there's still more than me prowling around, and every one of us ready to cut Snoffs up for the pure pleasure of it."

"Why the demons' toenails do you keep calling us that?" the swordfighter gritted out, as the science-witch pressed a wad of rags to her wound.

"And why attack us?" said the science-witch, pushing the wad down hard to stop the bleeding.

"For all the times you've come pillaging our ruins before we could mine 'em ourselves, us who need the stuff and you filthy Southern Snoffs who don't!" It was true they didn't get raided so much out here in the boondocks, not anymore, anyway, but they still got news from wanderlusters and refugees. "For shooting us down with your fancy timmyguns and grenades when we try to save some of the stuff for ourselves. Old Jake Sirney's gran was in Hegwish when you dropped the Just Kills People bomb on what was left of Chicagy, just so you could loot it. And for kidnapping our healthiest breeders when you don't kill 'em outright, for taking 'em back south to be your slaves or science-lab stock."

"Great Giver of Justice!" exclaimed the science-witch. "What sort of world is this?"

"The worst we've blundered into so far. Calling on a farmers' god, Frost? Now look, bogbrain," the swordfighter went on, turning from the science-witch back to Tiryn, "'we' haven't done one damn pinch of all that. We just stumbled here by accident and we'll be overjoyed to stumble out again and leave you mushheads to kill each other off without our help. Just point the way."

✦✦✦✦✦✦

After a moment, the wild woman said slowly, "You're not rich-better-than-anyones?" By the movement of her lips, she pronounced that term in a single syllable, but it always came to Frostflower's ears as four words.

The sorceress shook her head and tried to smile. "We are poor, lost travellers."

"Downright impoverished," Thorn grumbled. "But as good as anybody else otherwise. What the hell did you do that for?" she added as Frostflower allowed the prickly "bom" to disperse with a crackle.

"To demonstrate our good faith. Now," she told the wild woman, "we ask only a corner where I can treat my friend's wound. As soon as possible, we will leave. Meanwhile, is there any sign, any token we can use to show your friends that we mean no harm, that we have stumbled here by purest mischance?"

"Stumbled in here how? You sure couldn't have stumbled in through the cordon, not without killing somebody, so you *must've* landed one of your fancy Southern airwagons on the roof!"

Frostflower sighed. How explain Dathru's Circle, the wonderful gold ring a hand's-breadth across? Concentration combined with a touch to a certain point on Dathru's wooden pendant caused images of countless worlds to replace one another slowly within the Circle's circumference. There must be a way to hold one world long enough that she and her companions could step through into it, as the Circle enlarged momentarily into a misted portal. Each time thus far, the world in which they found themselves had been different from the last one they had seen imaged. But what could Frostflower say of this without either breaking her vow of truthfulness or alienating the wild woman?

Thorn grinned—or grimaced—and said, "Sorcery, child. We stumbled in with simple, harmless sorcery."

However the wild woman understood that word, she seemed slightly less unwilling to trust them. "Well . . . any other time, any other place, you could try the old white flag, but—"

"Tiryn?"

At the new voice, Frostflower stiffened. Thorn sucked in her breath, Dowl whined, and they all turned instantly to look.

A young man was coming toward them, out of the shadows, stepping softly, his feet bare. In his right hand he carried a drawn dagger, dripping blood, and in his left hand, a rather large, roundish thing, very faintly luminescent. Because of that feeble glow, Frostflower supposed it must be an artificial head. Until she noticed that it, like the knife, was still dripping. She had to call on years of sorcerous discipline in order to control her nausea.

"Tiryn O'Dunhew of Shipwafa?" the youth went on, raising his voice slightly. "Who the inferno are these?"

"Steevie! Steevie Garder of Oaklair." There was relief in the wild woman's voice, tinged with . . . regret? There was nothing resembling disgust. "So you put poor little Cobbin out of his misery, did you? I'm glad, Steevie. For the both of you."

Thorn muttered, "More scramblebrained here than in the last world!"

"Who are these?" Steevie Garder of Oaklair repeated, brandishing his knife. "They're not in the Game!"

As Thorn tensed visibly, Frostflower prepared to gather a second ball-lightning of green prickles.

◆◆◆◆◆◆

Tiryn decided, right then. They might be what they claimed, but even if they were Snoffs, she might as well let them kidnap her. There wouldn't be anyone left in the Game she much cared about being killed by, now Steevie had his passport out, and if her disappearance screwed up the even numbers, that'd be no scabs off her own sores —let Sainie and the Teach figure it out. Some folk said that Snoffs lived so rich, even their slaves had it soft, down there in the South, and who knew? They might heal her birth-shrivelled arm.

"They're okay, Steevie," she said. "Not Snoffs, just some poor science-witches who stumbled in here by accident."

"How come that one looks ready to slice you, blood-ied and all?"

"Jaycey! but you can be a stupe sometimes, Steevie Garder! So nobody else'll come up and slice me before I finish conversing with 'em."

"Here beneath the Holy Clock?"

"May be my last conversation this side of the Divide, you know," Tiryn hurried on, riding rough over his last objection. To the swordfighter, she muttered, "Get up off me, you damsilly. Sign of trust."

Scowling, the swordfighter sort of rolled off her, the science-witch helping.

But Steevie still hesitated. "Jillie Stack was left in the Game, last I saw. You could take her easy. Or even Saggin Jeans of Ryeslick."

"Yeah, I could get 'em down all right." Easy as I got you, she added in her thoughts, but those wouldn't be any words to end a friendship on. "Maybe I will, at that," she lied. "So long, Steevie. One way or the other, you'll be seeing my face outside any time now."

After another moment, he said, "Well, okay. And don't worry. I won't say anything about the science-witches, if that's how you'd like it."

"Thanks, Steevie. That's how I'd like it."

He might have stepped up and shook hands, if she hadn't still been in the Game. As it was, he just said, "Roger, over easy and out," and headed for the EXIT around the next turn.

"Over easy and out," she whispered after him, brushing a tear away with her fused right fingerstubs. The only kind of thing they were good for.

◆◆◆◆◆◆

"One more 'sign of trust,'" Thorn grumbled, "and somebody gets it right up the—ouch! Dammit, dog!—right up the left nostril. Can't you keep him off me, Frost? I'm a wounded woman."

Frostflower gave Dowl a gentle push on the hind-quarters. A little to Thorn's surprise, the mongrel took the hint, stopped trying to get in the way, and lay down to practice thumping his tail against the floor.

"We can hardly leave until your wound is closed," the sorceress informed her.

"Why the hellbog not?"

"Because I might bring us into an even more danger-ous place," Frostflower replied with a touch of impatience, "where we would need you whole and able to protect us."

"And what about the bloodthirsty scramblebrains prowling around in here?"

"I'll stand guard," Tiryn offered unexpectedly. "You get over there behind those planters, and I'll hunker down in front and keep a peeled eye out."

"Peel your eyes is what I'll do if you try any tricks on us," the warrior guaranteed. She tried to stand, but things went boggy, so she ended up getting to the indicated shelter on knees and one hand, Frostflower supporting her on the other side and Dowl trying to lick her face again.

Settled at last, she wisely kept her attention on Tiryn. Frostflower would need to concentrate, first on adapting her sorcerous powers to the present world and then on applying them to speed up time for the wounded part of her friend's body. Thorn, however, was as free as pain permitted to keep her wits focused on their sur-roundings.

One way to focus her wits, and also keep their self-declared watchgirl's mind from betrayal schemes, was talking. "You, Tiryn. From the beginning. What the hell are all you people doing in here, cutting off each other's heads?"

Of course, getting straight answers couldn't be that simple. Tiryn acted as if she had trouble understanding that anyone might stumble in knowing nothing at all about her world, while Thorn felt sporadic stutters of pain—all twinges and itches of normal healing condensed into a few moments and complicated by her friend's problems in adapting Tanglelands sorcery. Also, they kept their voices down, and from time to time broke off conversation completely so that Tiryn could peer around at some building noise or distant shout. But question by question and answer by answer, Thorn drew it out.

Three hundred years ago, more or less, this building had been an indoor marketplace of shops, one or two large and many small. With fountains playing and plants growing in the sunlight that fell through windows set high in the ceiling, it must have been as beautiful as the priests' city of Thorn's own Tanglelands. Tiryn's people thought that most of the shops had been open to the broad central walkways, but the doors and partitions could simply have vanished during the generation of looting before this Center was made a consecrated place.

What had happened, as nearly as Thorn could understand, was a series of incredibly big raids and battles, aimed at destroying everything.

Insanity must run in these people's bloodlines. All the gods of the Tanglelands abhorred warriors who burned crops or attacked anybody except fellow warriors, and one of Bloodrastor's first rules was to disarm first, wound if necessary, kill only as the last resort. Peel Thorn if she could understand what gain any intelligent leader could hope to get out of destroying lands instead of assimilating them. She had had her quarrels with the gods of the Tanglelands, but if any one of them had pushed for the kind of "Arm-and-get-'em" that Tiryn's Wrathful God Jevah had apparently demanded, Thorn guessed that Great Jehandru the Giver of Justice would have seen to it there was one less god for the farmer-priests to name.

Anyway, in order to destroy their opponents without singeing their own fingertips, they made weapons called "boms," like huge spearheads without shafts, that they could somehow hurl over very great distances. Tiryn had never seen a bom. That was how she managed to mistake Frostflower's little green ball-lightning for one. Whatever they had really been like, wherever they fell they gouged out pits, started fires, knocked down buildings and killed life for many days' journey in all directions. They had also filled everything they left with a sort of hot, long-lasting smoke that got into any survivors and made them sicken and die for generations afterwards.

The smoke had its uses. Clotted into the glowing green things up there in those clear globes, it was giving them the light Frostflower worked by. But Tiryn blamed it for causing her withered arm and for the color of that severed head her friend Steevie was carrying. By now Thorn felt twitchy, and hoped Frostflower would be able to purify them as soon as they got safely away.

The southern half of Tiryn's world had escaped the boms. It was too far away for Tiryn's people to walk there, but the Southern "rich-better-than-anyones" had boats and wagons that flew through the air faster than the fastest horse could gallop on level ground. Nice people, to loot instead of helping. If Tiryn's tales were true—Thorn half-suspected they were exaggerations if not plain superstitions—no wonder Tiryn's folk hated the Snoffs.

More to the present point, every two years Tiryn's people held one of these head-hunting "Games." Who played? Everyone, male as well as female, who wanted to generate children and hadn't qualified in some other way. For whole and healthy females, there were strings of other tests they could pass instead, but Tiryn had not been allowed to take any of them because of her arm. For young women like her, playing this Game was the only chance. For males, there was no other test. A young man either had to get into the first Game that came along after his eighteenth birthday, or let himself be gelded. Anyone who bore or was suspected of engendering a baby before qualifying got forced into some even bloodier version of the Game, and the baby was put into a special Compound— Thorn did not ask for any further explanations about that.

Besides the eighteen-to-twenty-year-olds, every ungelded male older than fifty-five and every man or woman between the ages of twenty and seventy who had developed visible symptoms of the Green-Glowing Sickness had to take part. Whenever there was an odd number, they made it even with a volunteer who would not have needed to go in otherwise. All the players filed into the building in the late afternoon, went through some sort of last salutation inside at sunset, and had until full dark to spread themselves around. The cordon of watchers outside let nobody out who was not carrying another player's severed head.

The only civilized rule Thorn saw was that once you had somebody's head, you were not allowed to attack anyone else, and nobody else was allowed to attack you. At that point, it was straight to the nearest door out, the way Tiryn's friend Steevie had gone. Exactly half the players who went in were supposed to walk out again. And this was not the only suitable building within a day's walk where the Game was being played tonight.

Thorn guessed that a few of the unexpected pains stitching her shoulder came when something Tiryn explained filtered through Frostflower's sorcerous concentration.

✦✦✦✦✦

Tiryn began to think they really were what they said. Surely they acted too gentle for Southern Snoffs. Even the swordfighter, who might be a pro, but who made it clear she'd rather win without killing.

Beside Thorn, Tiryn would class as an amateur, trained for one Game only. But there was no other way to win except killing, and it turned out she couldn't do that. Now she felt sorry to think that the strangers were not Snoffs come to catch slaves. Maybe she could have played fighting games the way Thorn played them.

"Twenty-eight of you came in here tonight, you said," Thorn reckoned. "Take away two—your friend and his . . . kill. One more, you. Leaves twenty-five prowling around."

47

"Twenty-three, tops. I saw Jorj Vastik on his way out a while back with old Mathy Hanss' head. But if there's eight or ten left by now, it'd be running about par. There're eight EXITS to this building, all total."

"Eight to ten still on the prowl, maybe more. All healthy, because the sick ones will've been killed first."

Tiryn thought about poor little Cobbin.

"But the strongest will've made their kills earliest?" Thorn added hopefully.

"Not always. The strongest ones like fighting each other, sometimes hold off when they meet someone they could take too easy, let 'em go look for somebody else their own weight. But, look, if you're worried, these places near an EXIT are pretty safe. It's only because you're Snoffs—I mean, everybody will think—"

The dog yelped again.

Tiryn jerked around for a look.

She heard Thorn grumble behind her, "Cold damn and pigs' breath!"

The hulk who stood where two hallways came together had to be Moggie Hojboom. Face was shadowed, but nobody else wore spiked shoulderpads. If he was carrying his passport, Tiryn couldn't see it.

Anybody else would have called, "Who's there?" Not Moggie Hojboom.

Tiryn sighed and broke the ice. "That you, Moggie Hojboom uv Ryeslick?"

Moggie had a nasty chuckle. "Tiryn O'Dunhew uv Shipwafa! Lucky for you I'm in the market for Jorj Vastik or Mathy Hanss tonight."

"That so? Too bad one of 'em already got the other and skipped." As soon as she said it, she bit her tongue. Moggie was just the kind to fight beneath the Holy Clock, bad luck or not. But chances to dig back at him were rotten few.

"Y'know, girlie, I'd guess you're ribbing me, if . . . Who the Great God Jaycey is that behind you?"

"Leave 'em alone, Moggie. They're strangers, just

stumbled in by accident and don't mean any harm."

"The hell we don't," Thorn muttered. Moggie made people feel that way. But the science-witch quieted her friend.

"Nobody just stumbles into the old Shopping Center," said Moggie. "Especially not on Game Night. Not unless they're Sno—"

"Dammit, we're not! Smardon's bellybutton, Tiryn, give Frost two more minutes and I'll take on that muttonjaw myself!"

Could any science-medicine work that fast? "No, thanks," Tiryn told her. "You're not in the Game. I am. But Moggie's not about to fight anybody here beneath the Holy Round Clock. Are you, Moggie?"

"The hell I'm not. You think Moggie Hojboom uv Ryeslick gives a damn about old mad scientists' tales?"

Tiryn hated the thought of ending up as Moggie Hojboom's passport, but for all she knew they might be the last pair of players left in the building. Anyway, once he had her head, he'd have to leave the strangers alone. She hoped. He wasn't going to get it all that easily, though. Keeping a watch on him the whole time, where he stood unmoving and probably grinning, she straightened up, strolled down into the sunken area, jumped onto the wide rim of the old, dry fountain, and waved her knife. "Okay, Moggie, come and get me!"

The strangers were saying something else, but she didn't hear what. Moggie gave a shout and rushed for her, knife high and shoulders hunkered. Wanted to catch her calves on his shoulder spikes—a Moggie kind of trick.

She guessed he expected her to sidestep, so at the last minute she somersaulted over him instead. Not the best move, seeing he was two heads taller, but while she was at his back she made a spring for it.

That might not have been wasted motion, if she'd had a good right arm to clamp round his neck, or else the stomach to jab her knife into his head. As it was, her point caught in his quilted jackets—he must be wearing three or four, all flappy—ripping a lot of cloth but only enough flesh to make him grunt a little as he swung a backhand that knocked her three paces to land sprawling against a broken bench. Moggie was even stronger than he was mean.

He got himself turned around, and she saw he was grinning. "Nuke you, O'Dunhew, that got me mad," he announced. "I think I'm gonna cut it off a tendon at a time."

He'd do it like that, too. Unless the only way he could get her down at all was to kill her quick. One thing—big, strong, and mean as he was, he didn't have that much speed.

"Gave you a scratch, at least, huh, Moggie?" she ribbed him, getting to her feet. She felt like a walking bruise, but that was okay, she only had to keep moving long enough to get herself killed quick.

Another prickly green thing came flying at them to hover in front of Moggie's face. He squealed and stepped backwards, heaving up against the fountain.

Tiryn loved seeing Moggie spooked, but it wasn't fair play. Dammit. Sighing, she shouted out to the science-witch, "Thanks, lady, but it's gotta be one to one in the Game. Just him and me."

✦✦✦✦✦✦

Was that so? One to one in a fair fight Tanglelands style Thorn could understand. But one bogbreath big enough to make a pair of blacksmiths, wearing spikes on his shoulders, against one butterfly-weight with a withered arm? Fighting by rules that required the winner to take off the loser's head? "Go on, Frost. Keep tickling his nose with it."

"Thorn! What—Thorn, your shoulder!"

She felt it itch and twinge, all right, but it ought to hold long enough, and she couldn't wait around. Pushing herself up, she ran at him.

Unfortunately, what remained of her own ideals wouldn't quite let her jump him from behind. Not even after Tiryn had jumped her that way. She ran in between him and Tiryn, facing him, Slicer ready. "All right, you demon's turd, get out of here or I'll make you eat stones!"

✦✦✦✦✦✦

How could Frostflower blame her friend for following the same impulse that had made her gather and aim a new ball of green prickles? All she could do now was watch for the best way to use her weapon, and try to hold it steady meanwhile in the tingling air. Her sorcerous powers could be made to work in this world, but only by fits and starts, with sluggishness between, as if she waded through mud with occasional dry stepping-stones. Otherwise, she would have had Thorn's wound completely healed before now.

"What?" said the man whom Tiryn called Moggie. "What?" His back was to Frostflower, but she assumed he was staring up at her missive.

"Out, bugbite, or I'll make you eat *that!*" said Thorn, and slapped his thigh with the flat of her sword.

He swung in reaction, catching Thorn with a blow to the side. She staggered and sprawled, blood flowing again. Frostflower gasped, and the green ball wavered. Moggie poked his knife at it. Thorn's blood started glowing green on his blade, but nothing else seemed to happen.

With a laugh that sounded only slightly nervous, he turned again to Tiryn. "First you, O'Dunhew, and then your rich-better-than-anyone friends."

"You can't kill more than one, Moggie Hojboom! The Sacred Red Tape—"

"Snoffs don't count, O'Dunhew!"

"All right for you, Hojboom!" She ran at him and rammed her knife straight into his gut.

She did it so fast she hardly knew what happened, any more than he did, till it was done. He walloped at her, but she ducked and heard his arms hit his own muscle. Keeping in a half crouch, she backed away, pulling her knife with her. Blood followed it.

Moggie looked down, groaned, looked up again, and started toward her. She sidestepped and tripped him. He crashed face down.

She jumped on top of him, hesitated about one second, swallowed hard and started hacking his neck before her stomach gave out. She vomited afterwards.

◆◆◆◆◆◆

"I couldn't ever have done it," Tiryn told them, "if I didn't know he was going to kill you, too. I guess it made me too angry to think, too angry to be spooked anymore. But now I've got my passport out, I won't ever have to go through another Game Night, unless I start glowing. And I can have children. Maybe by Steevie Garder."

Frostflower nodded. "You ought to make a fine mother. You have shown the true protective instinct."

"Hey!" Thorn protested. "What did I show? And you know the kind of mother I make."

"Gently," said Frostflower. "Even in the Tanglelands, my sorcery could not make up your loss of blood without food in your stomach. Tiryn," she went on to their defender, "I regret being unable to heal your arm. Perhaps, if we were to spend several days here . . ."

Tiryn shook her head. "Thanks, but we'd spend the whole time explaining to everybody who you are. Anyway, I'm used to it. Had it all my life. I'll get along, and you'd better skip on out of here as soon as you can."

"Tonight," said Thorn. "So get out the Circle, Frost, and find us a world where we can eat in peace and quiet."

THE FORBIDDEN WORDS OF MARGARET A.

L. Timmel Duchamp

[N.B.: The following report was prepared exclusively for the use of the National Journalists' Association for the Recovery of the Freedom of the Press by a journalist who visited Margaret A. sometime within the last two years. JATROF requests that this report not be duplicated in any form or removed from JATROF offices and that the information provided herein be used with care and discretion.]

Introduction

Despite the once-monthly photo-ops the Bureau of Prisons allows, firsthand uncensored accounts of contact with Margaret A. are rare. The following, though it falls short of providing a verbatim transcript of Margaret A.'s words, attempts to offer a fuller, more faithful rendition of one journalist's contact with Margaret A. than has ever been publicly available. This reporter's awareness of the importance to her colleagues of such an account, as well as of the danger disseminating it to a broader audience would entail for all involved in such an effort, has prompted the deposit of this document with JATROF.

    Before describing my contact with Margaret A., I

wish to emphasize to the readers of this report (knowledgeable as they undoubtedly are) the constraints that circumscribed my meeting with Margaret A. Members of JATROF will necessarily be familiar with the techniques the government uses to manipulate public perception of data. Certainly I, going into the photo-op, considered myself well up on the government's tricks for controlling the contextualization of issues it cares about. Yet I personally can vouch for the insidious danger of momentarily forgetting the obvious: where Margaret A. is concerned, much slips our attention in such a way as to keep us from thinking clearly and objectively about the concrete facts before our eyes. I'm not sure how this happens, only that it does. The information we have about Margaret A. somehow does not get added up correctly. (And to tell the truth, I'm not convinced I've gotten it right yet.) I urge you who are reading this, then, not to impatiently skip over details already known to you, but to take my iteration of them as a caveat, as a reminder, as an aid to thought about an issue that for all its publicity remains remarkably murky. I thus ask my readers' indulgence for excursions into what may seem unnecessary political analysis and speculation. I know of no other way to wrest the framing of my own contact with Margaret A. out of the murk and mire that tends to obscure any objective recounting of facts relating to the Margaret A. situation.

To start with the most obvious: Margaret A. permits only one photo-op a month. The Bureau of Prisons (naturally pleased to make known to the public that the government can't be held responsible for thwarting the public's desire for "news" of her) doesn't allow Margaret A. to choose from among those who apply, and in this way effectively controls media access to her. The Justice Department of course would prefer to dispense with these sessions altogether, but when at the beginning of Margaret A.'s imprisonment they denied all media access to her, their attempt to sink Margaret A.'s existence into oblivion instead provoked a constant stream of speculation and protest that threatened them with not only the repeal of the Margaret A. Amendment,† but even worse a resurgence of the massive civil disorder that had prompted her incarceration and silencing in the first place. Beyond obliterating Margaret A.'s words, I would argue that the government places the next highest priority on preventing the public from perceiving Margaret A. as a martyr. That consideration alone can explain why the conditions of her special detention in a quonset hut within the confines of the Vandenberg Air Force Base are such that no person or organization—not even the ACLU, or Amnesty International, organizations which deplore the fact of her confinement—can reasonably fault them. The responsible journalist undertaking coverage of Margaret A. must bear these points in mind.

Selection for and Constraints upon the Photo-op

I've been fascinated by Margaret A. my entire adult life. I entered journalism precisely so that I'd have a shot at firsthand contact with Margaret A., and have systematically pursued that goal with every career step I've taken. (I realize that to most members of JATROF it is the implications of the Margaret A. Amendment and not Margaret A. herself that matter most. The words of Margaret A., however, for a brief time radically changed the way I looked at the world. Since losing it I've never ceased to yearn for another glimpse of that perspective. Surely of all people JATROF members can most appreciate that such a goal does not belie the ideals of the profession?) Accordingly, I

---

†This reporter knows the amendment is officially titled "The Limited Censorship for the Preservation of National Security Act," but since the only object the amendment sets out to accomplish is the total obliteration of Margaret A.'s words, surely calling it "The Margaret A. Amendment" places the emphasis where it belongs? And though their name for it is better than the anti–free speech activists calling it the "Save America Amendment," I don't particularly hold with the free speech activists calling it the "Anti–Free Speech Amendment," either. The amendment wouldn't exist if it weren't for Margaret A. herself. And both the anti– and free speech activists seem to forget that.

studied the Bureau of Prison's selection preferences, worked my way into suitable employment and then patiently and quietly waited. I lived carefully, I kept myself as clean of suspect contacts as any working journalist can. When finally I was selected for one of Margaret A.'s photo-ops, *Circumspection has been rewarded,* I congratulated myself. Reading and rereading the official notification I felt as though I had just been granted a visa to the promised land.

An invitation to meet Simon Bartkey had been attached to the visa, however. Naturally this disconcerted me: an in-person screening by a Justice Department official is quite a bit different from scrutiny of one's record. But I told myself that I'd been "good" for so long that my professionalism would see me over this last hurdle. Thus one month before I was due to meet Margaret A., my producer and I flew to Washington and met this Justice Department official assigned to what they call "the Margaret A. Desk"—an ^^expert^^ who cheerfully admitted to me that he had never heard or read any of Margaret A.'s words himself. I couldn't help but be impressed with the show they run, for the BOP has it down to a fine procedure designed to ensure that everything flows with the smoothness and predictability of a high-precision robotics assembly. Besides providing an opportunity for one last intense scrutiny of the journalists they've selected, to their way of thinking a visit to Simon Bartkey sets both the context journalists are supposed to use as well as the ground-rules.

Let me note in reminder here that Simon Bartkey has survived three different administrations precisely because he's accounted an ^^expert^^ on "the Margaret A. situation." Since the early days of the Margaret A. phenomenon each administration has fretted about the public's continuing fascination with her. Bartkey expressed it to me in these words: "This ongoing interest in her defies all logic. Her words—except for a few hoarded tapes, newspapers and *samizdat*—have been completely obliterated, and

56

the general public has no access to them, and certainly no memory of them. The American public has never been known to have such a long attention span, especially with regard to someone not continually providing ever new and more exciting grist to the media's mill. Why then do people still want to *see* her? Why haven't they forgotten about her?" (How it must gall politicians that Margaret A. has for the last fifteen years enjoyed higher name recognition than each sitting U.S. President has during the same fifteen-year period!)

Though it was the most important event in my life (I was nineteen when it happened), I can't remember any of her words. I was too young and naive at the time to hold on to newspapers and the ad hoc ephemera figures like Margaret A. invariably generate. And like most people I never dreamed a person's *words* could become illegal. One hears rumors, of course, of old tapes and newspapers secretly hoarded—yet though I've faithfully tracked every such rumor I've caught wind of, none has ever panned out.

For perhaps twenty of the fifty-five minutes I spent being briefed by him, Bartkey took great pleasure in explaining to me how the passage of time will ultimately eclipse Margaret A.'s public visibility. Leaning back in his padded red leather chair, he announced that the generational gap more than anything will finally isolate those who persist in "worshipping at the altar of her memory." His fingers stroking his mandala-embossed bottle-green silk tie, he insisted that Margaret A. can mean nothing to college kids since they were only infants at the time of the Margaret A. phenomenon. He might conceivably prove to be correct, but I don't think so. The kids I've talked to find the Margaret A. Amendment so irrational and egregious an offense against the spirit of the Bill of Rights that they're suspicious of everything they've been told about it. If no records of Margaret A.'s words still exist, neither do reports of the massive civil disorder their civics textbooks use to justify the passage of the amendment. The *fact* of the Margaret A. Amendment, I think, has got to fill them with suspicions of a cover-up. Consider: the only images they connect with Margaret A. now are the videos and photos taken of this U.S. citizen living in internal exile, a small middle-aged woman dwarfed by the deadly array of missiles and radar installations and armed guards surrounding her. I doubt that young people are capable of understanding that anyone's particular use of language could in and of itself have threatened the dissolution of every form of government in this country (much less provoked the unprecedented, draconian measure of a constitutional amendment to silence it). I've seen the cynical skepticism in their faces when older people talk about those days. How could any arrangement of words on paper, any speech recorded on tape be in and of itself as dangerous as government authorities say? And why ban no one else's speech, not even that of her most persistent followers (except of course when quoting her)? Young people don't believe it was that simple. When I listen to their questions I've no trouble deducing that they believe the government is covering up the past existence of a powerful, armed, revolutionary force. They consider the amendment not only a cover-up but also a gratuitous measure designed to curtail free speech and establish a precedent for future curtailments.

Needless to say I didn't share such observations with Bartkey any more than I offered him my theory that the new generation is not only suspicious of a cover-up but dying for a taste of forbidden fruit. While doubting its vaunted potency (or toxicity, depending upon one's point of view), they long to know what it is they're being denied. This sounds paradoxical, I admit, yet I've heard a note of resentment in their expressions of skepticism. The dangers of Margaret A.'s words may not be apparent to them, but by labeling the fruit forbidden—fruit their *elders* had been privileged enough to taste—the amendment—which they consider a cover-up to start with—is provoking resentment in this new generation coming of age. Rather than developing amnesia about Margaret A., the new generation may well become obsessed with her. In fact I wouldn't be at all surprised if new bizarrely conceived cults didn't spring up around the Margaret A. phenomenon.

I don't mean to imply that I'd approve of bizarre cults and obsessions with forbidden fruit. The fascination I and others like me feel for Margaret A. is probably as incomprehensible to young people as the government's fear of her words. (Our diverse reactions to Margaret A. seem to mark a Great Divide for most people in this country.) But something about the very *idea* of her—regardless of whether *her* ideas are ever remembered—the very *idea* of this woman shut up in the middle of a high-security military base because her words are so potent . . . well, that *idea* does something to almost everyone in this country, including those who find the Margaret A. phenomenon frightening (excepting, of course, the anti–free speech activists). If I were Bartkey I'd be worried: it's only a matter of time before the Margaret A. Amendment is repealed. And if Margaret A. is still alive then, things could *explode.*

Margaret A.'s "Security"

All we ever saw of Vandenberg proper was its perimeter fence and gate. Even before we'd handed our documents to the guard three people wearing nonmilitary uniforms converged on us and ordered us out onto the tarmac. One of them then climbed into the van and turned it around and drove it somewhere away from the base; the other two ordered us into a tiny quonset hut off to the right. This at first confused me, and I wondered whether there had been a foul-up of some sort, or whether the background checks had turned up something about one of us the Justice Department didn't like (and I even wondered—fleetingly— whether for some convoluted tangle of reasoning they kept her there in that quonset hut, outside the base's perimeter fence).

What followed in the hut rendered my speculations absurd. Bartkey had of course made us sign an agreement that we be subject to strip searches, that we use *their* equipment, that all materials be edited by them, and that we submit to an extensive debriefing afterward. I bore with the strip and body cavity search without protest, of course, since journalists are commonly obliged to endure such ordeals when entering prisons to interview inmates. (I'm sure colleagues reading this know well how one attempts in such circumstances to put the best face on an awkward, uncomfortable situation.) Nor did I protest the condition that the Bureau of Prisons be granted total editorial power, for obviously the Margaret A. Amendment might otherwise be flouted. But their insistance that we use their equipment—*that* bothered me for some elusive, hard-to-define reason. Bartkey had explained that their equipment ran without an audio track, and since no one by the terms of the Margaret A. Amendment could legally tape her speech, my conscious reaction focused on that obvious point. But as I was putting my thoroughly searched clothing back on I learned that I could not take my shoulder bag in with me, and realized that not only would there be no audio tape, there would also be no pen and paper, no lap computer, no note-taking beyond what I could force into my own ill-trained mental memory. Naturally I protested. (I am, after all, the woman who relies on her computer to tell her such things as when to have her hair cut, what time to eat lunch and how long it has been since she's written to her mother.) It made no difference, of course. I was told that if I didn't choose to abide by the rules they'd take the producer and crew in without me.

After hitting with another review of all the ground-rules, they herded us into the windowless back of a Bureau of Prisons van and drove us an undisclosed turn-filled and occasionally bumpy distance. The van stopped for at least a minute three separate times before pausing briefly—as at a stop sign, or to allow the opening of a gate

(I deduce the latter to have been the case)—and then moved for only two or three seconds before coming to a final halt. When the engine cut it only then came to me in a breathless rush that what I had been waiting for nearly half my life was actually about to happen. Margaret A.'s words are forbidden. Yet for a few minutes I (!) would have the privilege of hearing her speak. Only "trivialities," granted, they would allow nothing else—guards with radio receivers in their ears would be on hand to see to that— but still the words would be Margaret A.'s, and even her "trivial" speech, I felt certain, would be potent, perhaps electrifying. And I believed that on hearing Margaret A. speak I would remember all that I had forgotten about those days and would understand all that had eluded me throughout my adult life.

This pre-contact assumption derived not from romantic dreams cherished from adolescence, but from what I had (discreetly) gleaned about the conditions of Margaret A.'s life of exile. I had learned, for instance, from a highly reliable source formerly employed by the Justice Department, that the Bureau of Prisons had run through more than five hundred guards on the Margaret A. assignment, all of whom had quit the BOP subsequent to their removal from duty at Vandenberg.† What continues to strike me as extraordinary about this is that the guards assigned to Margaret A. have always been—and continue to be—taken exclusively from a pool of guards experienced in working in high-security federal facilities. Each guard previous to meeting Margaret A. is warned that all speech uttered within the confines of the prisoner's quarters will be recorded and examined. Before starting duty at Vandenberg each newly assigned guard under-

---

†Though the Margaret A. Amendment does not prevent the press from reporting on publicly available facts on the conditions of Margaret A.'s internment, the major U.S. media have never addressed the startling data about the high turnover in personnel assigned to Margaret A.'s "security." Considering how fascinated the public would be by such details, what then keeps the media from openly reporting such facts? Surely the entire industry cannot share the reason I had for hiding my interest in Margaret A.!

goes rigorous orientation sessions and while on duty at Vandenberg reports for debriefing after each personal contact with Margaret A. Yet no guard has ever gone on to a new assignment following contact with Margaret A. Another curious statistic: those assigned to audio surveillance of the words spoken in Margaret A.'s quarters inevitably "burn out" during their second year of monitoring Margaret A.†

Consider: Margaret A. is forbidden ever to speak about anything remotely "political." How then can she so consistently corrupt every guard who has had contact with her and disturb every monitor who has been assigned to listen to her (non-political: "trivial"!) conversation?‡ It never occurred to me to wonder what Bartkey meant when he said that all conversation with Margaret A. must be confined to "trivial, non-political smalltalk." He and other officials outlined for me the sorts of questions I must avoid raising—ranging from the subject of her confinement, the Margaret A. Amendment, and the public's continuing interest in her to the specific points upon which, according to rumor (since documents no longer exist, one can refer only to rumors or fuzzy nodes of memory), she had spoken during the brief initial period of the Margaret A. phenomenon. I think I assumed that the corruption of her guards had more to do with Margaret A.'s personality than with the ^^smalltalk^^ she exchanged with them (never mind that this did not address the monitors' eventual termination by the Justice Department). Thus as our escort opened the back door of the van I in my wild state of excitement told myself I would now be meeting not only the most remarkable woman in history,

---

†It is a matter of public record that in one case a monitor incurred a felony charge for attempting to smuggle a Margaret A. surveillance tape out of the listening post at Vandenberg.

‡Informed readers may recall that the Bureau of Prisons initially eliminated all verbal communication between Margaret A. and all other human beings until the Supreme Court ruled that such treatment would virtually amount to perpetual solitary confinement, a condition they judged unnecessary for obtaining reasonable observance of the Margaret A. Amendment.

but probably the most charismatic, charming, and possibly lovable person I would ever have the pleasure of knowing.

Contact with Margaret A.

While my producer and crew unloaded the BOP's equipment from the van, I—the one who would later be asked on camera for my observations and impressions of Margaret A. and the conditions of her confinement—strolled around the tiny compound surrounding the quonset hut I presumed to be Margaret A.'s. At first I noticed little beyond the intimidating array of surveillance and security equipment and personnel. The twenty-foot steel fence reinforced with coils of razor wire and topped by a glass-enclosed visibly armed guardpost cut off view of everything outside the compound but the hot dry sky. (The southern California sun in that environment seemed stiflingly oppressive.) Several hard-eyed uniformed men carried automatic rifles. Was it possible they thought we might attempt to spring Margaret A.? My consciousness of the eyes of such heavily armed men watching waiting anticipating shook me, making me feel like a jeweler opening a safe for robbers, fearful that with one "false" (i.e., misunderstood) move I would be a dead woman. Because Margaret A. is not a "criminal," one forgets how dangerous the government has decreed her to be.

Yet the weight of this official presence exerted a subtle impression on me I became aware of only later while "chatting" with Margaret A. The uniforms, the guardpost, the overdetermined regulation of our every movement and intention conspired to make me forget that Margaret A. has never been arraigned before a judge much less stood trial before a jury.† Thus when I spotted

---

†Technically speaking, Margaret A. is considered to be held in preventive detention—since even one word spoken by her would constitute a violation of the Margaret A. Amendment. Though constitutional scholars have argued that the amendment itself violates the letter and spirit of the Constitution, its solidly reactionary composition ensures the Supreme

the scraggly little plants growing in a corner of the compound's coarse dry sand, I instantly perceived an "extra privilege" generously bestowed upon her by the BOP, and so rather than enter Margaret A.'s quarters with a sense of how intolerably oppressive it would be to live immured within that steel fence and guardpost with its glaring mirrored windows and menacing weaponry permanently looming over one, I thought how fortunate Margaret A. was to be able to walk around outside in her compound and "garden."

I make this confession in order to illustrate how subtly perception can be influenced. It strikes me as counterintuitive that the heavy presence of surveillance and security would contribute to a perception of the legitimacy of Margaret A.'s incarceration, yet apparently the Justice Department's experts believe this, for that oppressive presence is never censored out of videos and stills, while a variety of small concessions that Margaret A. has won for herself have *never* survived the BOP's editing.‡

Thus when I entered Margaret A.'s quarters accompanied by three guards and a crew grumbling over the antiquation of the BOP's equipment, I looked at all I saw through peculiarly biased eyes. It's *not so bad*, I thought as I surveyed the first of Margaret A.'s two rooms. I noted the cushions softening the pair of wooden chairs with arms, and was astonished at the beautifully executed woven tapestry covering a large part of the ugly tooth-

---

Court's ongoing adherence to its earlier ruling against judicial interference in security measures undertaken jointly by the Executive and Legislative branches. For a brief summary of the legal peculiarities of Margaret A.'s incarceration, see the ACLU's pamphlet *When the Rule of Law Breaks Down: The Executive, Judicial and Legislative Conspiracy Against Margaret A.*

‡Anxious to preserve a clean profile that would stand up to Justice Department scrutiny, I did not make the inquiries that would have informed me of these concessions before observing them with my own eyes. For a complete log of Margaret A.'s battles for these concessions, contact Elissa Muntemba, her principal attorney, through the California branch of the ACLU.

paste-green wall. *It's not as bad as most jail cells, and is certainly far better than the underground dungeons in which most political prisoners are kept,* I reminded myself. It occurs to me in retrospect that probably I wanted to believe that Margaret A. lived in tolerable circumstances so that the chances of her hanging on as long as it took to achieve her release would be reasonably high. And so before Margaret A. came into the room, my eyes fixed on the small computer sitting on a table near the outer door while I mused on how because of that computer Margaret A.'s way with words (and perhaps even her words themselves) might have a chance to survive, and rejoiced that in spite of the Margaret A. Amendment the BOP wasn't sitting as heavily and oppressively on her as they did on most political prisoners.

But then Margaret A. appeared and for a few crazy, breath-stopped instants time seemed to halt. After greeting the guards (whose faces, I mechanically noted, were suddenly suffused with wariness and dis-ease) she simply stood there, a small stout figure in gray cotton shirt and pants, looking us over—as though we were there for her inspection rather than the other way around. I struggled a few agonized seconds with the frog now in my throat and glanced at the guards in expectation of an introduction. But looking back at Margaret A. I realized the absurdity of my expectation, and scorned myself for taking the guards as hosts at an arranged soirée. Though I had no idea of it at the time (and I still don't quite understand how it worked), that moment marked the loss of a professional persona that had hitherto sustained me throughout my career in journalism.

My producer finally took the initiative: "Allow me to introduce myself," she began as, holding out her hand, she advanced towards Margaret A. Margaret A., however, shattered this moment of returned normalcy, for she ignored the proffered hand and commented that creating a façade of social conventions would cost more than she herself could afford—even if we felt ourselves able to afford it.†

Margaret A.'s pointed refusal to shake hands opened another edge to an already tense situation, and jolted me into a more sharply critical attitude towards everyone and everything around us. It was at that moment, for instance, that I understood to the marrow of my bones a bit of what this detention must mean to Margaret A. Previously I had felt an abstract outrage at her silencing and detention. But at that moment when Margaret A. mentioned the cost of social pretense, I *felt* the reality of her situation, I dimly sensed how apparently small things could exert enormous pressure on even a psyche strong enough to withstand the weight of official oppression such as that so constantly forced upon Margaret A.'s senses.

Having learned from my producer's embarrassment, I merely smiled and nodded at Margaret A. when my producer introduced me to her. Still Margaret A. rebuffed me, for the slight twitch of her lip (not amusement, for her ancient frozen eyes remained just as wintry and distant) made me feel foolish enough to blush (thus making me feel even more foolish). The rebuff and my reaction to the rebuff in turn provoked first resentment in me—for a moment I felt indignant at her lack of manners—and then, seconds later, abashment as it occurred to me that Margaret A. must take me for a lackey of the system that had specially targeted her.‡

The crew did not bother with introductions, they

---

†My reconstruction of our conversation with Margaret A. is, unfortunately, not verbatim. Neither my producer, myself nor the crew have eidetic memories (and if any of us had it is likely the Justice Department would have discovered such a fact and consequently disqualified us from contact with Margaret A.), and thus all recollections of Margaret A.'s words have come through a concerted effort by the group to remember, though even this was hampered by our separation from one another for the first forty-eight hours following contact with Margaret A. in accordance with the Justice Department's debriefing procedures.

‡For most of the time of my contact with Margaret A. I wondered, disillusioned, how I could have spent so many years yearning after a meeting that was proving to be such a letdown. Margaret A. did not stir me, she did not even warm me towards her, personally: I not only found it impossible to pity her—even though for the entire time I was in her quarters I glimpsed out of

simply set up shop and began taping with the equipment they despised. The producer reminded them to shoot without regard to our conversation, to scan everything in the two rooms of the hut and to be sure to get a shot of Margaret A.'s "garden." And then she nodded at me, as though to remind me that I should be getting on with my part of the affair, too. I looked back at Margaret A. and frantically tried to recall the first question I had planned to ask her. But nothing came, my mind had gone blank. (This hadn't happened to me since my first interview as an intern, but as I've already mentioned, Margaret A.'s entrance had so nonplused me that I'd lost my journalist's persona and the aggressiveness and cool that went with it.) Panicking, I blurted out the first question that popped into my head: "Who cuts your hair for you?"

Margaret A. flicked her eyebrows at me and snapped something to the effect that that was the sort of information the BOP would gladly provide me with. My entire body went hot with embarrassment; glancing around me I caught my producer frowning and the guards rolling their eyes. It was at that moment that it hit me: though Margaret A. is black, all the guards I had seen at Vandenberg were, to a person, white. (I suspect it was a combination of my noticing Margaret A.'s closely clipped woolly hair and my thinking that I could not imagine any of the guards whom I had seen—male or female—ever cutting it.) I wished then I could ask her if her guards had always been exclusively white and if so how she felt about it. But apart from worrying about such a question getting me into trouble with the BOP, I felt uneasy about what *she* might make of such a question. I had no idea whether the racial identity of one's guards would be relevant to someone to whom the imposition of any guards at all was an outrage . . .

---

the corner of my eye the steel fence confronting the room's single window and constantly snatched covert glances at the rifles the guards carried— but several times felt a flare of resentment towards her. Margaret A. has not a charismatic cell in her body.

Fortunately, I recalled one of the questions I had prepared, a question I thought could pass as personal (and thus "trivial"). "Has incarceration and the prospect of a lifetime of incarceration changed the way you feel about yourself as a human being?" I queried. Margaret A. looked straight into my face, as though to check out where that question was coming from. Uneasily I glanced around at the guards; though they paid no special attention to me (thus indicating the question to be acceptable, since if it weren't the BOP official monitoring the interview would have passed orders to the guards through the receivers I could see in their ears), I felt menaced by their presence as I hadn't before. *This room*, I thought, *is too small for so many bodies and machines.*

I wish I could remember Margaret A.'s exact words, but all I can give you is a paraphrase. She started with a humorous comment to the effect that one thing her incarceration had done for her was to indicate to her how seriously the official world took her, and consequently to make her take herself more seriously than she ever had before. Imagine, she said with a wry not quite sardonic smile, I was a nobody until people I never met started listening to me. Just imagine if people took every word that came out of your mouth as seriously as they take every bullet fired out of a gun. I don't think I ever took myself particularly seriously until after they threw me into solitary confinement and allowed me no human contact. They told me it was dangerous for anyone to hear anything that came out of my mouth. For several weeks I lived in the kind of quarantine you might dream up for the deadliest, most mysteriously contagious of diseases. I was sure I was going to crack up. But can you imagine the ego trip? Can you imagine your own words being considered that potent? This official reaction made me a uniquely powerful person, accorded powers never attributed to any other mortal in history that I've ever heard of. At first I couldn't take it that seriously myself. Later I got a little scared. But how could I go on being scared when there's not a chance in a million I'll ever be allowed to speak freely again? I've nothing to lose now for going as far as my sanity permits.

This reply took me entirely by surprise. I had expected her to talk about her bitterness at the unfairness of the system in denying her due process (which she could have done, I think, without necessarily mentioning the issue overtly), at the wreck her incarceration had made of her life, at the horror of her exile from friends and family. But because of the point of view she presented to me I suddenly comprehended afresh how extraordinary the apparatus of her silencing was—that so many resources were being devoted solely to that end, and how much credit, actually, they granted her by finding it necessary to protect themselves against the words of a woman who had been a simple mother and middle school teacher without organization (for the formation of an organization around her came only in the last three months of her freedom) or party affiliation. The Margaret A. phenomenon had streaked into brief exhilarating visibility like the first unexpected flash of lightning crackling across a late evening summer sky.

I asked her next about whether she missed her daughter (who, it is well known, moved to New Zealand subsequent to her mother's incarceration) and other family members. Margaret A. took several minutes in replying to this question, and such was the complexity and unexpectedness of her answer that I'm afraid I cannot vouch for the accuracy of my paraphrase.† The press and other institutions in our world consider privacy to be a privilege, Margaret A. began, a luxury, not something that must be respected of every person. Human society would not be the same were privacy not considered a privilege. Consequently my daughter has paid a price for my frankness, a price exacted by the press and other institutions. I imag-

---

†And indeed our joint attempt to reconstitute this answer resulted in such acrimony that in the end we finally agreed not to discuss it at all.

ine most people would lay that exaction at my door, working on the assumption that my frankness invited disregard of my own—and therefore my daughter's—privacy. But for me the issue with regard to my daughter becomes a matter of whether or not my self-censorship would have been worth the maintenance of the status quo of my daughter's life before my words attracted widespread attention. Could I have afforded to pay the price silence would have exacted from me? It is always a question of determining what lies at stake in what one does or omits to do. Undoubtedly you yourself forfeited to a considerable extent your privacy for the sake of taking part in this photo-opportunity. I wonder if you have weighed the price of your presence here today.

It surprised me that the guards did not interrupt this speech. I myself heard some of the subversion in her reply even as she spoke, for I felt certain she was referring not only to the strip and body cavity search I had had to submit to, but to the years of keeping myself "clean" of suspect contact, years of playing the game as primly as Simon Bartkey himself could wish. I suppose her fingering of the press "and other institutions" and her references to "human society" and "our world" sounded vague enough to the monitors that they didn't grasp exactly what she was talking about. But the expression on my producer's face indicated that she had no trouble understanding Margaret A.'s words, and that like me she considered them subversive, too.

We then had only three minutes left of the allotted time. Though the camera crew had been in and out of the other room, Margaret A. and I had so far remained in the one room. I asked her if she would show me her other room while answering my last question or two. She flicked her eyebrows at me as though to deride my asking her permission while my colleagues had been aiming their cameras at whatever caught their fancy, but then gestured me to go before her through the doorless opening in the wall. I had wanted to ask her about her gardening, but when I saw the books piled on the linoleum floor beside the patchwork quilt-covered mattress I instead asked her if she read much and if so what. She said she read only poetry. I snatched a quick look at the book on the top of the pile and caught only the name Audre Lorde. Aware of time ticking away I glanced at the bath fixtures taking up most of the room and wondered at the water standing in the tub. I asked her about it, and she said she was allowed one bath a day and that her bathwater was all that she had to water her garden with. Frantically, aware that only half a minute remained, I asked her how she spent her time. Instead of answering she told me that there was no point in her attempting to reply to that question, that she knew the guard would stop her before she had finished since they had done so on the two other occasions she had attempted to answer it.

A guard then told us our time was up. This was a moment I hadn't prepared for, hadn't begun to imagine. My entire adult life had been leading up to this time spent with Margaret A., and suddenly it was over, never to be repeated, and I would never again have a chance to listen to this woman whose words were forbidden.† I stood frozen for a few seconds, staring at Margaret A. as though to memorize the moment. Looking at her impassive, aging face I realized that our meeting meant nothing to her, that we were only another media crew come to gape, that after a few months she probably would not even remember me, that surely she considered all the media people to be faceless robots playing the game that mattered not at all to her (except, perhaps, as insurance against excessively abusive treatment by her captors).

During the next few hours I slipped into a dull numbness, mechanically answering questions and listening to the debriefers' comments, hardly caring about what might follow. I had done the only thing I'd ever aspired to,

---

†The BOP has a rule that prohibits media personnel from more than one contact with Margaret A.

and now it was over. The interview had been a disappointment and the future looked like an anticlimax—gray, dull, pointless.

The Question of Professional Standards

After the debriefing while en route to the L.A. affiliate that had lent us the van, we joked for ten or fifteen minutes about the transparency of the BOP's "deprogramming" techniques. For me at least it had been an ordeal (and I suspect it had been for them, too, since we found it necessary to joke about it). Not only did I need to keep my wits about me in order to give the debriefers the answers they considered correct, but I just as importantly needed to preserve intact (as much as that was possible) the memory of Margaret A.'s words. All of us apparently passed muster without a glitch, for our producer assured us that the official in charge had let her know that he was pleased with our debriefings.

When finally the joking had worked some of our disease out of our systems, the crew began complaining about the pointlessness of the whole Margaret A. situation. They said they couldn't see what the big deal with Margaret A. was, they contended that the Margaret A. phenomenon must always have been a super media hype since there certainly wasn't anything special about Margaret A. herself. They groused, too, about the BOP's deleting their shots of the computer, the "garden" and the partially filled tub and saucepan for bailing: touches that they had hoped would lift our photo-op above the mediocrity of those that had come before (when of course ours would show as almost identical to the others). Those particular cuts perplexed and perturbed them more than the BOP's cutting every shot in which Margaret A.'s lips were moving. They joked a bit about the BOP's fear of lip-readers, but then segued into a discussion of the government's paranoia in making such a big deal of a woman who was, they thought, simply boring.

After several minutes of listening in silence to the discussion, our producer disagreed. "The woman's a destroyer," she declared. "She's so damned sure of herself and her opinions that only the most confident people would be capable of resisting her subversive incursions."

The crew snickered. "What subversion?" they wanted to know. "You mean her refusing to shake your hand?"

The producer ignored this below-the-belt crack. "Those idiots monitoring us were too slow to catch what she was talking about. When she used the word 'institutions,' only an idiot would have missed what she was referring to." That counter-put-down shut them up—and ended the conversation about Margaret A.

No one seemed to notice my silence. And in fact I managed to talk to Elissa Muntemba and even negotiated my own on-camera interview without raising suspicions of myself.† The suspicions came later, in other contexts—after I had begun to ask of myself the very questions I believe Margaret A. in my place would insist upon asking. Not surprisingly the producer of the Margaret A. photo-op was the one to suss me out. *She* knew, even if no one else could trace it back to Margaret A.'s "influence." "You're a Margaret A. convert," she accused me. "She really got to you, didn't she?" I so detested the language she used that without considering the consequences I launched into a discussion of our complicity with the BOP. But she cut me off before I'd even finished my second sentence. "Professional journalists can't afford to be susceptible to subversion," she scathed at me. *Does she understand at all what she's saying when she uses the word "afford"?* I wondered. Of course she didn't, for she went on to berate me for being a gullible fool, for betraying professional

---

†It would have been pointless for me to have attempted serious analysis in the interview, for anything "radical" would have been cut, or the interview itself trashed. I consciously chose to toe the invisible line because I considered it important to get out the word that Margaret A. still had juice in her, that far from having been discouraged by her silencing rather she took it as a sign that she was on the right track.

standards—and then told me I was terminated. "I won't mention this in your file," she said—but later I wondered what such an assurance could mean since she obviously made a point of sabotaging every attempt I made at securing new employment within the mainstream media industry.†

This question of professional standards is a troubling one for JATROF members. The position of journalists like my producer amounts to using the government's contextualizations for determining the parameters of objectivity. Any considerations of facts outside of such contextualizations then become acts of subversion. If my contact with Margaret A. has taught me anything, it is that the self-censorship demanded of journalists is too high a price for me to pay. The question then becomes one of how the journalist reconciles the ideals of the profession with the practice my producer insists reflects "professional standards."

Summary

First, for those concerned with Margaret A. herself, I can attest to the fact that her incarceration and silencing have not demoralized or disempowered her. On the contrary, the government's efforts to obliterate her words seem to have strengthened rather than weakened the particular, distinctive articulation that characterizes Margaret A.'s speech. Should the day come when the government cannot resist public opposition to the Margaret A. Amendment (for as time passes more and more people will consider the government's fear of Margaret A. either hysterical paranoia or a cynical excuse for its tight control of the news media), Margaret A. will likely be prepared.

Second, my experience doing a Margaret A. photo-op suggests that as journalists we need to question the

---

†Like other journalists who have crossed the invisible line of self-censorship, I now face the choice of changing professions or emigrating out, and choose the latter.

conflation of the government's contextualization with the parameters of objectivity and professional standards, especially when such contextualization demands the obliteration not only of words but of facts. Journalists currently work in an environment in which their asking even so simple a question as "What would the harm be in showing a shot of a bathtub?" can lead to charges of subversive lack of objectivity. The "limited censorship" of Margaret A.'s words has thus demonstrably altered journalists' definition of objectivity and professional standards. Following the Margaret A. photo-op I learned to the cost of my career—thinking that since I had achieved my goal of interviewing Margaret A. I need no longer be "careful"—that this censorship process extends beyond the coverage of Margaret A. into other areas. JATROF members, I feel certain, will want to consider the cost to themselves and the profession of their continued submission to the principle of self-censorship the Margaret A. Amendment has so clearly spawned.

ROAD RUNNER

G. K. Sprinkle

Jacqui Brannon stood at the edge of the woods. She looked at the area around the weigh station through her binoculars' nightvision lenses. It was a good night for a run—moonless and warm. A breeze, smelling of honeysuckle and fresh-cut grass, blew through the cornrow braids in her hair. It was dark, except in the west where the lights of Des Moines cast an ugly orange blur in the sky. The open area around the station was empty. She stuck the binoculars into her jacket and zipped it shut. She slithered out of the woods on her belly toward the access road. She didn't have to; she did it for practice. She had to be perfect. Blacks who weren't perfect were bums; she'd learned that lesson from Stasiu Nalaski's mother.

Stasiu was crying; his cat had crawled under the porch. He was such a baby. She told him he wouldn't get hurt, only dirty crawling under a porch. He wouldn't do it. She crawled under there, all the way to the foundation, even ripped one of the knees in her jeans; her mother had yelled at her. Stasiu was happy when she'd come back out with Fluffy, but his mother dragged him away. "Dirty nigger," she said. "Can't play with dirty niggers." Jacqui yelled, "You can't crawl under a porch and come out clean." It didn't make a difference.

She was still crawling, but now she had clean clothes in her backpack. She paused, gauged her position by the lights on the weigh station, and continued. The lights scared her. Long-distance trucks had detectors hooked into their road computers. Only people needed lights. Running the truck out of the Illinois weigh station was always the worst part of her trip. Her heart pounded. She had to make it tonight.

Not that tonight was different. Every run held the possibility of being caught. Arrested. Jailed. Lonnie would love it. She could just hear his sleazy lawyer at yet another custody hearing. "Your honor, the petitioner," he would pause, pretending to hold back tears, "loves his children. He only wants what's best for them. Whereas, the defendant," then he'd point a finger at her and sneer, "is a criminal. Yes, a criminal." He wouldn't need to say any more.

She had reasons, but no one wanted to hear them. They were part of being a mother. Whereas, Lonnie's problems were a terrible obstacle to being a good father. The grass cuttings made her sneeze. She took out the binoculars—five more feet. That was the closest she'd ever gauged the distance. She wiggled forward. If she only didn't have lawyer bills, she could afford a car to get to Chicago. Of course, she wouldn't need to go then.

She heard the hiss of the air brakes first. Must be the California fruit run. She checked the license plate with her glasses, then flattened to the ground as the headlights came on. She often thought they programmed the lights just to wake the station clerk up. Watching the automated weighing procedure must be as boring a job as hers was keying the dispatch data into the network. The tires squealed as the truck slowed to a stop before the gate. The gate slid open, and the truck moved inside.

She was next now—five more minutes. Jacqui put on her left gripper glove. She scanned the interstate. Traffic was heavy for a Tuesday. Probably parents taking their kids on vacations. God, she'd love to take a vacation with the kids. She imagined the four of them reclining in a car as the autocomputer guided them down the road—going a steady speed, keeping them the right distance from other cars. She could see herself reading a story in the glow of a small reading light. She looked at her watch. Eight minutes gone. She'd never had a run come late. The sound of air brakes snapped her back into action. She looked at the license plate; it was the Toys R Us truck. Where was her run?

God, please, oh please don't let it be scrubbed, she thought. The truck's headlights came on. Its tires kicked gravel in her face as they passed her braking into the station. While the station went through its cycle, Jacqui checked her book for the next Brannon truck. She only ran Lonnie's trucks. She figured it was the alimony she should have received. She'd earned that money. Everyone used to say it was her job staying home with Lonnie and the kids. Suddenly, it wasn't worth anything.

She moved the pocket flashlight down the page, the anger making her hands shake. The next truck wasn't due until five thirty—a risky run at best with dawn close by, especially since it wasn't carrying electronic parts. They'd wave it. She'd have to catch it at the exit. She'd gotten lazy. She put the book into her jacket, swallowed, and took several deep breaths.

The sound of the air brakes startled her. A quick check showed it was hers. She shoved the binoculars in her jacket and stuck the magnetic lock pick into her mouth. She was up and running while she jammed her right hand into the gripper glove. She jumped to the side of the cab, pulling herself up to the step with the grips. She walked behind the cab, avoiding the exhaust stock. She stepped over the air hose and electrical connectors, and choked on the diesel fumes. Holding the grab handle with her right hand, she attached the grips on her left hand to the door. She slipped her right thumb and index finger out of the cut in the glove and moved the lock pick between the door and the frame.

The air brakes quit hissing when the truck stopped at the gate. She opened the door, stuck the pick in her mouth, and climbed into the driver's seat. She closed the door behind her. Her eyes darted around for a safe spot. The cab was the old-fashioned kind with a sleeper in the back. She scrambled between the seats and lay flat on her stomach, her nose pressing into the remains of a mattress mildewed from disuse. The truck started moving into the station.

She took several breaths—through her mouth. "You're all right; everything is all right," she whispered to herself. The truck positioned itself over the scale and hissed to a stop. It shook, dropping slightly as the scales engaged. Time passed. Sweat beaded on Jacqui's forehead. Had the station clerk changed the program when the truck was late? Were they going to put it through the sterilizing wave?

Jacqui heard a key in the lock of the passenger door. The clerk never walked out to the scales. Catching a wave was dangerous. Of course, this truck wasn't supposed to be waved, that's why she chose it. The door opened. She froze. He rummaged around on the floor, then sucked in his breath. Through the crack between the door frame and the seat, she saw him reach out and pick something up from the seat. It was a grass clipping. A Klaxon sounded twice, paused, and then sounded again. The clerk shut the door, jumped off the step, and ran into the office. The scales disengaged, and the truck moved toward the exit. She let her breath out.

She shrugged off her backpack, stuck it against the cab, and turned over on her back. The truck started accelerating along the access road toward the interstate. She heard the bump and knew what it was before the distinctive sound of the grips moved up the passenger side of the cab. She swore. If the police were watching the exit . . . her mind refused to finish the thought.

She heard three soft thuds, followed by a low strangled cry. *It can't be gunshots,* she thought. Something banged hard against the cab door like a loose screen door slapping open and shut in the wind. The tires ran over a bump in the road. Outside the cab, it was silent. Jacqui shook. The truck accelerated to move into the traffic, surging forward and braking a couple of times before settling into a steady speed.

What was going on? They locked you in jail for running; they didn't shoot you. She dug the flashlight out of her pocket. Gripping the sides of the seats, she pulled herself between them, and shone the light into the front of the cab. On the floor of the passenger side was a box, neatly tied with string.

Jacqui did not hesitate. If she was going to die, she wanted to know what she was dying for. She climbed into the front. Sitting in the passenger seat, she untied the box. It wasn't a difficult knot. She sucked in her breath.

The box contained money—lots of money. Though she hadn't hesitated to open the box, it took her a long time to touch the money. It was stacked in bundles like at banks. Each one contained a hundred old twenty-dollar bills. She counted the bundles—two hundred thousand dollars. If she threw everything out of her backpack, she could take it all.

She was rich. She had money. She laughed. It was like being with Lonnie again—flashing money at the best restaurants; walking into Marshall Field's and charging anything she liked. She picked up one of the bundles and kissed it. The first thing she was going to do was buy a car to get to these stupid hearings. No. The first thing was to get a good lawyer—Karl Marlberger. Yes. She would hire Mr. Society Lawyer himself; the one who stripped ex-husbands of all their money. She wanted it all. When she got through with Lonnie, he'd have to run the roads to get to work. She laughed again.

She imagined the scene. Marlberger, five diamond rings on each hand, would grab the witness box like Perry Mason. "So tell me, *Mis-ter* Brannon, if you love those children so much why don't you ever pay your child support on time? Don't you know they can't eat without that money?"

"Yes, of course," Lonnie would say. "But, *she* wastes my money."

"On what, *Mis-ter* Brannon. Clothes? Rent? Well?"

Lonnie would pull on his shirt collar with his finger. Sweat would drip down his face, and his eyes would dart around the room.

"Your honor," Marlberger would say, pounding the bench. "This man is impoverishing his children to get back at his wife. This man, your honor," an appropriate pause for moral indignation to rise, "this man is a bitter man."

Yes, he was a bitter man. She'd always known that even with everyone pretending it was love. What she hadn't realized was the depth of her bitterness over it. Not that his attorney hadn't said that, many times, hers too for that matter.

"You're mine, baby," Lonnie'd said when she told him she was getting a divorce. "You can't make it without me." He laughed. "Think you can live like this," his arm swept around the den with its built-in bar, antique mirror, and complete entertainment center, "on the salary a clerk makes, *if* you can even get a job. Think you can afford clothes like this, baby?" He stepped close to her, fingering the gold chains around her neck. He moved his face within an inch of hers. "You'll eat my shit if I tell you to 'cause I'll have you in court every week if you leave. You won't ever see a penny of my money." He twisted a chain, tightening it around her throat. "You drop the divorce and get my money back from that slut sister of yours, or I'll kick your cute little ass 'til it bleeds." He let go of the chain and strutted out of the room.

He'd kept his word. He'd put her back where she started from, and she was moving down like an avalanche from a mountain peak. He had all their money. He was spending it on other women instead of their kids. He laughed at her every time he dragged her into court. He'd take the kids from her, but it was too much fun making her jump any time he wanted. She hated him. Yet the hate was destroying her, not him. All the money in the world wouldn't change that. And this money would just bring her more problems. She put the bundles back, re-tied the knot, and returned the box to the floor.

While she cleaned the grass clippings from the front seats, she considered what might happen between here and the yard. There were several possibilities, none good. She examined the computer. It was supposed to be easy to work these things, but truck programs were more complicated than those on cars, especially long-haul programs. She gave up after a few minutes. The brakes hissed. She scurried into the back and flattened on the mattress.

The truck exited the interstate and stopped. The passenger door opened. She froze, not even breathing. She heard scraping, then the door closed. An eternity passed, then the truck accelerated back onto the interstate. She looked between the seats again and saw a small red box on the floor. She was lucky, twice lucky. It wouldn't happen again. Her watch showed forty-five minutes left. She decided to jump the truck before it entered the yard.

She lay down. The stress and worry, not to mention the smell, should have kept her awake. It didn't. She woke to the alternating acceleration and braking as the truck queued up to leave the interstate. Steel grey light lit the cab. The box was still in position. They might be watching the truck. She decided to jump the driver's side, to be safe.

As the truck made the turn into the side street leading to the yard, she climbed in front and opened the door. The air brakes hissed, the truck slowing behind a line leading into south station. She stood on the step, closing the door behind her. Her heart pounded hard in her chest. She jumped, and rolled across the street into a pile of trash cans. Her right hand scraped the concrete; one pant leg tore open at the knee.

She lay there amid the oily rags and 10W-40 cans like a wino. A tear rolled down her cheek; she wiped it away with the back of her hand. A police car passed her, lights flashing. The driver glanced at her, then looked away. She could imagine him saying "another deadbeat nigger" to his partner. She was not a bum. It would be so easy to give up; let Lonnie have his way. No. She wouldn't do it. She'd take a gun and shoot him in his evil heart first.

She glanced at her watch. The kids would be waking up about now. She saw them yawning, moving slowly. She smelled their warm bodies; saw their smiles. She heard them say, "I love you, mommy." Lonnie was a lout, but it didn't do her any good thinking about it all the time. She'd worked her way up from the bottom before; she'd do it again. She sat up. A second police car passed her, then a third.

What was happening? She picked herself up and limped a little closer to the yard. She stood behind a dumpster, the smell of soured beer making her gag. From there, she could see three cars ringing her truck. She took the nightvision lenses off her binoculars and looked. Lonnie stood next to the truck, talking and gesturing like he was Jesse Jackson. Two men stood beside him—stony faced, their hands crossed over their chests. They wore suits with white shirts, and their hair was cut short.

She put the binoculars back inside her jacket and turned away. He deserved it. She limped back down the street toward the interstate. She felt no joy in his troubles. She stopped and leaned against a crumbling brick wall. She examined her feelings. Lonnie's fate didn't matter to her. He was just another obstacle to overcome, another challenge to meet and beat. She'd do it no matter what happened to him. Another police car passed her by. She ignored it. She continued walking. The area around the interstate used to have restaurants and gas stations for the long-distance truckers. Now a self-service station and a diner held the only signs of life. She walked toward the diner. The hearing would be postponed today, again. She'd still have to go downtown or they'd wonder how she knew of the delay, but she didn't have to be punctual. Some eggs would be nice, maybe a small glass of orange juice. EATS—catchy name for a restaurant.

PICNIC DAYS

Cleo Kocol

After they passed the Natural/Bio Laws, I saw gray. I seldom see color now. Sometimes I catch the sun slivering in past the condo cubes. If I angle my head proper I glimpse rays laying a beam down the back alley. But mostly, I get the light from remembering. When the smell, the smog, and the noise close in, I recall picnic days so fine it hurts good remembering. Lugging baskets of food and our first-born, Radonna, we climbed the cliffs to see the view spread out below. Boats with white sails skimmed over sparkling blue water, fingers of land were green with trees, and from all around laughter flowed. Oh, how people lived in those days!

When the changes first sneaked in, I shouted anger words on the street. Then the childer came one after the other, and I had no time for protests. Priding myself on being a "good" mother, I tried to shut out thoughts of the past. But they kept sneaking in. The street we live on used to be a park.

Today before they leave for school I remind Lally and the other morning-goers to be careful crossing at Traffic Grid One. "Easier crossing at Fourth," I say.

"I ain't got time to go to Fourth." Lally stares at me, a make-me-if-you-can look on her face.

I stare back. "Okay, get yourself run over. See if I care."

The other childer, who go afternoon and evening shift, burrow deeper into their sleep boxes. Paradise only knows we got enough of us in these two rooms, eighteen counting me and Ralph.

I watch her and the others head out. We live in Sector A. Lately, they been talking about sectioning off the city with no travel between sectors. Said it would lessen the chance of ill-spread and be good for business, too. Make people shop in their own areas.

The whole idea frightens me. Radonna, my first-born, moved to Sector E when she married Bronley. My, I do miss her. She ain't like the other childers with their pale eyes and paler memories. Radonna remembers the early days. At least once a week she says, "Hey, Mom, let's go on a picnic."

"Where to?" I shoot back.

"To that place where they had roofs over the picnic tables. And there was ducks in a pond. And swings, and swimmin' and . . ."

"Okay, okay," I say, laughing and cuttin' in. Already my mind is picturing the past. I hang up and get out the old photographs of Radonna when she was little. All around the room I place pictures of places and times that aren't there any more. Then I get veggies from the window boxes and wash them sparkling clean before I sit down in the doorway to wait for her.

I spot her hurrying up the hill, a package in one arm, a baby in the other and toddlers clinging to her skirts. I hate the thought of her with six childer and she not twenty-one yet. But when she is with me it's almost like she's my babe again. Now, when she gets even with me I put on an everyday face and reach for the package. "So what you got?"

"Apple cake and cream pudding." Trying to see if anybody else is home, her look angles past my shoulder.

"Just us today," I say. "So you brung sweet tastes

from the high mucks' store!" I almost laugh out loud with glee, but I wait until we are inside before I smile. Then she puts the childer down and I shove at her and she shoves back. That's how glad we are to see one another. Otherwise, there's never any touching any more.

"Them look like really good sweet tastes," I say as I divvy up the veggies. She puts her childer on the roof and hands them carrot sticks through the window. Then me and Radonna munch our greens slowly before we savor the sweets. Licking our lips and picking up crumbs with our fingers, we remember out loud.

"There was a path clear around the hill," Radonna says. She eyes the photos, looking for things she'd missed before.

"At the top was where'd we see the water."

"I always wanted to take one a them boats."

"Me and your Dad was gonna rent one one day. When you fell asleep."

"Sure nuf?"

"Had it all planned."

We grin at one another and look away. From the hall voices echo up and down the landings where childer play when they ain't in school. Her little ones crawl to the edge of the tarpaper roof. At the last minute she goes out and hauls them back. I gather up the pictures. She looks through them again before she gets ready for the long walk back to her own place. "Well, I'm off," she says.

Today, it ain't so bad watching her leave cause I'll fone-a-vis her tomorrow. I come up with a way to call without going through Gov Lines and having to pay. No matter what happens, I aim to try it. If it looks like they're on to me, I'll disconnect or say, "Excuse the fone-a-vis" like I got a wrong number. I won't tell Radonna about it, though. She gets upset when I twist by the law. "Mum, that's cheating," she said once.

"What you mean, cheating?" Lally asked.

Radonna had a hard time explaining. Anymore there's just regs. You follow them or you find ways of getting around them.

Making plans occupies my mind, so it's almost night when real life sets in again. Ralph is reading the paper and when I look up he tosses it down and says, "I don't care what they say. I know there's gonna be walls and barbed wire between city sections. Everybody says so." Sighing deeply he turns up the communicator box.

That kind a talk scares me bad. I hardly hear the communicator.

"Extra attention," the audio blares. Colored lights flash and marching music floods the room until we all pay attention, including a couple kids I don't recognize.

"You kids bringing in loners again, you're gonna get it sure," I holler, fear scratching at my inwards like mice night-footing it through our cupboards. Loners eat you out of house and home.

Lally pale-eyes me, and the rest shout for me to shut up.

"It's a Directive," Ralph says.

He used to be a good sort when we got married. Made pretty good wages for a non-skill. Clever with his hands, he said. Clever with his mouth, I say. He talked me into his bed. Now all he wants is his meal and a Sour Swill. Sometimes his breath smells so bad I can hardly stand it. When the kids were fewer I'd go sleep with one a them. Now there's no escape. When he mounts me, grunting and groaning, I turn my head and pray to Paradise there won't be another childer.

We all turn to the screen.

The speaker is an approved gov ank. No mustache or beard. No accent. He says the rumors about sectioning off the city are just that, rumors. Only Sector D will be sectioned.

I feel such relief I have trouble concentrating on the rest of the message about traffic guidelines drawn up to conform with the Natural/Bio Laws. Nothing will impede the natural flow of traffic. Rules, regulations, and drivers' licenses will be eliminated.

"What's it mean?" the childer demand.

Three gov anks interpret the message for everybody. "If a person can afford a ground tran, they should be allowed to drive without restrictions," one says.

Another says it's bound to help with the population problem.

The third says it's a way of defusing centralization of govment.

"Big deal," Lally says. No one we know has private tran or ever did have.

"Please," I beg. I want to hear the latest population figures. Twenty million in the city sectors. Another twenty in the surrounds. It was a million and a million when Ralph and I got married.

In the morning I tap the fone-a-vis lines and make a free call to Radonna. She almost flips, me calling so soon after a picnic.

We plan another outing next week. For days I stay happy getting extras. Like a real tablecloth I find at the Old-Time Store. It took quite a bit of running around. At Street Grid One all the stop, merge, caution, and cross-walk signs were gone. As far as I could see there were no stoplights.

"You kids got to be extra careful now," I warn. "You take Fourth. Or go all the way up the hill to the fifth Grid, the one that was Mountain View when Radonna was little."

"Radonna, Smadonna," they chorus.

Lally laughs.

That night when she is late getting home, for a minute I hope she's run off. Never could get close to that childer. Then I get torn up with guilt and go down to First and wait for her. Gas guzzlers and elec sav tran whiz by and people thread in and out like it's a game. Then I watch as ground tran splatters Lally all over the pavement.

A woman next to me says, "One less mouth to feed."

"More room at home," another chortles.

The crowd laughs.

I'm glad they were the ones that said it. The bad feels are working at me hard. I go home and call Radonna, but even picnic talk don't help.

The next day and the next I wait at First for the morning-goers coming home from school. One day Bretna gets it mid-stream. A week later Ragid and Fex are dragged down the block, and Gog and Gig are run over until there's no identifying marks.

Ralph buys them all urns. I take one of the veggie boxes out a the window, and he lines the urns up on the sill. They got their names on them, and they show up real pretty when I turn on the lights at night. Looking up there I can figure out which childer are left.

Radonna seldom comes picnicking any more now that she has to go around Sector D. I go see her as often as I can, puffing the long way up the hill to Fifth and then waiting until four or five other people want to cross. Then I take off with them. I figure the ground tran don't like to ram into a whole bunch of adults. Usually though I visit with Radonna on the fone-a-vis. First she exclaims about the expense to me. Then we settle down to remembering.

I tell about school reunions and Sunday School picnics. "And nobody would believe I was old enough to have you."

"Tell me about the chicken," she says.

I give her my recipe, and we talk for hours about whether it's best to pan-fry or broil chicken, although you can't buy nothing but protein steaks and corn drumsticks in the market nowadays.

I hang up when I spot a gov snoop eyeing our condo cube. He goes to all the doors and asks about me.

"We got to go easy on the calls," I say to Radonna the next day.

"Ain't that what I been telling you?" She laughs, as if nothing I do is really wrong. She's got such a sweet way about her.

Twice she comes to see me in the next four weeks.

Leaving home before dawn, she threads her way past the blocked off sector, climbs to Fifth and down the hill. I spot her and get out the photos and the sweet tastes I been hoarding, and we gobble that food and spit out those memories in the hour before she has to leave.

When she's preggers again it's impossible for her to make the trip, and Paradise only knows, I'm too old. We make new picnic plans.

"I'll go to First," Radonna says. She's been timing it. There's a lull about two-fifteen when most people are at work. Three days in a row she counted thirty seconds without ground tran passing the corner. "At least we can see one another," she says.

That's how it started. For weeks we waved and shouted. She and her childer on one side and me and sometimes mine on the other. But it was like it was only Radonna and me.

"Picnic," I'd shout.

"Ants," she'd say, and we'd laugh.

And we'd stand there until we both felt better.

Today as we shout encouragement, I count to eighty without a car coming by. Maybe there's an accident up near Main slowing the racers down. The swish and roar is softened, and there are long gaps between four- and eight-wheelers passing First.

Suddenly, Radonna yells, "Ma, I'm coming," and she begins to run.

Such a fine looking woman, hardly bent, even though she lugs two childer and carries one in her belly. Her eyes are flashing, I can tell, even though I can't see them. None of them washed out eyes like the rest. Oh, she is fine. I tell her to hurry.

"It's gonna be all right," she says and points as if to say, see, I'm half way there already.

I feel tears smart my eyes, and I hold out my arms in a way I ain't held them out since she was little.

"Oh, Mum," she says, and she pauses a second and shakes her head in amazement, a smile lighting up her face so that I see color everywhere. It is warm and loving and beautiful and kind. I step from the curb. I can hear the traffic's roar now, but it don't matter. I see picnic days so fine there's no repeating them. White cloths and crystals and champagne bubbling in a never-ending river. I hold out my arms again, and Radonna rushes into them, and the light shines everywhere. It touches her face with glory before it blazes one last time.

I ain't never had such a fine picnic ever. Then I hear someone say, "She's gonna live," and I close my eyes tight.

NET SONGS

Elaine Bergstrom

"You have IF-4. Your blood analysis allows you two days . . ." The doctor paused to read my name off the terminal screen. ". . . Allison. You have that long to get your will in order."

"Will? Listen, you son of a bitch, this has to be the dumbest mistake a machine has ever made."

"You must have arrived with some symptoms." He actually sounded hopeful. So much for the promise of socialized medicine.

My hand shook as I held the computer card against the isolation glass. I always shake when I'm angry and I was in full rage now because a half hour before I'd been lying on an examining table with my bare legs spread and he'd been feeling me up. Did he really think he was going to catch something if he spent five more minutes in the same room with me? Hell no! He just wanted me scared. "I got this in the mail," I told him. "It said I should come in for a physical . . . I figured so what if it's early, it's free."

"There must have been some reason for Med Central to send it, Allison. Your lifestyle perhaps?"

I caught my reflection in a mirror. The overhead light shone through my lacquered bangs throwing warpaint shadows on my cheeks. Fitting for the sneered lie, "I despise men."

I thought that would get a rise out of him but Doc didn't even blink. "Women?" he asked.

If my life weren't at stake, I might have laughed. "Vow Certified, turkey. Check with Legal. The last review was two days ago. Virginity . . . front, rear, and mouth . . . noted."

While we waited for Legal to respond, Doc's eyes rested on everything but me. Last man who acted like this tried to mug me but Doc was probably jumpy. After all, I'd hit him with the best ammo a sweet young thing can have. Every two weeks a team of polygraph experts drug me, wire me, and ask questions that would turn a sex therapist the color of boiled rock shrimp. And I pass. Twenty-two and intact.

The data clicked in and Doc punched a few more buttons. "You came into contact with someone who had visible symptoms, Allison," he finally said. "We haven't made a mistake."

Neither had I and I'd spotted a liar through two inches of safety glass. Besides, if there were danger of an epidemic, I'd be the first to know. I tried to look miserable. Given the circumstances, it was easy. He dropped a card through a narrow slot in the partition. "Report to this address on the 21st. In the meantime, don't break your vow. See my nurse on your way out for your prescription."

"Pills?"

"Mood elevators. Most victims find them beneficial. Should you experience any of the following . . ."

By the time he'd finished the printed warning, huge tears were rolling down my cheeks. I slouched out of his office with what looked like resignation, my legs rubbery from the certainty that, if I didn't act the part of victim to perfection, he'd never let me leave.

I went home and told Evie I might be dying of the world's most lethal disease. Nine out of ten people would find a way to say bye and not politely, but Evie only stretched, the thorough stretch of a cat getting ready to head out on a warm spring night. "Bull . . . shit," she said and gave me a long friendly hug. I reminded myself this was Evie and tried not to stiffen. To tell the truth, if we weren't both VC I might have . . . well, I rewarded her confidence with Doc's pills instead. Evie likes El's and she'd been dry for a while.

Within an hour her pretty eyes were contemplating the bottom of the toilet bowl we only thought of cleaning when our faces were in it. She looked up at me, kohl and mascara darkening her frightened tears. "Remember how you were coughing last week? Now look at me. These are symptoms, aren't they? Maybe we're both . . ."

"I had a cold. I got better. I'm fine!" Even so, I grabbed Doc's prescription and ran to the chemist.

I won't mention his name except to say he's the only dealer I know mixing his own drugs and they're worth the price. I told him about the crazy diagnosis and he waved me to a far corner while he ran some tests on my pills. "Sweet Buns," he said when he'd finished because he knows the nickname pisses me off, "Sweet Buns, what did you do to that doctor to make him want to kill you?"

I looked down at the bottle in my hand. "With these?"

"Nah, but if you'd took one instead of Evie, where would you be headed now?"

The ovens! Oh shit, I'd be heading for the ovens!

Now I may be a foul-mouthed bitch dressed to camouflage in the nearest dumpster. My lifestyle is usually illegal . . . the razors I have strapped to my thighs certainly are . . . but I wouldn't be Vow Certified if I didn't have dough. I'm on a trust fund dole now but I inherit plenty if I stay VC until marriage then pick a male with the same vows. After the wedding, it's monogamy and babies and if the kids are lucky they'll live to claim their pieces of my parents' pie. Damned dull future but I understand my folks' concern. Pop had a fling when I was 14, passed the results on to Mom. They died within days of one another but not before they made plans for me.

Not that they needed to. After all, sex is a pretty easy itch to scratch on your own and it's suicide to sleep around.

There's four strains of untreatable gonn, two of syph, and a C-lam that would make me sterile in a week. AIDS is still with us, too; but about the time health departments were drafting rules for enforced isolation, the virus glitched into something less serious than mono. I'm too young to remember the rejoicing but Mom told me that the summer of 1995 was marked by sexual heights—and depths—not seen before or since.

Then came IF-4 and the end of promiscuity . . . as well as heavy petting, kissing, all other manners of oral perversity and, when the risks are high, hugs and handshakes. I avoid crowded elevators myself; no reason not to play it safe.

I don't know what happened to 1, 2, and 3, but Netnews says IF-4 started in Russia fifteen years ago when some limp flu bug got spiderpowered in the second round of Chernobyl fallout. Anti-nuke garbage maybe but what's really bending is the disease is a lot like exposure to heavy radiation . . . nausea, bloody shits, collapse of main organs, quick and horrible death.

And it spreads. First sexually like common VD but symptoms show in a matter of weeks and soon the virus passes with any contact. Every time there's danger of a plague, I report to the VC center in La Pas to ride it out while the non-C families seal their doors and windows with the latest fad in "total protection" and pray the bug didn't ride home with them.

You can blame the Hospice Program for that big disaster two years back. Since doctors refused to approach the dying, new victims were ordered to tend them. The program ended like anyone with a gram of common sense would have expected . . . break-outs, panic, and eight thousand stiffs in New York alone. Now we have the ovens. Quick, humane, painless . . . that's what Netnews calls them but I've heard rumors the Meds don't wait to see the symptoms. Exaggeration? Probably, but I sure as hell didn't want to risk my hide to find out.

I had 45 hours left before I became the star of every TV channel, every security screen in every country in the world. I could hide, change my haircolor, or dye my skin but the net has my voice prints. Any time I make a phone call, talk too close to a security sensor, or try to get money from a voice response teller, I'll set off an alarm. Then if the police don't get me the mob will.

All I could do was clear my file fast. I went to see my lawyer.

I sat in his office looking like I do for VC grillings: feminine tones of blue and coral and strippy sandals over white nyloned feet. A simple swept-back hairdo. A dot of Classic Joy behind each ear. Allison Wonderland Harper, strangling the damp hankie in her hand.

I gave him my VC card and told him everything. He said something reassuring and went to his terminal, punching buttons furiously until he halted and began responding to system input. When I walked around his desk to see what was coming down, he backed off, his expression 200-proof fear.

—.. infected, dangerous, antisocial ..— the screen read.

"You believe this? THIS!" I screamed. His hand inched towards an office intercom. I kicked, one of the cute mid heels on my sandals connecting with the soft spot on his temple. Antisocial? When my life's at stake, you bet!

I used his phone to call Evie. "Come with the car," I whispered. "I'll meet you at . . ."

Something caught my eye. My own words were appearing on the computer screen. The office sensors blinked twice then began to screech. I wedged a chair underneath the doorknob and left by the fire escape. Keeping to empty streets, I walked back to the doctor's, hoping his files would give me some clue about what was going on.

Though it was after six, Doc's door was unlocked and he sat in his private office talking on the phone. I picked up the nurse's extension and listened in.

". . . doing the best I can," the voice on the other end whined. "They won't listen. They don't care."

"Four this month, Maxwell. Four just from me. And this last one is VC. She knows we lied. Even with those pills, she may not show."

"Then maybe it's over for all of us. I sometimes think that would be just as well."

They lied! They LIED! THEY LIED! I swallowed all my cheers of relief, hid until the doctor left then pressed his phone's redial button.

"Med Central," the man named Maxwell said.

I hung up without a word and flipped through Doc's files. Nothing but bills and receipts. My records must be on his machine and I didn't dare try to claim them.

I was outside trying to think of my next move when the public alarm sounded.

I hadn't heard it but I knew. All around me people who wouldn't say good morning to one another were buzzing around Netnews terminals. I got close enough to a screen to see my own face staring back at me. Damn the Net! Damn it! I wasn't even getting my two days. I could feel the panic around me and I found myself looking down at hands and feet, trying to act like it wasn't me they hunted. For the second time in my life, I prayed as I picked my way slowly through the crowd and into one of those skin houses that dotted New York like some hot new hamburger chain. Sensors carpeted the house ceiling but I could wait out the hours until dark if I kept my mouth shut.

I plunked down a twenty, grabbed a paper sheet from the ticket taker, and pushed my way past the couples

lined up at concessions, purchasing everything from Milk
Duds to the latest fad in disposable vibrators. Inside, I
chose a double's seat because it was closest to the emergency exit but before I could figure out how to raise the
privacy shades a man walked over from the center aisle.
"Are you alone?" he asked nervously.

Luck was screwing me . . . and brother, after what I'd
been going through it felt like heaven! No one would
suspect me now; after all who in their right mind would
spend time with Allison Harper? I nodded and pointed to
the spot beside mine. As our seats reclined, the transparent skin rose between us, distorting the gratitude I saw on
his face.

The movie began to roll. It had a contemporary plot
and the latest big names but when the time for the sex
scenes came, the actors were perfectly positioned for the
cut to X-rated footage shot before I was born. Studios had
bought porn rights for millions because they knew what
the public wanted and today's actors wouldn't provide it
even if the penalty weren't blacklisting and six-figure
fines. After what IF-4 did to Hollywood who can blame
them?

Though I prefer old romances to outright smut, I had
to give this flick four stars. In spite of my fugitive status, I
started to heat.

So had my new best friend. He'd undone the buttons
on his shirt, unclasped his belt and slid closer to me.
When he reached through the skin, it yielded like a soap
bubble. His finger brushed my lips and I felt the rough
edge of its nail, the thick callous on its side smoothed only
slightly by the thin protective membrane. I thought of the
gloves Doc had worn this afternoon and refused to let it
turn me off.

I could have come here any time without changing
my status but books and videos had been enough. Not
now. I might die within hours and I wanted to feel a real
man, wanted to see a real man, not stare at some air-
brushed picture and fantasize some too-perfect hands

and lips and prick. I touched the band of his white cotton shorts and he slipped them off. To keep myself occupied, I did the same with my underwear.

When I looked I was disappointed. His penis was so small, so soft, and his legs were too hairy. No muscles on him; I was probably stronger but I reminded myself I'm nobody's fantasy either. Above us, the lean, perfect actors were tangled together, screwing with impossible enthusiasm. In disgust I raised the front shade to block out the picture.

And touched him . . . no, almost touched him because though I could feel even the fine hairs on his stomach there was this horrible barrier between us. Sex here was worse than celibacy; worse than anything I had ever imagined. If I hadn't thought there was some way I could escape the death Med Central planned for me, I would have taken my razor, cut the skin, and crawled through to him . . . or anyone, anyone at all. For the first time, I understood why I had never gone to a skin house before.

He brushed away the tears falling off the bridge of my nose and I saw he'd been crying as well. "I'm sorry," he whispered. "You looked so much like Whitney I wanted to try. I can't. I'm sorry . . ." He held up his hand, the platinum wedding ring reflecting the dim yellow light. "She died ten weeks ago. I wasn't even able to say goodbye."

We got into our clothes without looking at one another. But when the skin was down and the shades lowered, I took a chance and put my mouth close to his ear to whisper, "I wish she were still with you. I really do."

Even that soft sound was enough. The alarm shrieked, a beam of light struck my face. "Allison Harper?" The man mouthed the word. I couldn't look at him, couldn't bear to see his recoil and hate. I broke his grip on my wrist and ran.

The thunder of feet, of shouts, of curses rolled after

me. I fled into a narrow alley and saw a rusty Volvo pull up and block the far end. As I scanned for another way out, I stumbled and the mob caught me, spinning me around, ripping at my clothes. I pulled out a razor and cut my arm, waving the bloodstained blade at them, forcing them back. "My blood. MY blood. The first one of you who gets too close gets cut and you're dead the same as me."

I backed up slowly, hoping my knees would hold me if I had a chance to bolt, and hit the open door of the Volvo. Someone must have pulled me inside and drove away but I didn't remember anything until my eyes focused on the cracked windshield, then on my friend from the skin house.

"Why'd you play hero?" I asked.

"Why did you run?" When I didn't answer, he shrugged and went on, "I'm Jeffrey Chapman. Ten weeks ago my wife died of IF-4."

"And now you're suicidal?"

He watched only the traffic as he continued. "I was in France on business. We were both VC and more than careful so I didn't bother to keep in touch. Whitney tried to reach me but I'd taken some time off to see the sights. IF-4 and she went to the ovens alone." He wiped his eyes with the back of his hand. Bogie he wasn't though he'd sure shown balls when he'd dragged me away from the mob. "I'll drive you to Med Central," he said, "I'll stay with you until the end."

"The hell you will!" I explained my status, then told him everything that had happened to me. He didn't believe me, so I asked, "Your precious Whitney, the girl who was more than careful, who poked her while you were gone?"

He looked like he wasn't sure he should be mad. Then he exploded. "Nobody. So you just shut . . ."

"Then think, come on, think! Has Netnews even whispered plague in the last two months?"

When he finally answered, he sounded like he'd known the truth all along. "They killed her, didn't they?"

"I heard Doc say I was the fourth one this month just from him. THIS MONTH!" My voice rose, furious at all the dumb slobs like Whitney who'd never questioned the verdict.

"Where will we go?" I asked after I calmed down.

"My apartment." I began to object but he cut in, "This is a borrowed car and the owner's out of town. We have time and you shouldn't be seen on the streets like this." He ran a finger down the tear in my sleeve and I slapped his hand away. Jeff looked confused. "I was only . . ."

"Listen, just listen!" I pointed my thumb in the general direction of the skin house. "I was hiding; that's all. I won't ask what you were doing there."

He smiled sadly . . . and I've got to admit my scrawny savior had a damn pretty smile. "Whitney and I spent a lot of time there before we were married. By our wedding night, we knew one another real well."

I wondered if they'd used rubbers on their honeymoon for that old familiar feel. I decided not to ask.

Jeff had a hot tub in his bathroom. I tried to relax in the foamy water while Jeff brought me chamomile tea laced with peach schnapps and a thick terry robe. I slipped it on and padded into the bedroom.

A change of clothes lay on the bed . . . a classic denim skirt, a red flannel shirt and a scarf to cover my hair. I dressed, then stretched out and looked at the photo on the nightstand. Whitney, in a similar sporty outfit, smirked back. I pictured Jeff bringing her flowers . . . the two of them drinking champagne in bed, curled up close with love, real love, in their eyes. "Oh, you bitch," I whispered in envy, "you had it all even if it was for just a little while."

I closed my eyes. When I woke, the bedroom door was swinging open. My hand dropped to the strap on my thigh but it was only Jeff with a printout in his hand. "Know the enemy," he said and passed it to me.

102

Nothing had ever seemed as ugly as the figures on that sheet. IF-4 New York deaths had fallen to less than four per month by the end of last year then in March a sudden jump to 14. April, May and June had 16 each. And not even rumors of plague!

"Med records are sealed," I said suspiciously.

"I collect data for Netnews. I plugged in my presscard and requested this." He went to the bar and poured us each a drink, saying more to himself than to me, "Did you know we use the same sensors as security? Any computer files are fair game. Freest data access in the world and I never even thought to check it. Christ, was I a fool."

I stared at the figures, his grief making me remember how my parents had waited for the end in the isolation room. They'd asked me not to come but I showed up anyway; some twisted fascination forcing me to watch them die. I never knew what I'd expected—maybe love or at least forgiveness—but I saw only pain and, later, the hate when they looked at one another. They'd been so trapped by it, they never thought to tell me goodbye. I tried to never think about it but now the whole scene came back like it had happened yesterday. I swallowed hard, hoping Jeff hadn't noticed my weakness.

But he had. He thrust a drink into my hand and said, "There's more." I turned the page and scanned the data on the victims, then gulped down the brandy. It tasted strong and oddly bitter, a perfect chaser for my rage.

"Twenty! Twenty goddamn doctors referred all these patients!"

"I don't think all of them are doctors, Allison."

"What?" I studied the sheet. Sixteen had referred one or two patients. Four had referred twelve or more.

"I tried to pull the four's biosheets. They have no backgrounds, Allison. As far as the Net goes, they don't exist."

My own doctor was one of them. It must have been the thoroughness of the morning exam that made me flush. "World figures . . . are they . . .?" I had trouble turning words into a question.

"About the same patient to doctor ratio as here. I don't think there's anywhere you can hide." He glanced out his window, then added, "I'm sorry we don't have more time. If we're separated and you're able, try to make them talk."

My cheeks were getting redder and the blood pulsed through my ears. I could hardly hear the pounding at the door or feel Jeff unbuttoning my blouse, pulling me close and kissing me. The room filled with faceless goons in white uniforms, gloved hands pulled Jeff away from me and I couldn't raise my arms to fight. As my eyes closed, I heard someone, a man, growling, "Christ! First he calls and says she's here. Then he drugs her and tries to fuck her. Take the crazy bastard in and let him die with her."

I woke alone, strapped to a metal table in a med isolation room. There were no pictures, nothing to break the loneliness of the white tile walls except a window of one-way observation glass and two doors. The exit was closed, the oven door open and waiting. An IV bottle hung above me, its saline solution dripping slowly into my arm. Attached to its tube was the narrow vial of bright blue poison. When symptoms showed, the vial would open, the liquid would fall and I would be dead before the table rolled into the oven.

But there would be no symptoms! I choked back a scream of unfamiliar terror, tested the strength of the leather straps and felt the cold handle of the razor against my thigh. The goons hadn't searched me!

I called for help, then begged someone to tell me why I was here. When nobody replied, I took a chance and began inching up my skirt. By straining on the straps, I was able to reach the razor, twist it around and free my wrist. I would have sliced the other straps as well but I heard a mic switch on.

104

I lay still recalling for an instant that this agnostic was petitioning the Almighty a hell of a lot today. A man said my name and I scorched my own ears with a reply.

When I stopped for air, he went on. "We are sorry you have seen part of the truth, Allison Harper. It would have been easier for you if you hadn't."

A sensor above me began to blink. I decided it was busted and tried to ignore it. "I was a mistake, wasn't I?"

"An error was made, yes. Your VC status was missing from our files. Otherwise you are a perfect candidate."

"Listen, I wouldn't be a slut even if . . ."

"Perhaps. But no one would have stayed with you. No one stays with any we choose."

"I'm not the first mistake, am I?"

"If you are referring to Whitney Chapman, her husband had left her. When she wired him about the diagnosis, as we expected, he did not come. Now he has sheltered you and you have infected him. It will be a sad but well-published story when he dies."

So much for Whitney's torrid romance. Though I had every reason to wish it were Jeff on this table instead of me, I actually pitied that guilty son of a bitch. After all, I was getting about what I expected . . . but him? Well, if I had the time, I might have tried to figure out what he'd thought he'd gain by turning me in. Instead I worked on the bigger puzzle and the answer hit me fast and hard. "Was there ever an IF-4?" When he didn't say anything, I remembered Jeff's final words to me and added, "Come on, I'm not going anywhere. At least tell me what I'm dying for."

He hesitated, then began to speak, his words coming faster and faster as if he'd wanted to spit out the truth for a long, long time. "There was an IF-4 and in the last decade it killed over a half million people. To find a vaccine, we had to study the virus. It could not be cultured nor transmitted to animals. It did not live more than an instant after the infected died. We, therefore, observed IF-4 in those who had run or who had come here alone.

105

We restrained them, hooked them to monitors and took blood and tissue readings until they expired. Our success was incredible and we were ready to announce both vaccine and treatment when we determined how disastrous the consequences of that announcement would be.

"We would even have discarded our findings had it not been for the danger of unchecked plague. So instead our drugs were included in every medication Med Central dispensed. Though we intended to control the virus, not destroy it, there have been no reported cases for months. IF-4 is gone but the fear remains.

"And we thrive on this fear. In this city alone, rapes have fallen 82%, physical assaults are down 56%. The divorce rate is now 4% and only 2 out of every 100 births are illegitimate. The birth rate itself has fallen 20%, saving the globe from almost certain disaster. If our projections are correct, in 10 years worldwide prosperity will . . ."

Not only was the man justifying murder—MY murder—with statistics but he didn't hang his feet in the real world at all. A rape is nothing compared to the social suicide that comes with reporting it. As for purity, I could take this maniac to half a dozen safe houses where blood samples are taken from the johns in the waiting room and the girls they poke have tracks on their arms to justify someone else's addiction. And if this city is so peaceful, why did I carry the weapon I gripped so tightly now?

But it's useless to argue with a schizoid so I considered my few possible exits until I heard him saying, ". . . just weeks, we'll be able to release an altered IF virus. Victims will die far more painfully but there will be a longer incubation and more marked initial symptoms. Before the disease becomes virulent, victims will be forced to seek help. There will be few plagues, no need for a cure."

It didn't take brains to read between his lines! As long as there's any risk of plague, there'll be the VC program, the skin houses, the home and portable filtration systems and all the other dubious preventative devices that have already turned buck-heavy neurotics into condoms with feet.

Though the body count will go down, public fear will rise. After all, victims will suffer in their homes and hotel rooms and in alleys and street corners and we can read about their agony on Netnews screens and catch face-to-face interviews during the TV family hour! One thing was certain: the bastards who'd dreamed up this scheme wouldn't be the ones to fry. "Who ordered this!" I bellowed. "Just tell me their names so I can make sure there's a place reserved for them in the seediest part of hell!"

No answer. The mic switched off. The table started to roll and the poison slowly fell through the tube. Not giving a damn who saw me now, I hacked away at the straps. At the last possible moment, I yanked the IV, rolled free of the table and, gripping both razors, I faced the door, ready as I'd ever be for their next move.

But when the door banged open it was Jeff who rushed me, dragging me into the oven and slamming it shut behind us. I pulled and pushed on it, unable to force the automatic lock. There was no exit, not anymore. I went from furious to freaked in half an eyeblink, turned back to Jeff and croaked, "Why?"

"Because we didn't have a chance out there. Look around you and try to understand."

I looked. We were in a glass cube, protected sensors patterning all six sides. The onyx mirrors behind them multiplied their twinkling lights into the infinite straight lines of an accountant's universe. "It's a machine, Jeff," I said in a whisper approaching hysterical. "You trapped us in the guts of a goddamn machine!"

Jeff swayed and, for the first time, I saw the blood dripping from the deep slash I'd made on his shoulder. He held his presscard close to a sensor and recited a series of numbers. At the end, he had to force the words, "Emergency security. Override local commands. Begin taped broadcast."

107

"Affirmed," the Net replied in its polite interested tone.

I dropped my bloody knife, wrapped an arm around Jeff and stared up at the sensors. "Taped?" I asked.

Jeff might have been pale, but he was still able to dredge up that smile. "I submitted the whole story while you were asleep. Netnews is running the figures now. I thought they'd put us together but it looks like you didn't need any help breaking loose. Did they record you while you were in the outer room?"

"The sensor sure had its eye on me."

"Good. Netnews will run that tape after my story. Then it will plug into the Med Central system and cut to us. We have about 15 minutes before Med Central can override the computer controls and stop us. I guess this is your speech. Better make it a good one." He slumped against me and I lowered him carefully to the floor.

Outside I could hear people pounding, their attempts to open the seal no more effective than mine had been. "At least nobody can get in," I said.

"The door might have to open when Med switches to manual controls. Be ready."

Though I wouldn't bet good money on our escape, I did begin to slide Jeff closer to the door. "Broadcast," the Net ordered and when I didn't bark on cue it repeated the command.

I didn't think about where my voice was going, only that this was my chance . . . my only chance to expose the madness that still infected the world. I began by giving my status and Med Central's address. Then, picturing the rabble that might be coming to save me, I recited all the justifications the goon had used and finished with the news of the altered IF-4.

Afterwards, I tried to say something else, stammered with delayed stage fright and fell silent. But I hadn't said enough; I hadn't hit the truth. I looked around me and thought of my parents and of Whitney and of all the victims of the lies, all those who had died bitter and frightened and alone. I started to shake and when I could finally speak, I aimed for the heart.

"What about love," I screamed. "Where will love be in their pure panicked world. Look at me. I'm obsessed with sex like an addict without his next fix but how can I love anyone when I can't even touch him, when he might die from a one-night stand or a plague or because Med Central decides to kill him!" I stood and raised my fists to the sensors. "Before IF-4 the world had something precious and Central planners want to keep it from us. Damn them! Damn every one of them!"

One hell of a speech but I might never know if anyone had been moved by it. The room went dark and I heard only Jeff's forced whisper, "Want a job, Allison Harper?"

"Ask me tomorrow." I sat beside him and waited for the door to open. But Jeff must have been wrong because the walls began to glow. Sparks patterned the ceiling, bouncing from edge to edge like ripples on water. The heat began to rise and the ozone reeked heavy in the thinning air making me dizzy and sick. But when I heard the lock click open, the adrenaline hit me like I'd shot it up. I jumped over Jeff and pushed the door out.

I sent one goon tumbling but the others were ready for me. A stun dart hit my side and I folded slowly forward with the edges of my sight spiraling in. Jeff called my name. I tried to reach for his hand but the door shut, trapping him inside. There was a roar, a scream cut off as quickly as it began, then silence . . .

When I opened my eyes, I saw my hand soaking in a puddle of blood. More painted the isolation walls and seeped from the bodies surrounding me. Though I have a strong stomach, I gagged when I saw what had been done to them.

The oven door was open, the oven empty except for the wedding band the fires had not claimed. I slipped it on and walked slowly down the long hall towards the exit. Doors hung open on either side of me, but nothing moved in the labs and offices except the smoke rising from smoldering piles that had been papers and machines and chemicals and men. Rage—not frustration or fear—had fueled the world for far too many years and it had supplied the perfect finale to the 15-year Reign of Terror of IF the Fourth.

One nightmare was over. Another had just begun.

On the early morning streets, crowds milled around the newscreens reading the morning headlines and feeding in quarters to get the facts. VACCINE! VACCINE!

A daring pair shared an ice cream cone, then a long passionate kiss at a bus stop. Their example was contagious as the old plague, and soon couples and groups began disappearing into apartments, hotels, and skin houses. I turned a corner and skirted a crowd gathered around a pair who had decided to seize the moment and one another and go full at it in the middle of 56th Street.

Someone reached for me and I cringed with the face of the lonely man in the skin house forming beneath the tears in my eyes. I thought of the past, then of the future as I had always dreamed it could be. Looking straight ahead, I headed home to where Evie might still be waiting for me.

SHARK-KILLER

Carol Severance

Iuti squatted motionless near the edge of the reef flat, her still body washed time after time by the wave's ceaseless action. Her golden brown skin and the faded skirt and long-sleeved man's tunic she wore for warmth against the evening chill blended perfectly with the tumble of coral stones and boulders.

Only her eyes moved as she searched the incoming swells.

"Come to me, brothers," she chanted softly. "Come fill my nets before I turn to a cold stone here in the sea." She did not use a true beckoning spell—she dared not with Pahulu lurking nearby—she only said the words in time with the shifting waves.

Flickering color caught Iuti's attention, and she shifted her gaze to follow the erratic paths of two blue-green parrot fish. They began feeding on the living coral, and Iuti watched patiently while they darted here and there among the colorful growths, turning and drifting together through the clear water as if they were one.

The parrot fish turned away from the reef, and abruptly, Iuti dashed forward. She leapt a gap in the coral and scooped the startled fish into her hand nets. As quickly as one touched and tangled itself in the left net, the other did the same in the right. Struggling for footing in the wave's strong backwash, Iuti lifted each of the fish to her mouth, biting them just behind their eyes. It killed them instantly and removed them forever from Pahulu's power.

It was a game these two played, the island sorceress and the mainland warrior: one forever lurking in the background, the other meticulously avoiding all use of the magic that would give the sorceress entry to her soul. Pahulu's sorcery was particularly powerful in and around the sea, Iuti knew. The sorceress could send her soul into the living fish and other sea life, binding them to her will and enchanting them so that their flesh would cause terrible nightmares, even death for any who ate it.

Iuti glanced back toward the beach as she disentangled the fish from her nets. She knew the sorceress was there somewhere, hiding in the shadows, waiting for the chance that Iuti might break her resolve never to use magic on this isle. Iuti wondered if the islanders knew that their healer gained her power by draining it from other living creatures, if that was why so little magic was in evidence here. She stuffed the fish into her woven waist pouch and wiped the slickness from her hands.

Casually scanning the reef flat, Iuti saw that the girl, Tarawe, had crept closer while she was busy with the fish. Tarawe was lying prone in the water now, with only her head above the shifting waves, no doubt thinking herself well-hidden. Iuti restrained a smile; her unacknowledged apprentice was getting better.

Iuti supposed she would have to do something about Tarawe soon. Send her away. Make her angry or afraid enough to stop her spying before the others, especially Pahulu, decided to take notice. It was too bad, for the teenager showed great promise and was obviously interested in learning. Often, Iuti came upon her practicing some technique learned only from distant watching.

A change in the air brought Iuti's full attention back to the sea. The rhythm of the waves had not changed. Nor had the wind, but something was oddly different. She listened carefully above the rumbling surf, wishing she could call on Mano's power to amplify the sounds. She had lived so long under her totem's protection that at times she distrusted her own natural senses.

Iuti grew taut as she recognized the soft splash of canoe paddles and the barely audible cadence of a whispered war chant. Quickly, she sank down again and turned her look toward the open sea.

No islander would be outside the lagoon at this hour. It was near dark, the sun had almost set. Iuti had only stayed on the reef this long to teach Tarawe a lesson—and to irritate Pahulu. She hoped the girl, at least, would have sense enough to remain hidden.

The chanting drifted off with the wind for a moment, then returned, just loud enough for Iuti to follow the beat. Through squinted eyes she made out a shadow on the water, then the wavering silhouette of an outrigger paddling canoe bearing steadily toward the island. As it reached the breaking waves, the steersman dug his paddle deep into the sea, turning the canoe parallel to the reef's edge. The chant changed. The beat became stronger, the voices deeper so that the sound carried clear and clean through the night air.

"Mano, protect the girl," Iuti whispered softly. She did not ask the shark's safety for herself—she no longer held that right—but dread crept like mainland cold across her back. The chant was a ghost song, sung only by crews of the dead. She could see now that the canoe carried only seven paddlers. The place before the steersman was empty.

The canoe moved steadily closer. It would pass just yards away from where Iuti hid. She braced herself as best she could against the surge, and breathed sporadically between the sweep of the deepening waves. The tide was reclaiming the reef, so she would have to move soon or risk drowning.

The sudden thought that the canoe might have come

for her made Iuti shiver, gave her a taste of brine through inadvertently parted lips. The great warrior Ser Iuti Mano, one of the Teronin War's bloodiest survivors, dead with a sackful of fish on her back. There was a joke to test the gods. She sucked in a slow, deep breath, tucked her chin to her chest, and slid beneath the water while the canoe glided past.

As soon as she dared, Iuti lifted her head again. There was something familiar about the canoe, though it seemd to be made in the island style. Wood thunked on wood and a muffled curse reached Iuti's ears, causing her to choke in surprise. She dropped quickly underwater again, holding what little breath she had left until it could be held no more.

This was no ghost canoe! Not unless dead men now cursed in the gutter tongue of Teron. Iuti shifted and peered again through the near darkness. Knowing now what to look for, she recognized the slightly higher prow and extended outrigger of a Teronin war canoe, It had been altered to appear island-made from a distance, and certainly the death chant was real enough, sung in the island's own dialect. But the men aboard, she would wager, were as alive and warrior-wise as she. Iuti remained as still as the growing coral until the canoe had completed its passage along the windward reef.

As soon as the canoe was gone, Iuti slipped back across the reef flat. She startled Tarawe from her hiding place and urged the soaking, shivering girl back to the village. Pahulu was already there, talking excitedly to the gathered islanders.

"The only lives that vessel seeks are those too foolish to prepare a defense," Iuti told them all when Pahulu insisted the ghost canoe was real. "It's an old Teronin trick. They use some local superstition to frighten their intended victims into huddling together unarmed. Then they attack when you are most vulnerable. If you insist upon hiding in your homes to avoid a nonexistent ghost canoe, Teronin warriors will walk ashore unchallenged two nights from now. They will slaughter you in your own homes."

"We have no quarrel with the Teronin," Tarawe's uncle said. He was chief of the leading clan, and he spoke for all the others. "These islands are neutral territory, more valuable left alone than destroyed by roving warriors. We pay regular tribute to the Teronin to leave us in peace." Iuti wondered, not for the first time, what these small islands had to offer that kept the Teronin away. Perhaps it was only their isolation and their seeming poverty that provided their protection.

"No, warrior, it was a true ghost canoe that came tonight," Tarawe's uncle went on. "Pahulu saw it from shore. We all heard the chant right here in the village."

"But Pahulu was far up on the beach," Iuti said. "I was at the reef's edge, so close I could have reached out and touched the canoe." She explained again about the shape of the vessel, repeated the whispered war chant she'd heard, and the Teronin curse. She implored them to aid her in preparing for the island's defense.

But they would have none of it.

"Go back to your hut," Pahulu said, "before your foreign ways and tales of bloodshed corrupt our children." Her black teeth glistened and her eyes flashed triumph. Iuti knew she could never convince the others while Pahulu denied her warning.

"You gave your word not to bare your sword on our soil," one of the younger men said.

"Aye, and you killed your own family totem to seal the bargain," another added. "How can you even think of taking up that blade again?" Iuti lifted a hand to her neck, where she had once worn a strand of mano's teeth to signify her shame. She had drawn the great gray shark to her with an ancient family song, then slit his stomach with her fine, metal sword, relinquishing his protection so that she could live for a few short months without further bloodshed. The necklace was gone now, but the feel of the shark's lost strength still burned against her skin.

"We are not interested in war here," Pahulu said. "Go away and don't speak about it further. We will remain inside at night until the canoe completes its third passage. We will provide no opportunity for untimely accidents, and the ghost canoe will go elsewhere to fill its vacant seat."

Iuti cursed then—the islanders for their stubbornness, Pahulu for her duplicity, and herself for having so foolishly accepted the conditions of these people's peace. She was enraged by the casual reference to her disgrace. She dumped her pouch of fish at Tarawe's uncle's feet and stalked off, taking little satisfaction from the envious comments concerning the size and quality of her catch.

"Fools," she muttered.

"Shark-killer," she heard one of the women reply.

She pointedly ignored Tarawe, who had entered the canoe house and was measuring the height of the largest canoe's prow.

The girl came to her early the next morning. She sat cross-legged just outside Iuti's small cookhouse, watching in silence while Iuti moved the boiled breadfruit from the kettle to the wooden pounding board. Iuti slammed the heavy *po* down onto the mound of softened breadfruit.

"What are you going to do?" Tarawe asked after a time.

Iuti did not look up. "You can see very well what I am doing." The stone pestle crashed again and again into the wooden trough. Had this been an ordinary day, the sounds of similar pounding would have echoed across the island. But the islanders were performing only silent and safe duties today, those which could be done in or near their homes.

"I mean about the Teronin."

The *po* struck with enough force to splatter white breadfruit paste.

"If you keep swinging like that," Tarawe said drily,

"you'll bash yourself right in the head. Then a ghost canoe will come for sure."

Iuti bit back a sharp reply, smiled slightly and lightened her strokes. "I'm not afraid of ghosts," she lied.

"Are you afraid of the Teronin?"

Iuti sighed. "Go away, girl, you know I can't speak to you of the Teronin."

Tarawe leaned her elbows on her knees, chin on crossed hands. "If they're going to kill us all tomorrow night anyway, what does it matter if you talk to me now?"

"It matters because I gave my word not to," Iuti said. She met the girl's frank stare. "I killed my own family's god, gave up my right to his power and his protection, to prove my word was good and gain your elders' permission to live here in peace. Do you think I took that oath lightly?"

Tarawe was the first to glance away. Iuti returned to her pounding.

"My uncle and the others will be eager enough for your sword tomorrow," Tarawe said after a time.

Iuti snorted, wondering why the girl was being so persistent. "Even if I were released from my vow, my sword arm would be of little use after the entire Teronin fleet arrives," she said. "The Teronin don't engage in contests of honor. They won't stride across the reef one by one tomorrow to meet your island champion."

Tarawe's hesitation was very slight. "Then you must meet them tonight," she said, "when they are but a few."

Iuti blinked, glanced around to be sure they were not being overheard. The girl was right, of course, that it no longer mattered, but her word had been given and the habit of caution was strong. She sucked a wad of breadfruit from the side of her hand.

"You could surprise them," Tarawe said, her eyes sparked with sudden excitement. "They won't be expecting you on the reef tonight. You could kill them all before they even knew what was happening."

Iuti took a deep breath and resumed her pounding.

"I'll help you!" Tarawe cried. "I know the reef, and I know how to use a knife."

That brought a laugh. "You know how to slice breadfruit and gut fish, girl."

"I can cut the inner muscle of a giant clam with a single stroke!"

Iuti dropped the *po* and leaned forward. "Have you ever cut through *human* muscle?" she demanded. "Killing a man is not the same as killing a shellfish, girl. It is not so easy, nor can it be done with so little consequence." Tarawe pulled back and Iuti forced herself to speak more calmly.

"When a warrior takes the life of another person, even an enemy, she exposes her own soul to the evil that surrounds all violent deaths. She becomes vulnerable to the darkness, and without careful training and the protection of her family gods, has little defense against it."

"But you're a trained warrior," Tarawe said. "You've fought the Teronin before. You have a real metal sword and a chance against them."

"I have a metal *sword* which I cannot *use*, girl." Iuti lifted the *po*, then began to pound again, striking the breadfruit to the beat of her words. "A sword that I *will* not use even if your elders *ask*." A gob of sticky paste stuck to the pestle and flew off with the next downward stroke. It splatted on the ground near Tarawe.

Tarawe stared at the breadfruit for a moment, then angrily kicked sand over it. "I thought you were different," she said. She jumped up and settled her fists on her hips. "You're even worse than the others! You just sit here and take what comes. They at least had the excuse of being tricked into giving up their strength before the Teronin came. You're still whole and strong, and—"

"What *others?*" Iuti demanded.

Tarawe hesitated again. Then she laughed, her voice became a mocking parody of Pahulu's. "Did you think you were the first to be invited to our island, warrior? Oh no, you're not that special, despite your great reputation. We offer our hospitality to many people—as many as it takes to keep the Teronin recruiting ships filled. They prefer those already trained to war, but they care little for their prior loyalties."

"By the very gods!" Iuti breathed. "The tribute! You buy your freedom by selling human lives!"

"Not lives," Tarawe corrected. "*Souls!* Pahulu strips them of their power while they rest here in 'peace,' and then the elders sell their empty shells to the Teronin."

Iuti stared at her, then down at the pounding board, remembering suddenly those early weeks on the isle, when she had thought her exhaustion and restless, dream-laden sleep were the natural result of her healing wounds and overall weariness. Pahulu had been too eager, however, and Iuti had become suspicious. She discovered that each time she attempted a simple sleep or self-healing spell, each time she sang the fish into her nets instead of simply waiting for them to come near, Pahulu was using the opportunity to drain her strength away.

"A miscalculation," Pahulu had said when Iuti confronted her. "I sought only to test your intentions, to verify that the fish you provide the villagers are not tainted by any mainland sorcery."

"Aye," Iuti had replied, "a miscalculation," and from that day on, she employed only her physical skills. She lived and fished as she had in her childhood before being trained to the ways of power and war. The nightmares ceased and her strength slowly returned. She looked up again at Tarawe.

"Even the most powerful and practiced of warriors must leave the battlefields at times," Iuti said. "The darkness and the blood and the horror all blend into one after many killings or after we have been weakened by injury or exhaustion or simple disgust. The approach to evil becomes irresistible."

"I thought you were different," Tarawe said. Her voice sounded again like that of a young girl. "You resisted

Pahulu from the beginning. That's why I came to warn you, to help you."

"I came here because I was too well known to find any mainland hideaway," Iuti said. "I came here because I was desperate. I accepted your elders' conditions for my stay only because I was too weak and horror-filled to do otherwise. Freedom from evil carries a heavy price, youngster." A shadow, darker than the surrounding shadows, flickered near the edge of the clearing. Iuti straightened.

"Go away, girl," she said very softly. "Go away now, and do not come near me again."

"But —"

"Go!"

Tarawe blinked back tears, then spun and ran off between the trees. The shadow disappeared as Iuti's next stroke split the wooden pounding board in two.

Later, hidden inside her sleeping hut, Iuti opened her private box. The locking spell had not been of her own devising, although it yielded easily enough to her touch, and was thus safe from Pahulu's influence. Iuti tossed her cold weather cloak aside, sneezing at its mustiness. Powdery sprays of mildew blossomed on each of the leather clasps and on her torn mainland boots. Rust lined the edges of her forbidden sword's scabbard and Iuti winced as she pushed it aside.

It pained her to see so ill-kept a weapon, but, even if her oath had not been given, she would not bare that blade again. She had used it to kill mano-niuhi, the great gray shark, protector of her clan and family. It had been the price of her stay on this "neutral" island—that and her honor.

A package lay at the bottom of the box. Iuti untied the coconut twine bindings and folded back the woven wrappings to reveal a heavy, wooden war club. Lifting it in both hands, she carefully inspected the double row of shark's teeth that lined the weapon's jagged edges.

They were mano's own teeth, stolen from his body to earn herself this brief time of peace. Iuti ran her fingers along the glistening, white surfaces, tested their seatings in the firehardened wood and twisted coconut fiber.

"Mano," she whispered. "It is time. Tonight I will take you back to the sea. I claim no right to your protection, but I still owe you vengeance. Tonight we will taste again the blood of our enemies."

She lifted a shield from the box—it, too, was studded with mano's power—and placed it along with the war club atop her sleeping mat. Iuti had honored her pledge to set aside her mainland war tools, but no one had suggested she not create new ones with the island's own resources. They assumed that because there was no metal here, there was no way for her to create replacements. And, Iuti realized now, the islanders had expected her to be helpless under Pahulu's dark influence.

After hiding mano's weapons and setting the box and its other contents out to air, Iuti walked to Tarawe's uncle's house and tried again to explain the danger. Pahulu arrived just behind her and whispered into the chieftain's ear so that he simply frowned and refused to listen to Iuti's warnings. She called him a fool, him and all his people, then did what she had really come to do.

"Keep your niece away from me," she complained. "I'm tired of her following me about the island, watching everything I do. She belongs with the rest of the children." It was cruel to shame the girl so, but this was not a time for a warrior to have an untried teenager at her back. Besides, if Pahulu joined in the battle tonight, as Iuti knew she must, Tarawe was safer locked away with her siblings. The sorceress would not hesitate to kill the girl if she could gain power by doing so.

If by some chance I survive this night, Iuti promised Tarawe silently, I will take you from this place and find you a home among people who pay their debts honestly.

Returning to her own hut, Iuti twisted her long hair into a topknot and donned her faded brown trousers and tunic. She hid the war club and shield within the bulk of her skirts and the bundle of her nets and set off through the jungle.

"So, warrior, you think to defy the gods and fish on the reef despite their clear warning." Pahulu stepped into the path and reached out to touch Iuti's bundle of nets. Iuti stepped back.

"If, indeed, it is a warning as you claim, I am in no danger until tomorrow," Iuti said.

"A ghost canoe rarely departs without filling its empty place," the sorceress replied. "You could be injured on the reef today and die on the morrow." She reached for the nets again. "Perhaps I can offer a small warding spell . . ."

"If you touch my nets again, sorceress," Iuti said without moving, "it will be *you* for whom the ghost canoe comes."

Pahulu smiled tightly and refolded her arms across her chest. Her eyes and her very stance pleaded with Iuti to defy her, to use some small spell to set the battle in motion. Iuti knew that that way led only to death. Her one chance lay in the surprise of her weapons and the arrival of the unsuspecting Teronin. Not even the sorceress would expect her to act tonight. Iuti stepped around the old woman, shivering as the old woman's cackling laughter followed her along the shaded path.

Iuti chose a place on the reef near where she had been the evening before. Squatting in the waist-deep water, she freed herself of the skirt and anchored it along with the war club and shield beneath the waves. Setting her fish spear atop a coral stone, she dismantled the wooden frames of her hand nets and tied the two nets together, testing them with a yank before draping them across one shoulder.

Finally, she pulled a leaf-wrapped packet of dark paste from her waist pouch. The dye had been boiled down months ago from the sac of a giant octopus, and she used it now to draw dark lines along her cheeks. The

122

marks of mano would provide her no magical protection during the coming battle, for even if the shark still acknowledged her, she dared not use his magic while Pahulu was nearby. Still, the Teronin had no way of knowing she had forsaken her totem; the marks might slow them at least for an instant.

As the sun began to set, Iuti listened for the distant beat of the paddlers' chant. Several times she thought she heard it, then realized it was only the waves and the wind. When the faint sound finally came, she was stiff from not moving, growing cold in the late evening air. Shifting carefully, she stretched what muscles she could without revealing herself, and adjusted her height to the rising tide.

The whispered war chant halted sooner than the night before, as if the Teronin were taking more care this time not to be overheard. Iuti fingered her nets. Even though she was waiting for it, she started when the eerie ululation of the death chant began. The sound was like winter ice slicing through her soul.

Something moved to her right, and abruptly Iuti sank down so that only her eyes were above the water line. There was a thud and a startled cry, cut off quickly, then a splash as one of the Teronin toppled from the canoe.

Instantly, the death chant stopped. A shout came from the canoe, then a shrill keening wail from the beach.

"Mano's teeth!" Iuti cursed. The call had been one of question; the wail—Iuti recognized Pahulu's voice—an answering Teronin attack command. The sorceress had given Iuti's position away.

The canoe drifted for a moment, then a frantic, whispered command brought it closer to the reef. Before the Teronin could get near enough to leap directly onto the coral, Iuti jumped up. With a great shout, she slung the fish nets across the front of the canoe. Making use of the incoming surge, she yanked hard, bringing the entangled bowman crashing into the prow and turning the canoe itself into the reef. As the canoe sped toward her, she threw her spear.

Her aim was true, and thanks to endless hours of pounding breadfruit, her arm proved as strong as ever. The thin, wooden spear sliced easily through the neck of the nearest warrior and lodged solidly in the shoulder of the one behind. Two slivers of cold touched Iuti's soul, and she knew that the bowman and the first of the speared warriors were dead.

She felt Pahulu slip a wedge of darkness into the opening the deaths created. Without Mano's protection, Iuti had little defense against the evil cold, yet she dared not call upon the sea god. She could feel the sorceress circling, waiting for the chance to enter fully and take control.

"I'll give myself to the Teronin before I give myself to you, old woman," she muttered.

But Iuti was too well battle-trained to stand quietly while the Teronin killed her. There were only three left, possibly four if one was hiding under the empty seat. She sealed her mind as best she could, and scooped up her club and shield.

"I am mano!" she screamed and flung herself at the two warriors now leaping onto the reef. One man stayed aboard, trying to save the canoe from the waves. Iuti laughed aloud when the others hesitated before shrieking their own battle cries in reply. Even in the growing darkness she read recognition and fear in their eyes. It was clear they had not expected a battle on this night, and certainly not one with a fully armed and aware warrior. It was clear, too, that they now knew who she was.

She warded a blow from the nearest man's sword, twisting her shield as the blade turned so that mano's teeth dug deeply into the Teronin's sword arm. He cried out, stumbled. A wave washed away his footing. Instantly, Iuti brought him down with the war club. Blood from his arm and the back of his crushed skull stained the twilit water black. Warmth swirled at Iuti's ankles while

Pahulu's darkness and images of horror forced a deeper gouge into her consciousness.

The second warrior's blow caught Iuti as she rose, still disoriented by Pahulu's oily thrust. She deliberately collapsed under the blow to lessen its force, but still the warrior's wide metal blade slid across her shoulder like a branch of fire coral. She fell, rolled painfully, and crouched to meet him again. She called on the honest pain in her shoulder, the true pain of ripped skin and torn muscle, forcing it to take precedence over the chaos in her mind. She met the Teronin's second thrust with mano's shield, raking it downward along the man's arm and chest. Then she killed him with a sweeping blow of the mighty war club.

Iuti staggered under Pahulu's immediate attack. Her mind squirmed away from the darkness like an eel tying itself in knots to escape a fisherwoman's hook. Gasping, she slid the back of her hand along her shield's jagged edge and focused on the pain to keep from calling out to mano.

Iuti felt rather than saw movement on the canoe. She spun around, loosening the shield. The canoe had pulled off the coral and was drifting slowly just beyond the line of breaking waves. There were two people on board, facing each other with drawn swords.

Tarawe! Iuti realized with horror that the girl had somehow managed to get aboard the disabled Teronin vessel. *Of course,* she thought, and cursed herself for a fool, *it was Tarawe who downed the first Teronin.* With a fish spear, no doubt, thrown from the edge of the reef. Iuti had seen the girl practice the move often enough. But how had Tarawe escaped her uncle's vigilance and where had she gotten the sword?

The Teronin crept forward, balancing with practiced ease on the bobbing canoe. Tarawe crouched, waiting, sword arm close to her side. Iuti could not throw the shield for fear of hitting the girl. There was a movement behind Tarawe as the man Iuti had speared earlier struggled to pull the wooden spike from his shoulder. He yanked it free just as the other Teronin lunged at Tarawe.

The girl dipped neatly beneath the warrior's sword arm, and Iuti sent her shield sailing, knocking the man with the spear into the sea. Again, ice grabbed at her soul. Another death. Iuti pushed Pahulu back. The last Teronin stumbled as he passed Tarawe, caught himself, then abruptly slumped forward across a blood-soaked hull. Tarawe had killed him, gutted him as smoothly as if he were a tuna.

Tarawe stared at the dead warrior for a moment, then gave a ragged cry and bent to jump into the water. A swift, dark shape slid beneath the drifting vessel.

"Stay in the canoe!" Iuti screamed. Another dark form approached the canoe, and another. Mano had come for the taste of blood.

"Stay in the canoe!" Iuti called again. She could hear the panic in her own voice, see it in Tarawe's stance. Pahulu ripped at her mind's raw edges.

Then abruptly, Pahulu pulled back. The darkness faded, disappeared, the nightmare images ceased. Startled, Iuti turned back toward the beach. Pahulu was standing in knee-deep water and as Iuti watched, she lifted both hands to point at the Teronin canoe. The shrill keening began again and Iuti heard Tarawe cry out, a long shuddering wail.

"No!" Iuti shouted. "Leave the girl alone!" She turned back to see Tarawe drop her sword and clutch her head in both hands. The girl swayed, stumbled, reached again for the side of the canoe. The sharks circled, waiting.

"You may not have the girl!" Iuti shouted across the reef to Pahulu. The sorceress's black teeth shown wet in the twilight, she grinned and Tarawe screamed again.

"The girl killed twice," Pahulu laughed. "She has no warrior's protection. She is mine!"

"No!" Iuti cried. She lifted her own arms and flung a powerful warding spell toward Tarawe. The strength of it knocked Tarawe back against an outrigger strut.

126

"Stay still, Tarawe," Iuti called. Above the rumbling surf, she heard the sorceress shriek with laughter, while in her mind, rotten black teeth grinned in triumph. The nightmare images swarmed back, filling the gap her use of the power had provided. Pahulu's shrill voice lifted again above the waves, and Iuti poured more strength into the warding spell.

Pahulu used her power over the sea creatures then. Small fish thrashed at Iuti's feet, their sharp, poisonous spines raked against her bared skin. Eels and other dark things slid from their holes and sank their teeth into her ankles. Iuti battered them away with the war club, but for every one she killed, a dozen more appeared. The very coral itself burned.

Iuti knew she could not maintain the warding spell around Tarawe and fight off Pahulu at the same time, not without her family god's help, and that was no longer hers to request. Her only chance was to swim to the canoe and paddle both Tarawe and herself beyond Pahulu's power.

Iuti stared at the blood-darkened sea and felt the numbing weakness of true terror. She had swum in this place before. As an honored member of Mano's clan, she had mingled unharmed among the lesser cousins while she conspired to slay the great mano-niuhi, himself. Staring at the blood-darkened water, she knew that no family song or sword, however strong, could protect her from the sharks' vengeance now. The small cousins were already ripping at the Teronin, and mano-niuhi had yet to appear.

The sucking tentacles of an octopus wrapped around her ankle, tugging her against the sweeping waves. She smashed the creature away. The blow struck Pahulu as well; Iuti felt a slight ripple in the sorceress's power. But it did nothing to diminish her attack. And Iuti could not kill all the creatures of the sea.

Iuti glanced again at the canoe, then threw her war club as far as she could into the sea, knowing she could never use it against the sharks. She dove into the next wave and started swimming. Something bumped against her leg. She screamed and sank, choked on foul-tasting brine. Fighting back to the surface, she saw that it was only one of the Teronin, torn almost in half by the sharks. She pushed the ravaged body away and swam on.

Pahulu smashed at her, forcing her deeper in the water. A school of tiny needle fish swarmed around her face, making it impossible to breathe. In desperation, Iuti attempted an attack spell of her own, ripping in the manner of mano at the sorceress's mind. She had a swift taste of acrid bile before Pahulu twisted away and jammed her own wedge of control deeper.

Time and again as Iuti swam and fought and swam again, the racing sharks startled her into choking down yet more of the blood-slimed sea. "Take me quickly," she tried to sing, "before Pahulu sucks my soul dry." Her arms felt like stones, she could barely lift her head high enough to gasp in air.

Suddenly, a great gray shadow appeared beneath her. It rose to her side.

"Mano!" Iuti gasped, then screamed as mano-niuhi bumped against her, sliding like crushed glass along her wounded shoulder. She thanked mano for the pain, focused on the sharp agony to drive away the ebony horrors in her mind. Pahulu's attack receded in the great shark's presence.

Smaller sharks circled, darted close, then dashed away to feed on the Teronin. They returned again and again, churning the water to a bloody froth. Would mano-niuhi take her himself, she wondered, or would the smaller cousins tear away her soul piece by bloody piece?

"Mano," she whispered through frigid, terror-tightened lips. The shark continued to swim beside her, to watch her steadily with one shining eye. "Brother, I stole your strength to gain a few months of peace," Iuti slipped unconsciously into the singsong of an ancient family chant, "but I did not steal your soul. I did not eat your flesh nor share it with others on the land."

"I do not call on your protection now," Iuti sang to

the shark. "But I beg you, take back my family's power now. Take it quickly, before Pahulu wrests it from me and uses it against the girl and later against all others who cross her will."

Tarawe's shout tore Iuti's attention from the shark. She lifted her head, gagged again on foul-tasting water. The Teronin canoe was still beyond her reach. But there was a second canoe floating just beyond it. Iuti thought for a moment that it must be another of Pahulu's illusions, for it flickered and wavered with the movement of the waves. But then she heard the cadence of the death chant and realized a true ghost canoe had come at last. It had one empty place, the other seven were filled with the still flickering images of the dead Teronin.

The last place is mine, Iuti thought in despair, I will spend the rest of eternity paddling empty seas with a crewful of my most hated enemies.

Without warning, mano-niuhi veered away, scraping once again along her side. For an instant, Iuti thought the end had come, that mano would kill her at last. But the great shark merely circled, then swam back toward the reef. As the distance between them grew, Iuti felt Pahulu's crippling attack return. She swallowed brine, coughed, and gagged her way back to the surface.

Tarawe cried out again and pointed.

Pahulu had moved further onto the reef, standing now in water up to her waist, waves washing as high as her shoulders. Her arms were still lifted toward Iuti, and her eyes were squeezed shut. Iuti caught her breath as she recognized the phalanx of dark forms streaking through the water toward the sorceress.

Pahulu cried out when the first shark struck, more in startlement than in pain. The twisting darkness in Iuti's mind shivered, then strengthened. A second small cousin raked its razored teeth across the sorceress's hip, and a third ripped a gouge from her side. The darkness shattered. Suddenly, Pahulu was thrown back into the water, screaming, shrieking in surprise and agony. The myriad sea creatures she had controlled tore from her mental grasp and fled, abandoning her to the famished sharks.

When mano-niuhi struck, Iuti was with him just as he had been with her on many a battlefield of old. She tasted the slick tartness of Pahulu's blood, twisted her head from side to side as she shredded the sorceress's flesh between her doubled rows of teeth. She thrilled with her brother at this momentary pause in his endless, ravaging hunger.

And then, suddenly, she was alone.

Iuti reached frantically for mano-niuhi's mind, attempting to re-establish the bond. But there was nothing. The tie was gone. Only emptiness and cold remained, and a feeling of terror that she had never before experienced in the sea. She grabbed for the paddle that Tarawe thrust toward her and pulled herself hurriedly toward the canoe. Something stabbed her foot as she clambered aboard, and she almost collapsed in relief when she saw it was only mano's war club, bobbing in the waves beside her. She lifted it onto the outrigger.

Tarawe stared at her, then back at the place where Pahulu had stood. The ghost canoe had drifted into the blood-smeared shallows, and the old woman's image was slowly reforming in the vessel's final empty place. As the image solidified, the last of the nightmare images disappeared from Iuti's mind.

Iuti stumbled toward the canoe's bow and dumped the remaining Teronin warriors overboard, shuddering as her lost brother and his cousins raced to take the kill. Leaning over to inspect the damaged hull, she saw that the wooden war shield was tangled in the hanging fishnet. She brought it aboard and laid it carefully, teeth down, in the bottom of the canoe.

"Where did you get this?" she asked, picking up Tarawe's bloodied sword and turning back. She recognized the blade now by the rust that marred its edges.

"Pahulu." Tarawe's voice trembled. "She brought it to

my uncle's house. Later, the auntie guarding the door looked away long enough for me to escape with it. I didn't realize until too late that Pahulu meant for me to come so she could use me against you."

Tarawe glanced away, then straightened and looked defiantly back. "But it wouldn't have mattered. I wanted to come. I would have found a way even if Pahulu hadn't provided the means."

Iuti remained silent.

"I will pay my own debts from now on," Tarawe said.

And, almost, Iuti smiled. She rubbed her hand across her injured shoulder, glanced at the frenzied sea, then wiped the blood away on her wet trousers.

"I no longer carry the shark's protection and power," she said. "I have only a warrior's natural skills now. Still, I have debts of my own that need to be settled." She offered Tarawe the rusty blade's hilt. "You may join me if you wish."

Tarawe's dark eyes flashed in triumph as she took the sword. She grinned and quickly joined Iuti in turning the canoe away from the reef. Below them, alone in the starlit sea, mano-niuhi slid silently back into the deep.

FIREBIRD

J. L. Comeau

Concentration is the thing.

You have to block out everything but the task at hand if you want to succeed. In my mind, I am the Firebird, soaring above the ashes of my own extinction.

Ignoring the sweat pouring down my face, I stand before the mirrored wall, one hand lightly touching the barre. I bring my knee up steadily and lay it alongside my nose, then ever so slowly extend the calf, arching my toes toward the ceiling.

Technique, line, proportion, balance: these are the classical elements of the dance. Ballet is a celebration of the physical instrument, a ruthless, brutal discipline from which mastery of movement emerges. I try to think only of the dance as I push away from the barre and glissade to the center of the cold, silent studio.

I want to pretend that it is not nearly four a.m., that I am not exhausted, that I am not courting injury by pushing myself too hard. Going up on pointe, I turn a dozen mad fourettes, one-legged spins that confuse the mind and challenge the spirit. I want to forget what happened last night. I want to fill my empty soul with the dance.

I keep my balance by means of light and gravity. I

focus on the staccato *tock-tock-tock* of my toeshoes against the hardwood floor. I will myself to forget, but even as my body transcends exhaustion and pushes into the realm of pure bliss, I remember . . . I remember . . .

The dream is always the same: I'm charging through a long, dim hallway surrounded by shadowy blue figures running ahead and beside me. Blood crashing in my temples all but obliterates the thunder of our heavy boots as we approach a scarred metal door at the end of the hall. Amid angry shouts and confusing clamor, the door suddenly bursts open. (At this point in the dream, I start struggling to awaken myself because I can't bear to see what I know waits in that apartment.) My screams reach out of my dream and into my consciousness. I awaken on my feet, engulfed in a blind panic.

The dream is a remnant of the other side of my life. Of necessity, most dancers live two-sided lives. Foremost always is the grand passion—the dance—but unless one is a principal dancer in a large company, there is also a full-time outside job that pays the rent and buys the toe shoes.

When I'm not dancing, I work for the city. I'm one of a five-member tactical assault team the Detroit Police Department secretly calls "The Nut Squad." We're specifically trained to respond to barricade situations, which are often precipitated by emotionally disturbed persons, hence the nickname.

My given name is Julianna Christine Larkin. At the dance studio, I'm addressed as Julianna, but inside the police department, I'm often referred to as "Twinkletoes" or "The Sugarplum Fairy" behind my back. At one time, the guys on my squad gave me a hard time, making ballerina jokes and crude references to my gender. Now they simply call me Larkin, and that suits me just fine.

When I pack up my toe shoes and go out with my squad, the mandatory gear is decidedly different. Instead of a skimpy leotard, I wear heavy pads of flexible armor covering my chest, back and groin. A spidery two-way radio headset with multiple channels allows us to communicate quietly. We each carry a different weapon: a shotgun for support fire, an M16 A-2 automatic rifle for close-range management, a .223-caliber assault rifle for long-range control. I carry the A-2, which is relatively light but effective. We also have hydraulic jacks to crack open locked doors, systems to deliver tear gas canisters, and a contraption that shoots explosive diversion devices called "Thunder Flashers."

Like ballet, tactical police work requires agility, strength, endurance, and a rigorous training schedule, so the two are not quite so disparate as they might at first seem. These are the areas where I excel. It's a grasp of social competence that has so far eluded me.

For me, adolescence was a nightmare. Girls who reach a height of six feet by junior high school might as well have leprosy. But after a full day of peer indifference or outright scorn at school, I would become a swan in dance class, envied for my length of limb.

"Stand tall, Julianna! Reach for the clouds!" Madame Jedinov would bark from the back of the studio as she pounded her baton in time to the music. "Arch the neck! Extend the arm!"

In the grace and beauty of the dance I found pleasure in being me.

There is a certain grace and beauty to be found in the savage Detroit inner city streets as well. Instead of a joyous dance of life, it is a desperate dance of death, beautiful in its own wretched way.

My first police assignment was a barricade situation located in a shabby, drug-riddled housing project downtown. When I arrived, the building had been pinned to the night sky by spotlights and ringed by armed personnel.

Lieutenant Steven Brophy, my squad leader and veteran of two tours of combat in Vietnam, told me, "I want you to stay in back of the team, young lady. Don't want any trouble on this one. We've got our hands full and we don't need to be babysitting you."

His doubts about my competence did not annoy me—I was having my own misgivings. Everyone in the department was aware that I had received my placement in the unit to squelch a rash of sexual discrimination suits filed against the city. I thought I would be able to prove myself when the time came, but right then, I was just plain rabbit scared.

As I adjusted my radio headset, a sharp cry pulled my attention to the third floor apartment window where something dangled beneath the windowsill. Pushing my hair up under my cap I saw that it was a child—a baby!—being held by one ankle, bobbing precariously above the bleak tundra of the courtyard thirty feet below.

The baby screamed in terror, windmilling its little arms, arching its back. My heart froze. Seconds later, the child was jerked roughly back through the window and disappeared from view. Only its wails echoed in the cold night air.

"That's right," Brophy said as he motioned for me to follow him toward the equipment truck. "We got us a maniac, little girl."

After he handed me a heavy hydraulic jack, which I would carry during the assault, we joined the rest of the squad for a fast briefing. It was terrifying. Unconfirmed reports indicated that there was a psycho in apartment 302 named Ralph Esposito who had taken his former wife and children hostage. Sporadic gunfire heard earlier in the evening was shortly followed by the ejection of an object from the window which was later identified as his ex-wife's head. Of the six children presumed to be inside the apartment with him, it was unsure how many survived. The situation had been deteriorating rapidly for several hours and the life of the single known surviving hostage, the baby, had reached an unacceptable level of risk.

Our task: Full-Assault Scenario/Termination of

Suspect Authorized.

We crept into the building past a dozen uniformed officers and waited for one breathless minute at the end of the third floor hallway until Lieutenant Brophy gave the signal to move. At that point, I was so frightened and everything started moving so fast that the whole sequence of events always comes back to me in blurs and flashes:

Midnight blue figures hustling down the hallway—the sound of our boots against the linoleum floor—halting outside the door to 302—handing the jack to Fred Zaluta, second in command—dragging my A-2 off my back, throwing the safety—the door buckling and bursting open—gunfire—Zaluta on the floor, writhing—I know he's moaning, but all I can hear is my own blood crashing in my ears—a naked man, clotted with gore, pointing a rifle at me—NO!—the end of the barrel explodes with light and something punches me hard in the shoulder—I start to go down, sure that I'm already dead—automatically, I train the red dot of my laser aiming device on the center of the madman's forehead and squeeze off a fast burst.

As I go down, I see the top of the suspect's head lift off and explode in hundreds of shards and droplets that fan out in every direction—swiveling my head, I see another spray of dark blood pumping out of the torn meat of my shoulder—I think very clearly, "Where's the baby?" as I hit the floor—there is shouting and commotion—I lay injured and dazed, but not actually registering pain yet—the medical people swarm over me, lift me onto a stretcher that puts me at eye level with a strange object that looks like a raw roast beef pinned to the wall with a big cooking fork.

Time twists and stretches now, slowing to a crawl.

How odd, I think, running my eyes over the blue veins marbling the strangely shaped piece of meat. Rivulets of blood trace down the dingy wall beneath. How very, very odd.

People talk to me as I'm carried toward the door, but all I can hear is the hushed voice of one uniformed policeman addressing another officer.

"That's the way it goes with these screwballs," he was saying, shaking his head sadly. "The bastard killed every one of them. Skinned the baby alive and staked it to the wall with a fork right before the rescue unit got in. Five more minutes might have saved it. Ain't that a shame?"

When I start screaming, the ambulance attendant jabs me with a needle. Fadeout.

The first thing I thought of when I woke up in the hospital was that poor mutilated baby fastened to the wall, and I've thought about it every day for the past two years. I learned afterwards from the reports that the man I'd . . . killed . . . had a history of mental problems and had been released from a state hospital that same morning because of budgetary cutbacks. Ralph Esposito. The sound of his name makes my neck prickle. The baby he murdered along with his ex-wife and five other children was named Carmelita. Carmelita. Such a musical name. So full of laughter and promise. I can't stop hearing it in my mind.

Well, months of sweaty work in the dance studio and the department gym healed my shoulder. I've always been able to handle the physical demands of life. It's my head that keeps giving me trouble. If I could only banish the image of that poor child . . . poor Carmelita, from my dreams.

The guys on my squad welcomed me whole-heartedly into the unit when I came back to work. I was no longer considered an irksome political placement to bolster the department's image.

Lieutenant Fred Zaluta, who was also wounded during the raid on 302, became my champion. He still insists that I saved his life, but I don't know—I was just doing my job. He knows I live alone in a coldwater flat downtown, so he and his wife invite me over for a home-cooked meal with them and their three kids at least once a month. I love watching the Zalutas together. They're a volatile group, always fighting and bickering, but you can feel the love radiating from every cluttered corner of their home. I was raised an only child. My parents' house was cool and hushed, the corners immaculately bare.

My squad leader, Lieutenant Brophy, and the other two men on the team, Parks and Channing, treat me equitably, but we don't socialize. While we've become an extremely tight working unit, the prevailing wisdom is that it's dangerous to become emotionally involved. I guess Zaluta and I are just asking for trouble, but I can't imagine losing those wonderful evenings with his family. I'm willing to risk it.

When I first started having the dream about the raid on 302, I asked Zaluta if he thought I was going crazy.

"Naw," he said. I could tell by the way he wouldn't look me in the eye that discussing it troubled him. "We all get dreams. I heard once that the only way to get rid of one entirely is to replace it with something even worse."

"You have one, too?"

"Aw, sure. There was a raid back in seventy-two. A psycho twisted some pitiful old lady's head around two full turns while I stood there with my mouth hanging open. I always thought maybe I could have saved her if I hadn't been so green and scared. I don't dream about it as much as I used to, though. It gets better little by little, Larkin. You'll see."

I nodded, disturbed by the way his shoulders sagged and his broad face had grown pinched. I decided not to mention the subject again.

These past two years since the raid on 302 have rocketed past. I divide my time between police work and ballet and, usually, that's enough . . . until I key the lock to the dreary little closet I rent downtown. At some point, even cops and ballerinas have to go home. Maybe someday I'll buy some curtains, or a cat . . .

Detroit is often referred to as "Murder City" by the press, and from my own vantage point, the inner city resembles a monstrous, diseased organism that seems to grow exponentially by feeding on its own overabundance of poverty and rage. I don't know if a cure exists—I just help fight the symptoms: teenage gangs warring over drug turf, crazies strung out on crack and PCP, plus the usual family violence. Automatic weapons like Uzis and Baretta handguns equipped with 100-round banana clips are common in the rougher projects downtown. Drug turf battles are dangerous, but I would much rather respond to a gang war barricade than a nut barricade. Gang members usually surrender quickly—they're willing to trade their machismo for survival. But the whackos, they just don't give a damn, which makes them infinitely more treacherous.

Whatever the particular scenario happens to be, each assault is virtually the same, a tightly choreographed dance that never becomes routine. It's the part of my job I dread the most and love the best. The sweats and the jitters I experience seconds before an assault are indistinguishable from the butterflies I get backstage just before dancing in front of an audience. It's thrilling and terrifying at once.

When poised for an assault on a barricaded house or apartment, my heart is always in my mouth right before the door goes down. We never know what we'll find inside. When the door gives and we rush in, I go dead cool. Instinct and training kick in and, one way or the other, it's all over in a matter of minutes. Afterward, just like after a ballet performance, I experience an intensely gratifying rush of physical and emotional satisfaction we call the "afterburn" back in the squad room. It's what drives me, makes me push myself to the very limit of my capabilities, what clouds my judgment at times, but always, always satisfies . . . for the moment.

Zaluta says everyone is chasing the afterburn in one form or another, and I think he's right.

Sometimes I worry that I have some kind of weird attraction to brutality. Violence is integral to police work, of course, but not many people recognize the inherent self-inflicted violence of the ballet. Ballerinas look like fragile, fairy-like creatures who rest on satin pillows when not dancing—that's the illusion. Pink satin toe shoes and opaque tights usually conceal feet that look like raw hamburger and ugly surgical scars criss-crossing sprung knees and ankles.

Personally, I'm terrified of injuries and pain, but I keep running head-on at the possibility, nonetheless. I don't know, maybe there's something wrong with me. I've never been a particularly introspective woman, but after what happened last night . . . everything has changed. I've changed.

I had just showered up and was busy stowing gear in my squad locker yesterday evening when the call came in. It's unusual for an off team to get called back on duty since there are three other teams working on rotating shifts. When we arrived at the scene, it was already dark and cruelly cold as only a Detroit winter night can be. A large crowd had gathered across the street from a five-story tenement building, brilliantly hideous against the black winter sky lit by rows of huge, smoking kleig lights. The crowd was clearly agitated, surging behind the phalanx of uniformed police officers who were having some difficulty keeping them in order.

"They've got my Momma!" A young black man wearing a flimsy grey sweatshirt shouted, trying to break past the sawhorse barrier.

An elderly woman shrieked, "Help me, God!" and collapsed in a faint, disappearing into the rippling sea of bodies.

It struck me as odd that none of the people who had assembled across the street were behaving like the usual gawkers who always turn out for a barricade. Instead of the typical good-natured spectators looking for a little excitement, each appeared to have something personal at stake. Most of the women and a good number of the men were sobbing and moaning; none took their eyes from the floodlit building.

I knew then that it was going to be bad. Very bad.

When I heard Lieutenant Brophy summoning our squad for a briefing, I almost didn't want to hear what was going on. Christ, I thought, just let me do my job and get out of here. Then, as I was turning to join my team, the crowd stopped their frantic milling and shoving all at once. It made my flesh creep the way they stood like zombies, faces pale and distorted as they stared up at the building.

When I turned, I entered a waking nightmare.

Wailing in terror, little Carmelita Esposito, my nightmare child, was being dangled three stories above the sidewalk by a wild-eyed man. There was no doubt in my mind that the man was her father, Ralph Esposito, the man I'd killed two years before.

I went hot all over despite the frigid night wind. I felt like I weighed a thousand pounds, petrified.

I might still be standing there if Zaluta hadn't gripped my arm and started shouting, "Holy Jesus, Larkin! It's the old woman I told you about! Mother of God, her head's on backward and she's still alive! Oh, Jesus!"

I swung around and looked at Zaluta. His face was twisted in anguish as he watched the building. I shook his arm hard and he looked at me. I don't know how long we stood holding onto each other, but when we turned our eyes back to the building, whatever it was we'd seen had vanished.

All hell broke loose. The crowd behind us became a hysterical mob, screaming and pushing against the barriers, demanding that something be done. A two-way radio in a nearby squad car squawked something about assembly of a riot control unit. Curling clouds of frosty vapor rose before our faces as we breathed into the numbingly cold air, my own pumping fast and heavy. A couple of teenage boys broke through the police barrier and made a run at the building, but were stopped and strong-armed back behind the line by one gigantic uniformed officer.

"I don't see any of the other assault teams around," I

remarked to Zaluta as we headed for the equipment truck to pick up our gear. "I thought we were all supposed to be out here."

"I overheard the Chief telling Brophy that the other units were all getting in place and ready to go. They're just waiting for a signal from the point team."

"Who's on point?" I asked.

"I don't know, but I'm glad it's not us."

I nodded as we pulled on our armor. "I'd like to know what the hell's going on. We're hallucinating or something worse. I feel like I'm dreaming."

"I *wish* you were dreaming," Zaluta said, hoisting his Heckler and Koch 9mm submachine gun, a real brute of a weapon that was just too heavy for me to handle. "If you were dreaming, we'd all be at home."

While we were adjusting our radio headsets, the rest of our team, Brophy, Parks, and Channing, climbed into the back of the truck and joined us, their faces grim and pasty behind frosty crimson lips and noses.

"This is the deal," Lieutenant Brophy said, rubbing his hands together. "Something fucking weird is going on in that building."

Everyone snickered but Brophy, who cracked a sideways grin. Having successfully loosened us up, his mouth fell into a frown and his eyes narrowed. "Nobody knows what we've got in there. I guess I don't have to tell you that whatever is happening, we're all witnessing some pretty strange stuff."

Everyone nodded.

"OK. Here's the plan. Earl Cook's unit is the point team. They're going to make an assault in a few minutes. We're last up, so we're just here for backup. We won't be called out unless the other teams fail to resolve this situation."

We all fell silent for a long moment.

"Here's what I know," Brophy continued. "Around six this evening, the department started receiving frantic calls from a number of hysterical people, all claiming to have seen a different event occurring at this address. Four uniformed officers entered the building shortly after six-thirty. Evidently, they never came out."

Carefully adjusting the armor protecting his groin, Brophy said, "Let's not bust our nuts worrying until we get a reconnaissance report from the point team, OK?" He looked up at me. "And you, Larkin, don't bust whatever it is you got to bust."

We laughed and shook our heads, then slowly filed out of the truck. Parks went to get everyone some hot coffee, and the rest of us took positions behind the rows of squad cars parked in a semicircle in front of the building. Then we waited. And waited. The tension was bone-crushing. There was a lot of fidgeting, shifting, and dry-throated coughs.

Behind us, the crowd rumbled like thunder, their collective growl a continual roar that rose and fell, punctuated by shrill cries and hoarse shouts. At the time, I considered that unruly throng as much of a threat to life and limb as the situation inside the building.

As it turned out, I was very much mistaken.

Then things started popping. The first team went in like gangbusters, detonating a number of small, grenade-shaped devices called Thunder Flashers that explode harmlessly, but mimic miniature atomic bombs. You can't help but be disoriented momentarily, even when you know it's coming. Under cover of this diversionary blitzkrieg, they entered the building.

When the sound of the flash-bombs finally stopped reverberating in my ears, I could hear what was going on inside through the command radio hooked into the teams' two-way sets. There was gunfire mixed with the most gut-wrenching shrieks and screams I have ever heard, and which I suspect I'll be hearing in my head for a long, long time. I clenched my fists so tightly my fingernails punctured my palms. Wedged in between the screams were a few frantic words that I could just barely make out:

". . . outta here!" one of them yelled in a high-pitched

squeal.

". . . fuckin dogs! . . . *No!* . . . *Jesus!* . . ."

The gunfire finally ceased, but the screams continued for at least another minute. Then there was a crackling silence.

After that terrible pause, everyone started talking at once, and Brophy had to shout us down to make himself heard. Once we quieted, he said simply, "Unit Two is preparing to enter," and turned away.

Whispering close to my ear, Zaluta said, "That was Kellerman screaming about dogs on the radio. He's been scared shitless of dogs since a crack dealer holed up in a motel released a Doberman on him a few years back."

We stared at each other. Everyone in the vicinity was experiencing his or her own private nightmare.

"Are we being purposely manipulated? Is this even *real?*" I asked, hearing my voice becoming shrill.

Zaluta shrugged his shoulders wearily and patted me on the arm. He was only in his late thirties, but he already looked like an old man. "I don't know, Larkin. I don't know."

The crowd was working itself into another frenzy when the second assault team silenced them by plunging into the building amid another round of booms and flashes.

Again, the radio crackled with shouts and gunfire. But this time, when the chaos died down, one distinct voice rose out of the background hiss, a trembly but jubilant voice declaring victory.

"I got the murdering bastard!" he cried. "I'm bringing him back alive, folks, so don't blow my ass off when we come out. And send in the medics stat, people. We've got a slaughterhouse in here. OK, hold your fire now, we're exiting the building."

Hot relief swept over me. I spun around to face the building and began to cheer and clap with the others when two figures emerged.

"It's Delroy Stanton," Parks said.

The wild applause dwindled and died away slowly when it became apparent that something was amiss. Instead of driving a suspect at gunpoint, Stanton was dragging an inert, profusely bleeding man by the tattered collar of a midnight-blue shirt—an assault team shirt.

The prisoner appeared to be a member of his own unit.

"See?" Stanton shouted deliriously as a pair of medics rushed him and pulled away his prisoner. A group of officers, including Lieutenant Brophy, swarmed around him. His eyes were wild, rolling back to show white. "It's the *boogeyman!*" He fell to his knees and started to sob. "Oh, God! *It's not even HUMAN!*"

Too quickly for anyone to stop him, Stanton raised his handgun and placed it in his mouth.

"No!" Brophy shouted, charging at Stanton, hands stretching for the pistol.

I squeezed my eyes shut a split-second before the crack of the gun discharging racketed into the night, echoing through the cold streets.

Beside me, Zaluta moaned.

Complete pandemonium ensued. The crowd behind the lines went berserk, shrieking and throwing empty bottles and other debris as the policemen fought to hold them back. In our own camp, professional decorum evaporated. Angry demands for full disclosure raced through our ranks. Two of us were known dead, twelve more lives were probably lost inside the building.

A tenured officer named Detrick clambered atop a squad car with a bull horn and blared, "ASSAULT TEAMS THREE AND FOUR REPORT TO COMMAND POST AT ONCE!"

"That's us," Zaluta said.

Following behind Zaluta, I was struck by the surreal quality of my perceptions. Even the shiny black heels of Zaluta's boots flashing and ebbing as he walked ahead of me looked strange somehow. Brighter . . . more textured. Sounds lost their sharp edges and became rounded, hollow.

When we arrived at the command post, a jerry-rigged open-air office on the far side of the police lines, Lieutenant Brophy and his Team Three counterpart were busy talking with the Chief and his people. Amidst the chattering department personnel was an odd little man dressed in a long black tunic covering tightly fitted black trousers. He stood solemnly, clutching a battered leather portfolio case to his narrow chest. As I stared at him, he swiveled his head and looked directly at me, pegging me to the spot with his luminous dark eyes.

We surveyed each other for a long moment, until the spell was broken by the strident voice of Mel Anderson, a flashy, balding department spokesman whose job it was to deal with the media.

"All right, people," Anderson called out, waving his arms and making his storm jacket bunch up around his neck. "Let's have some QUIET! I have some information to pass along to you assault personnel, so listen up."

Lieutenant Brophy, standing behind Anderson, rolled his eyes and shook his head slightly, affirming his widely known dislike of the man we privately called "Captain Video."

"Now what we've got is this," Anderson continued, referring to a yellow legal pad in his left hand. "Two officers confirmed casualties, twelve officers missing in action, and an unknown number of tenants inside the building, condition unknown. Identity of suspect or suspects unconfirmed. Causative factors, unconfirmed." He paused, delivering his patented Concerned Countenance, which I'd often seen him wear on the evening news. "We don't know exactly what's going on, so what we've done is bring in an expert on paranormal occurrences."

Putting his hands up to quell the rising buzz of indignant murmurs, he added, "Now, you all know that Homicide Division occasionally employs the services of psychics when they've hit a wall with their inquiries—"

"Oh, come on, man!" someone shouted.

146

"We ain't no Ghostbusters!" someone else yelled.

"Look!" Anderson said angrily, pointing a finger at us. "If any of you hotshots have the answer to what's going on in that goddamned building, step right up!"

Silence.

"Fine," he said, adjusting his tie. "Now shut up and listen." He extended an arm toward the little man in the black tunic, who walked over and stood next to Anderson. "Mr. Chase has graciously consented to lend his expertise to the department and to work with us on this case. And it is therefore expected that all personnel will treat Mr. Chase with the utmost dignity and respect." Turning a baleful eye toward us, he growled, "Is that UNDERSTOOD?"

This is getting too weird, I thought, thanking Channing as he handed me a styrofoam cup of bitter-smelling coffee.

"I would like to speak to the young lady," Chase said in a thin voice tinged with a rolling accent.

Like everyone else, I started looking around for the alleged "young lady," but when my eyes returned to the strange little man the department had brought in, I was surprised to find that he was pointing at *me*.

I touched my chest and Mr. Chase nodded. "Oh, Christ," I said under my breath, gulping my coffee down in three swallows.

Amid much hooting and laughter from the guys, I followed Mr. Chase, Lieutenant Brophy and Mel Anderson to one of the squad cars and climbed into the back seat with Mr. Chase.

"This is Corporal Larkin," Brophy said, twisting around in the front seat to face me. I noted the silent apology in his eyes. "What do you want with her?"

"She is the only person I saw with the aptitude to remedy this unfortunate occurrence," Mr. Chase responded measuredly.

"What do you mean, 'aptitude'?" Anderson asked. "We've got plenty of men out there."

"My point exactly," Chase said. "Corporal Larkin's obvious aptitude, in this case, is her gender."

"Now, wait just a minute—" Brophy started, but was interrupted by Anderson.

"Mr. Chase," Anderson said, "we need some answers here. We're laying the department's credibility on the line by inviting you into this matter, so if you can tell us something, please be clear."

The little man nodded his head politely and cleared his throat. "It is my firm belief that this disturbance is being caused by a drude," he announced. "'Drude' is an Old English expression for a nightmare fiend. According to most authorities, a young witch becomes a drude when she reaches the age of forty and then assumes the power to haunt any victim she chooses with terrible visions. Sometimes, this new power drives them mad, which is precisely what I believe has occurred here. And in order to put an end to her malicious activity, she must be destroyed. That is your answer, gentlemen."

He inclined his lips slightly, apparently amused by our dumbstruck expressions. He patted my forearm and added, "Males are powerless against drudes. You are therefore chosen, Corporal."

"Oh, this is *nuts!*" Brophy shouted. "Do you think I'm going to allow Larkin to go in there after two heavily armed squads have failed?"

Anderson had just opened his mouth to respond when every single window in the barricaded building exploded outward with a terrible shattering sound and sprayed a hundred-foot perimeter with glittering shards of broken glass.

"Maybe we ought to hear Mr. Chase out," Anderson said.

After we'd listened to Chase's incredible plan, Brophy looked at me with tired eyes and said, "It's up to you, Larkin. It's your ass—you call it. I'm telling you right now that I think it stinks, but like Anderson says, the Chief will overrule me on this one for sure." He sneered at

Anderson. "You guys will try anything to protect your public image, won't you?"

Anderson ignored him. "Our next best alternative is to send the two remaining squads anyway, Larkin. What if Mr. Chase is right? All those lives . . .?"

"Hey!" Brophy said, his face red with rage. He grabbed Anderson roughly by the collar.

"You better cool off, Brophy," Anderson said. "It's out of your hands."

"We'll see about that!" Brophy shouted, releasing Anderson's collar before slamming out of the squad car.

I appreciated Brophy's gesture, but I knew even then that it wouldn't make any difference. I was going into the building alone. It was simply a fact. I knew it in my heart. I saw it in Chase's ebony eyes. Some things are inevitable. So I said, "All right."

After a few more careful instructions from Mr. Chase, I went over to the equipment truck to check out my radio and pick up some extra gear. If I refused the assignment and more people died as a result, it wouldn't be worth the effort to live. I had to do it.

But I was scared. Good Christ, I was scared.

Once I had made up my mind, Brophy and the rest of the guys quit trying to talk me out of it, but I thought I saw tears in Zaluta's eyes as I came down the ramp leading out of the truck. That's when I nearly backed out; I came so close to backing out . . .

But then Mr. Chase was affixing something to the collar of my shirt. "This is the only thing that will work," he whispered.

I lifted my collar and saw an old fashioned hat pin inserted through the fabric. It was silver, about seven inches long, and was topped with what looked like an enormous black pearl.

I looked down at Mr. Chase. "The heart," he said. "Remember the heart."

I nodded, wondering who was crazier, him or me.

"Keep your focus," Chase continued. "None of it is

real. Only the drude. But she cannot alter her own appearance before another formidable woman. Ignore everything else. Remember the signs I told you to look for and you'll find her."

Fastening a string of small explosive charges to my vest and snapping a clip into a 9mm Baretta semiautomatic handgun equipped with a flashlight attachment, I figured that I would be carrying nearly seventy pounds. My antiballistic armor weighed forty-eight pounds alone. The additional weight of the handgun, clips and my A-2 was finally the limit I could bear and still move.

I had never really considered the utter strangeness of what I do for a living until I walked across that cold lot toward the building, the arsenal I carried swaying in time to my steps. I'm sure I must have looked like a erstwhile Valkyrie, except there was no Valhalla waiting for me—I was going in after a deranged *witch* who had taken up residence in a Detroit project building.

The radio buzzed and cracked in my ears. I adjusted the earpieces one last time before I stepped across the lines and crossed the lot toward the building. Hustling as fast as I was able, I crossed the open area of the courtyard until I hugged the icy bricks forming the base of the building. I got a quick glimpse of Zaluta crouched beside a nearby trash dumpster, his face was turned up, his mouth open wide.

Across the street, the crowd convulsed.

I tilted my head back just in time to see a plastic trash can teetering on the ledge of a third floor window being turned over. Before I could move, I was struck full in the face with a splattering gush of hot, clotting blood. When I could get my eyes open, I saw my nemesis, Ralph Esposito, leaning over the windowsill, leering at me past the edge of the dripping can.

I turned away, revolted and terrified. I tensed my body, trying not to retch, ignoring the shouting voice on the radio. *Concentrate!* I told myself. *It's not real!*

My breathing slowed and I looked down at myself.

Clean and dry. Not a speck of blood. Chase had been right. It was going to be a battle of wills, not weapons. I looked up at the window. Nothing.

"It's all right," I whispered into the radio mouthpiece. "I'm going in."

Having thus committed myself, I trotted up to the fire-blasted front entryway and slipped into the building. It was similar to other project apartment houses I'd been in, except for one thing: a naked overhead bulb glared across the writhing floor of the entry hall. I found myself standing up to my ankles in snakes.

Something darted near my eyes and I instinctively batted it away with one hand. Panting, I watched my radio headset tumble into a thrashing reptilian mass at my feet. *Stupid!* I thought. I'd let myself be fooled into losing my communications. There were no snakes. Clamping down on my terror, I tried to concentrate, *concentrate . . .*

I blinked my eyes and the snakes vanished.

Not wanting to waste the time it would take to rehook my headset, I left it lying on the filthy grey linoleum and headed for the stairs. There wasn't sign of a living soul. The building was still as a tomb. Remembering Chase's instructions, I strained to hear a high-pitched keening sound, and I thought I could hear something fading in and out like a remote radio signal, a fluttering wail hovering on the far edge of my audial range. It was coming from above. I headed for the stairs.

When I reached the second floor, I edged around the corner and stood against the wall at the end of the corridor. Nothing moved. A coppery tang hung in the air, a salty odor I recognized instantly. Above it rode the sharp smell of cordite. Most of the lightbulbs lining the ceiling had been long since smashed or stolen, so the corridor lay in an eerie half-light. Hugging the wall, I inched down the corridor to find that all of the apartment doors had been left standing ajar.

Toeing open the first door, I discovered the bodies of several people strewn like smashed mannequins across the dimly lit living room. One of the dead, a large man with a rough beard, lay sprawled on his back, his hand still clutching a plastic-handled steak knife with which he'd apparently slashed his own throat.

Feeling sick and lightheaded, I turned away from the carnage, taking deep draughts of air into my lungs. Back in the corridor, I leaned against the wall for a moment trying to regain my bearings and wondered what my odds of escape might be if I made a dash for the stairs.

I was thinking, *shit on this—I'm bailing out*, when I heard something behind me move.

I couldn't help screaming when I turned and faced the dark, bloodied figures that shambled toward me from the interior of the apartment. They jerked and hobbled as if drawn along by some mad puppeteer, eyes glazed and fixed on nothing.

Flashes of fire began strobing in front of me and there was thunder in my ears. A bitter cloud of blue smoke rose near my face, through which I could see the advancing corpses exploding and flying apart. It wasn't until after I'd expended my entire 30-round clip that I realized I had been firing my A-2 through the apartment doorway.

And they were still coming.

I turned and made a panicky run for it, breaking for the stairs. Honor and duty be damned. I couldn't think of anything but getting the hell out. I didn't care what happened as long as I got away.

I only made it as far as the top of the stairs when I heard a familiar voice call my name.

"Julianna," it barked in a familiar tone.

And I knew goddamned well that if I turned around, it would be a stupid, perhaps fatal, mistake. But I couldn't help it. I just had to look.

There in the filthy tenement corridor, not ten feet behind me, stood Madame Jedinov, starkly majestic in her wispy dancing skirts, baton in hand, a fierce look on her stern Baltic face.

I stared, astonished, as a huge black tongue snaked out of her mouth like lightning, wrapping itself around my neck and yanking me off my feet. I hit the linoleum floor like a sack of cement and my A-2 skittered out of my hands and bounced down the stairs. As the constriction around my neck tightened, I could hear braying laughter booming over my head.

No, I thought as little lights danced in my head. *I won't go down like this.* Clamping down on every fiber of my imagination, I forced myself to concentrate. *It's not real. It can't hurt me.*

When the corridor swam back into focus, I found myself on my knees with my own hands clenched around my throat. Releasing them, I stood, coughing, and looked down the hallway. It was silent and empty. The buzzing in my head cleared until all that was left was that strange, electrical keening sound I'd first detected downstairs, stronger now.

I touched the collar of my uniform and found I'd almost dislodged the hat pin that Chase had inserted there. So that was the game: Get Rid of the Pin. The bitch was *scared.*

Jamming the pin tightly into my collar, I glanced down at my A-2 lying at the bottom of the stairs. I wouldn't be needing it. In my mind, I conjured up an image of a bent, hideous crone wearing a peaked black hat and focused on it. Placing my boot squarely on the first step leading to the third floor, I silently called out, *I'm coming for you.*

Soft laughter echoed above. A shimmering image appeared on the stairway, an abortive, half-formed horror that I was able to sweep away with a wave of my hand. *I'm wise to you now.*

Confident of my own power to dispel the drude's best efforts to fake me out, I jogged up the stairs, heart racing, hot for the game. *Go ahead,* I thought wildly. *Hit me with your best shot, honey.*

When I reached the third floor, I stopped dead in my

tracks. Suspended from the overhead fixtures that lined the ceiling were eight large, meticulously skinned human bodies. It was obscene. They swung like smokehouse hams in small, lazy circles spotlighted by naked bulbs above their dreadfully glazed, fleshy heads.

My hands flew to my mouth and I gagged. Looking away, I called back the imagery of the witch-crone and concentrated upon it, hating her, crowding out the revulsion and terror with rage. With a strangled cry, I turned and charged down the hallway directly at the swaying atrocities the drude had conjured to stop me. I would reduce them to vapor like the one on the stairs.

It's impossible to describe how horrible, how shocking, how loathsome it was when I collided with that cold, wet slab of human meat. I struck it hard, bounding backward off of it and hitting the floor hard. I lay there looking up, seeing that terrible dripping thing dangling over me, trying to get my breath back.

There was a soft popping noise and the corpse, evidently released from its mooring, toppled from the ceiling and collapsed on top of me.

A woman's shrieking laughter filled the corridor, drowning out my screams as I struggled to get out from under the inert body pinning me on my back, holding me in a repugnant embrace. Her laughter racketed in my ears, making it impossible to think. My heart pounded painfully hard, forcing great pulsing torrents through my body. My will and concentration had been pushed to the wall. I was unsure if I possessed the emotional strength to handle my predicament. Surely my spirit could not survive one more shock.

And then the lights went out.

Silence. Not a sound except my own breathing. I managed to push away the thing on top of me and it hit the floor with a wet, slapping noise that reverberated oddly, like in a cavern.

Grabbing the handgun out of my belt holster, I flicked on the flashlight attachment and swung the beam

154

out across a domed roof that undulated with the squirming bodies of huge brown bats. One of them disentangled itself from the seething mass and flew at me, striking my chest, snapping at my throat.

As I grappled with it, trying to tear it away, I dragged my left hand across the point of the pin in my collar, painfully ripping open the skin of my palm. *Remember the pin! The drude is trying to get the hat pin,* I thought wildly. *There's no cave, no bats. Concentrate.*

The cavern rippled and shimmered, then faded into the walls of the tenement corridor. Arcing my flashlight to the end of the hallway, I saw that the shadows pooling there seemed to be alive, thrashing like storm clouds. This was a sign, according to Mr. Chase. She couldn't bear the light, he'd said, and threw out darkness like a squid expels ink. Being careful to avoid contact with the remaining bodies suspended from the ceiling, I followed the beam to the end of the hall. I flashed the light on the door. The numbers on the scarred metal fire door read, "302."

I should have known.

This is it, I told myself as I pressed a small clay charge beneath the doorknob. Standing well to one side of the door, I triggered the charge. The door blew open and stood ajar, smoking.

Edging past the door, I played the beam of my flashlight around the room, but the darkness was so thick that the light scarcely cut three feet into the gloom. A bright pain blossomed in my heart with each breath I took. My soul was exhausted and damaged. I truly did not think I would be alive much longer, and the unadorned reality of that absolute belief somehow washed away my dread of death, filling me with one burning conviction: to make my last act on earth a meaningful one.

I was going to take that crazy bitch down with me.

"Where are you, you fucking *hag?*" I shouted, ignoring the tears blurring my vision. I whipped the flashlight beam back and forth, until it fell upon a pale figure standing in the whirling darkness.

His naked body was very white where it was not splashed with blood. My own personal nightmare, Ralph Esposito, stood with a viciously gleeful smile on his mad face. In front of him, he clutched a beautiful little girl by her dark hair, holding a dimestore pocket knife to her throat.

Little Carmelita begged me to save her with desolate brown eyes.

"I'll peel her like a grape if you take one more step," her father growled.

I didn't have the strength to banish the delusion, so I let it play itself out. Sobbing like a child, I moved forward.

Ralph Esposito drew the blade evenly across her smooth neck. She went rigid and shrieked as a crimson trickle necklaced her tender throat.

"Stop it!" I screamed. I couldn't stand it. I couldn't bear the child's agony, real or imagined. Dropping to my knees, I begged, *"please . . ."*

I felt the light touch of a hand on my back. I turned to face whetever new demon had been summoned to torment me and looked into the jet black eyes of a divinely beautiful golden-haired woman.

"You're tired," she murmured. "So tired."

Her sympathy drained me. I slumped at her feet, my face against the silken fabric of her long skirt. If I could close my eyes and rest a while . . .

I felt her hand slide to my collar and gently tug at the pin, but her soothing voice lulled me into a dreamy fantasy. I was wearing a crystalline costume, dancing on a mirror in a child's jewel box, spinning round and round—

A sudden thunder pounded overhead, shaking the floor beneath me, jarring me awake. I reached up and grasped the hand fumbling with my collar.

The drude screeched in my ear and tore at my face with her free hand. Feeling her nails tear deep furrows across my cheek, I jerked my handgun up until the barrel jammed under her chin and emptied the clip into her head.

The drude screamed with laughter and knocked the gun out of my hand, the flashlight beam pinwheeling through the roiling dark and coming to rest beyond my reach. If anything, she had grown even stronger, fighting like a wildcat. Though barely half my size, she possessed at least twice my strength. And she was choking the life out of me. I couldn't allow her to get hold of the pin.

The bass thrumming overhead increased, filling the room with its heavy pulsations.

The sound distracted her for a scant moment and I took advantage of it, knocking her off balance as she sat on my chest. Whipping my leg around, I caught her across her neck and levered her onto her back.

Above us, the booming throb increased to a deafening intensity.

I yanked the hat pin out of my collar and held it out before me. The drude disappeared into the shadows.

I spun around, my heart banging painfully in my chest. She could be anywhere, ready to pounce on me from behind. I edged over to where my gun lay and picked it up, flashing the beam around me.

The building pulsed and shook. *WHOP-WHOP-WHOP.*

I found her. She was cowering in a dark corner, shielding her eyes from the light, making pitiful mewling sounds.

She looked up, her lovely face stricken with pain and fear. "Please," she whimpered. "Please. Don't kill me."

Her anguish caught me by surprise and that one moment of hesitation on my part was all she wanted.

She sprang at me with blinding speed, but I was ready for her. When she grabbed my wrist, I felt bones splinter but held fast to the hat pin. It was her own hand that helped drive the pin up beneath her ribcage and into her heart.

She stiffened, her black eyes wide with surprise. Exhaling a gust of foul breath into my face, she went limp and her knees buckled. I went down with her, driving the pin hard, setting it deep.

Pulling myself to my feet, I looked down at her small, crumpled form. There was no victory here. The swirling darkness receded, leaving the room in its former dingy, trash-strewn verity. Above the thunderous pandemonium roaring over my head, I heard the wail of a baby.

Emerging from a cluttered corner, Carmelita Esposito, the most beautiful child ever born on this planet, wobbled unsteadily toward me on pudgy toddler's legs, arms outstretched.

An indescribably intense rush of joy surged through me when I picked that precious baby up and held her in my arms. She was safe. She was mine. I would never let her go. *Never.*

Hugging her close, I sidled up to a bare window where jagged shards of windowpane rattled in the casement from the bedlam outside. Gales of cold wind blew into our faces, bright lights shone down from overhead. I recognized the insectile outlines of the black shape hovering over us.

A Chinook helicopter hung above the building, its rotors roaring and throbbing.

What are they doing up there? I wondered, certain that any rescue operation would certainly be ground-based.

Something was being lowered from the side of a chopper, something that looked like a large coffee can on a wire.

A bomb. They were going to bomb the building! Images of the Philadelphia MOVE house bombing, the explosion and subsequent conflagration leaped into my mind.

The chopper eased up to a higher altitude, readying for the drop. There would be no time to escape from the building's entrance door. I screamed up at them, but my voice was lost in the chopper's backwash. There was only one alternative left for Carmelita and me, and not a very good one.

158

My mind set, I kicked the remaining glass out of the window and looked down. At least a thirty-foot drop to frozen turf. If I wrapped myself around the child and let my legs take the impact, she might not be injured. My legs would be shattered. The dance . . .

"Fuck it!" I shouted, ripping off my Teflon vestpiece and wrapping Carmelita in it. Her big brown eyes flickered with light.

Holding her tightly to my chest, I climbed over the casement and pushed out, leaping into the cold, cold night.

As if suspended, we seemed to drift like a feather. I saw the ground coming up slowly, slowly.

As we fell, the top floor of the building exploded behind us in a gigantic fireball of mortar and steel.

The ground surged to meet us. I felt a tremendous impact as my legs slammed into the ground. I could sense that the big bones had shattered on contact, but there was no pain.

Then silence.

Lying on my back, I couldn't raise my head, I couldn't move. Then I felt the light pressure of a small hand on my face and Carmelita's sweet face rose over mine.

I remember smiling, then spinning down, down into blackness.

I came around slowly, my blurred vision focusing itself on Zaluta's worried face.

"Is the baby all right?" I asked.

"Baby?" Zaluta said, then motioned to someone beyond my visual range.

A white-coated medic kneeled down beside me and flicked a penlight beam across my eyes. I pushed it away, angry now.

"The baby! Is she *all right?*"

Zaluta looked at the medic and shrugged. "Looks like she took a pretty hard lick from that bottle."

"What?" I demanded, becoming extremely upset with him.

"One of those jerks in the crowd lobbed a bottle at us and it caught you in the back of the head, Larkin. Knocked you silly for a couple seconds, but you're going to be OK," Zaluta explained.

"Wait a minute," I said, sitting up and rubbing the painful knot near the base of my skull. I looked at my legs: straight and healthy. I stood up. I was behind the barrier with the rest of the police personnel. "What's happened?"

Not understanding my question, Zaluta said, "False alarm, kiddo. They dragged us out here for nothing. The situation's been resolved."

"You mean it's all over?"

He nodded. "Team One went in and found the suspect dead. Suicide. They're bringing her out now."

"Her?"

"Yeah, some woman on the third floor caused a ruckus then offed herself. Stabbed herself to death with some kind of long pin, can you imagine? A neighbor said it was the woman's fortieth birthday. Happy birthday, huh?"

We watched them wheel out the gurney with the body bag strapped across it; I didn't need to see the dead woman. I knew her face. I just wanted to go to the studio and try to dance away the empty feeling in the pit of my stomach.

I dumped my gear and walked through the dark Detroit nightstreets toward the studio. A light sprinkling of snow drifted down from the swirling black sky and glittered like diamonds in the harsh glow of street lamps.

I stood out in front of the old warehouse housing the dance studio watching the snow obliterate the grey ugliness of the city, trying to remember how little Carmelita's hand had felt against my face. But I couldn't get it back. The dream was gone.

Sighing, I turned and unlocked the warehouse door and flicked on the lights. The stairs to the dance studio seemed unusually steep as I trudged up to the dressing room. Released from the confinement of my uniform, I pulled three pairs of legwarmers over my tights to protect my ankles and calves against the unheated chill of the building. There was a dull ache in my chest as I laced the pink ribbons of my toe shoes and tested the firmness of the pointes.

When I went to close my locker, I noticed a black velvet case resting on the top shelf. Picking it up, I found a plain white note card concealed beneath it. The note read:

> *Remember the heart.*
> *Your fond admirer,*
> *D. Chase*

Inside the case lay a silver hat pin topped with a huge black pearl.

Technique, line, proportion, balance: it is clear to me now that these things apply in all areas of life. I dance feverishly, spinning and leaping, thinking of my bleak rented room, my bleak heart.

Enough. Dripping perspiration, I cool myself down with a series of slow barre exercises. Mopping my neck with a towel as I leave the studio, I stop in the wardrobe room and inspect my costume for tonight's performance of Stravinsky's *Firebird*. It is exquisite; leotard and head-piece ablaze with flashing orange and red sequins and streaming yellow feathers.

Dancing the principal role this evening, I will feel like Pavlova. It makes no difference that this performance will take place in an elementary school auditorium. It's the dance that matters, not the stage. Zaluta and his family will be in the first row and, instead of dancing for myself, tonight I am going to dance for them.

And when the dance is finished, I will sleep. I will not wake up afraid in the night. There is nothing left to fear. And tomorrow . . . Tomorrow I will remind myself that life is more than a series of choreographed movements. I must learn to open my heart. It will be difficult, I know, but I have always enjoyed a challenge.

Concentration is the thing.

A CEREMONY OF DISCONTENT

Eleanor Arnason

Vusai woke at sunrise. The sky was overcast, and the air
had the smell of rain. She got up and took down her
hammock. Quickly she folded it and put it away. Then
came the curtains along the edge of the veranda. They had
come from Hui, the village with the best weavers. They
were thin and completely transparent, except where the
pattern was. The pattern was a zigzag, done in white and
green. At the bottom the curtains were tied to the floor, so
bugs couldn't fly in under them. She undid the ties and
pulled the curtains up. Then she went inside. The rest of
her family was there: her husband Mawl and Shaitu, the
wife who had children. Mawl was cooking breakfast.
Shaitu was doing nothing. She was pregnant again,
round, fat and pleased with herself. Vusai had never
understood her attitude. What was so fine about bulging
out and becoming clumsy? Who would want such a thing?
Vusai helped herself to a piece of bread, then looked
around for the children. They were in a corner: a green
heap of naked bodies, all tangled up with one another,
wrestling fiercely and silently. All girls and fine ones.
When the time for the choice came, she knew what it
would be. They were too independent to be mothers.

She sat down. Mawl gave her a bowl. She dipped the

bread in and took a bite. Ah! That burned like the sun! It took the bad taste out of her mouth, and it even lightened her mood a little. The day seemed less grey.

"I have made a decision," she said.

"Yes?" said Mawl.

Shaitu blinked and looked interested.

"I am going to ask for a ceremony." She finished the bread and took another piece.

"What kind of ceremony?"

"A ceremony of discontent."

Mawl looked surprised.

Shaitu asked, "But why? Your pottery is going well. Did you hear about the people from Hui? They asked for your work by name. They wanted pots by Vusai, they told the trading chieftainess."

"I know."

"Are you unhappy with the family?" asked Mawl. He sounded anxious. He was the kind of man who always worried about his wives and his children too.

Vusai told him, "No. I do not know exactly what is wrong. But nothing looks right to me. Everything has a nick or scratch or an imperfection of color. I hear false notes when you sing, Mawl. And you, Shaitu, the sight of you enrages me. I think, why is she happy?"

"Maybe it's the rain," Mawl said. "You have never liked this time of year."

"No." Shaitu leaned forward. "She is discontented. I know the signs. She has been restless since the harvest, and it was dry then. Remember when she broke the pot? The big one that was as blue as the sky? She said it had a flaw. It didn't. I have seen this before."

Mawl looked uneasy. Everyone knew about Shaitu's mother. She had gone crazy and abandoned her family, in order to make fishing nets. It was all due to uncertainty and discontent. No one had noticed the first signs, and by the time the ceremony was done, it was too late.

"Very well," he said. "Go to the chieftain in charge of ceremonies. I will contribute three boxes of dried fish."

"I will contribute food from the garden," Shaitu said. "And take him the pot that is spotted white and brown."

Vusai got up. "Thank you." She still felt angry. Shaitu was comparing her to the crazy woman who made nets. She was certain of it. She left the house. It was raining now, a steady drizzle. She walked down the muddy street. One of the village birds followed her. It was a big creature, almost as tall as she was. It had long legs and a long neck and a tiny head. It wanted food, and it was too stupid to realize she wasn't a mother. Only mothers fed the birds.

"Go away, you stupid thing!" she told it.

It followed her all the way to the house of the chieftain in charge of ceremonies. The chieftain was a man, of course. In every village, the work was always divided the same way. Men took care of the fishing and the ceremonies. Mothers took care of the gardens and the children. Independent women did the trading and made the most of the goods that were traded. There were a few women-men, who lived like the independent women. But they were comparatively rare. In some villages, they were thought to be perverted.

The chieftain in charge of ceremonies was on his veranda, sitting cross-legged and smoking a pipe. He was tiny and withered with a dark green complexion.

"Good day, grandfather." Vusai sat down.

"If you had my rheumatism, you wouldn't say this day is good. I can barely move! How I hate the rainy season!"

"I have come for a ceremony."

He stared at her. His eyes were black with a little yellow showing around the edges. "You are dissatisfied."

"Do I show it?"

"A little. I have also heard how you are behaving. You are rude and self-preoccupied. You break pots. You shout at children. You have come to me just in time. Help me up. As soon as we've agreed on a fee, I'll get the steam house ready."

She helped him up. They went inside and argued about the fee. He won. After that he hobbled out to the steam house. She drank tea with his wife. Only the mother in his family was still alive. She was as tiny and as withered as her husband.

"A ceremony of discontent, eh? He tried to make me go through one after my last child was born. I said, 'Leave me alone! I'm just in a bad mood. Strong tea and exercise will cure me.' And it did. But not all people are the same. For all I know, you really need his mumbo jumbo."

"Yes, grandmother."

He came back and told her the steam house was ready. She undressed and went into it. All morning she sat and sweated. He was outside, ringing a bell and singing:

"This person asks
for single-mindedness.

"This person asks
for a soul that leans
in one direction

only."

At last, when she was dizzy from the heat, he said, "Come out."

She ran down the bank and jumped into the river. The water was cold. "Ai!" she shouted. She dove under water, then surfaced and swam to the middle of the river. It was raining harder than before. She felt angry again. She hated this time of year. The sky was always cloudy, and the rain almost never stopped.

"Come back!" the chieftain called.

The current was taking her away from him. She swam back to shore, then walked along the bank till she reached him.

"Now you are purified. Go to the house of isolation. I will bring you water and the kind of tobacco that makes people see things. Stay in the house and smoke until something happens which makes you understand your situation. I will come by once a day and make a lot of noise."

Vusai said, "All right."

She went to the house, walking naked through the village. People looked away from her. It was never polite to stare at someone who was in the middle of a ceremony.

The house of isolation was on a hill at one end of the village, all by itself. It was small and windowless. There was a leak in the roof. Rain dripped in, and the floor was wet. This was going to be terrible, Vusai thought.

The first day nothing much happened. The rain stopped. She got hungry and thirsty. The chieftain didn't come till late in the afternoon. He rang his bell and sang:

"Whoever is responsible
for this situation—
listen to me!

"Whoever is responsible
for this situation—

give this person
some help!"

"Water!" shouted Vusai.

"Be quiet! You can have the water when I'm done singing."

He went on singing till the sun was almost down. Then he left. She heard him go down the hill, ringing his bell. She opened the door and brought in the water. She had made the pot. It was round and fat with a long neck. The glaze was black with streaks of reddish-brown. She drank some of the water, then sighed. "The old fool! I thought he would never stop!" She looked outside again. There was a pipe on the ground. It was a long one, made of green stone. Next to the pipe was a pouch of tobacco.

"Tomorrow," she said. "I will smoke tomorrow."

The next day she was even hungrier. She began to smoke the pipe. After a while, her mother came to visit her. She was a fat woman with an angry expression. She had been dead for years.

"Why did you choose to be independent?" she asked Vusai. "A woman should have children."

Vusai did not reply.

On the third day she felt less hungry. She smoked more tobacco, and her father arrived. He was dead too. He had drowned. He came to her with seaweed in his hair. Water dripped from his tunic. He carried a net, rolled up.

"I have been trying to decide if it was worth it," he told her. "I have plenty of time at the bottom of the sea. There's really nothing else to do, except watch the fish. And I can't catch them any more, so it makes me angry to see them—so fat, so lovely, darting right above me." He put the net down. Now she was able to see that fish thrashed inside it. The strands of the net grew thin like smoke and vanished. The fish flopped away.

"You see?" said her father. "I did everything the way I was supposed to. I made nets. I made songs. I caught fish. I helped to organize all the important ceremonies. What good did it do me? Now I lie at the bottom of the ocean. The tongue is gone out of my mouth, and I don't even have a real net anymore. Only a dream net, that won't hold fish. What was the point of my life?"

"I can't tell you," said Vusai. "I don't know."

Her father vanished.

On the fourth day she saw Mawl and Shaitu. It was early in the morning. The sun was out, a rare thing this time of year. A beam of sunlight came in through the hole in the roof. It touched Mawl right in the middle of his back. He was on top of Shaitu, having sex with her. She lay on her back on the floor, looking happy. Vusai watched curiously. It must be so much easier—to do it without worrying about making children. Independent women rarely had children, of course. From the time of puberty they ate a special diet and drank tea made from the root of the plant that prevents children. This kept them safe, most of the time. But every once in a while, an independent woman got pregnant. This caused terrible problems. It had happened to an aunt of hers. The poor woman was a trader and had been planning to go on a year-long trip. Instead she stayed home and moped. After the child was born, she gave it to the mother in her family. Then she got a divorce. The child got on her nerves, she said. She didn't want to be in the same house with it. She moved to another village and remarried. The child died young of a coughing sickness.

A sad story, Vusai thought. Why did she remember it? By this time, Mawl and Shaitu were gone. She smoked another pipe of tobacco. Now she saw people with the heads of animals. They came in the door, one after another. They spoke to her loudly. She couldn't understand a word they said.

"This is bad! This is frightening! Why is this happening to me?" She threw the pipe down and covered her face with her hands. The animal-people went away. After a while, she heard the chieftain, ringing his bell outside the house of isolation.

"I want to come out!" she called.

"Have you had a good dream?"

"No. All the dreams I've had were bad ones."

"Then keep trying." He rang the bell again.

"I want to go home!"

"You can't go home. Shut up and dream."

On the fifth day her father came back. He was still wet. There was still seaweed in his hair. But his net was gone. He said, "I wish I had become a woman-man. I would have gone traveling—not over the water, but up into the mountains. Like my second wife. I remember how she looked, so tall and strong, with a basket on her back and a long staff in her hand. Why don't you do that?"

"I don't want to."

He looked angry. "I think you are afraid to travel. Remember, someday you will be dead like me." He disappeared. She broke the pipe in two and stood up. She was a little dizzy. She stood for a moment, breathing slowly and evenly. The dizziness went away. She opened the door and went outside. As usual, it was raining. This time it was a downpour. Rivulets of water ran down the hill. "Enough is enough! I am going home!" She went toward the village, slipping and sliding in the mud. What a hateful time of year!

There was a person next to her, she noticed. He had the head of a bird. "Remember," he told her. "Without rain there is no spring. Without spring, there is no harvest. Most things have a purpose."

"Who are you?"

"A dream spirit. The effect of the tobacco hasn't worn off, though it will soon. Why did you leave the house of isolation?"

"I'm hungry, and I don't like the dreams I've been having."

"Well, I am a good dream, and my advice to you is this—go to the wife of the chieftain in charge of ceremonies. She is a wise old biddy. Ask her what she did, when she felt unhappy with her life. Her husband isn't home at present. He's down at the edge of the ocean, singing over a new fishing boat. Hurry up! He will be done soon." The bird-man began to change, growing thin and changing color. Now he was yellow instead of green. He was no longer human. Instead he was a bird. He stared at her, then squawked and stalked away.

She thought for a moment, then said, "What harm can it do?"

She went to the house of the chieftain in charge of ceremonies. His wife was inside, sitting by the fire. She had a blanket around her. It was thick and brown with a pattern of knots and tufts. Local work. It wasn't as fine as the weaving done in Hui.

"Come in," the old woman said. "Sit down. Have a cup of tea."

Vusai sat down. The old woman poured tea. It was the mild kind, that relaxed the body and filled the mind with peace—for a while, at least. Vusai drank.

"Why are you here?" the old woman asked.

"My dreams told me nothing."

"Ah! So the mumbo jumbo didn't work. Well, not everyone is credulous."

"Tell me what you did when you were full of doubt."

"I told you before. I drank strong tea. I worked in my garden. And I thought about the old stories my mother told me. Old stories are full of truth. That being so, I am going to tell you a story—about how the plant that prevents children was found."

"I know the story."

The old woman looked angry. "Shut up and listen."

"Yes, grandmother."

"Long ago, there was a time when we didn't have the plant that prevents children. Every woman was a mother. Every man had a house full of children to take care of. There were no travelers and no people who worked full time at perfecting a skill. Maybe this was good, and maybe it was bad. I don't know.

"In any case, there was a woman named Ashotai. She didn't want to be a mother, and she heard about the plant that prevents children. It grew in one place in the world: on top of a very high mountain, which was overgrown with brambles and guarded by monsters. The monsters had wings and large mouths, full of venomous teeth.

"Ashotai was brave. Off she went. She got up the mountain. I used to know how, but I've forgotten. On top of the mountain, she met a spirit. The spirit said, 'Well, you made it! Good work! But are you wise as well as brave? I have a final test for you. There are two plants here. One is the plant you seek. The other is a ringer. You can take one—only one—with you. Make your choice.'

"Ashotai looked at the plants. They were exactly alike. Then she smelled the flowers on the plants. One plant had sweet flowers. The blossoms on the other plant had a sour aroma. Finally, she broke off leaves and tasted them. The plant with the sweet flowers had a wonderful taste, light and sweet like fruit. The plant with the sour aroma had a terrible taste. It was both sour and bitter.

170

"Ashotai sat down and thought. Finally she said, 'The plant I seek will give people the ability to choose. And every real choice is bitter. If you choose to do one thing, then you lose the chance to do other things that may be just as pleasant or interesting. Because of this, it can be said—in every choice is the seed of regret, like the sour pit or core of a fruit. I think the bitter plant is the one I seek.'

"'Well, well,' said the spirit. 'You *are* wise. The plant you have chosen is the one that prevents children. And, as you say, every real choice is bitter. The other plant—the sweet one—is the plant that gives true peace of mind. If you had taken it, you and your people would have been happy forever. But you can't have everything. Take your plant and go.'

"So Ashotai came down from the mountain and gave the plant to her people. After that, every girl could choose whether or not to be a mother. And it was decided to give men a choice, out of fairness. Most men chose to be fathers. But a few become women-men. They act like the independent women in almost every way, and a man can take one of these into his house as a second wife."

"I know all this," said Vusai.

The old woman frowned. "No you don't. You have heard the story, but you don't understand it. Remember, every choice is bitter. In every choice is the seed of regret. Well, you have eaten the fruit, Vusai. And now you are biting down on the seed. When I was your age, I realized—I was what I was. I had six children to care for and a garden and a flock of birds. I would never be a traveler. I would never have a skill as fine as the one you have. Ah! How that hurt! But I pulled weeds and drank strong tea. In time I felt better. I advise you to go back to making pots. Eat well. Sleep well. Drink medicinal teas. Your mood will improve."

Vusai put down her cup. "Is every choice a trap?"

"No." All at once the old woman had a face like a prowler from the hills. Her ears were huge and pointed. Her eyes were green, and she had a muzzle covered with yellow fur. "A choice is a path. No one can walk down two paths at one time. And when you are far enough down one path, you cannot turn around. You are too old. You do not have the time to go back to where you started." The prowler stared at her. "Pay attention to what I tell you! Remember what I say! I cannot talk to you any longer. You are almost sober. Wake up and go home. This ceremony is over."

Vusai opened her eyes. She was in the house of isolation. Rain was dripping down on her through the hole in the roof. Light shone in through the cracks around the door. She could see the dream pipe in front of her. The stem was broken.

"Ah!" said Vusai. She got up and rubbed her legs. They were stiff and sore. Then she stretched and yawned. Finally she went home.

MAMUGRANDAE—
THE SECOND TALE

Merril Mushroom

One day, Vildachaya asked Mamugrandae to go out for her again. "Find the place where the purple flax grows," she said, popping Mamugrandae's soul into her own mouth for safe-keeping. "Gather the moon-shadows and bring them home, and I will make from them bleeding pillows to sit upon during our moon flows."

So Mamugrandae went out, and at last she came to a place that was strange to her, and she did not know her way any further. She sat down on a boulder and pondered what to do next. As she rested her left hand on the stone next to her thigh, she felt a squirming beneath her index finger; and a tiny, muffled voice said, "Pardon me, but would you please move your hand?"

Mamugrandae lifted her hand and looked down at the stone, and there she saw a little brown ant which the weight of her finger had pushed down. The ant wriggled about until it was able to get back onto six legs, then raised itself up on four legs and brushed itself off with its feelers. At last it stood on its two back legs and waved its four front legs and feelers at Mamugrandae. "Thank you," said the ant. "You have no idea what it's like to be crushed by anyone who decides to sit on this boulder and lay a hand on it."

"You are right, I don't," agreed Mamugrandae, "and I

am terribly sorry for being so careless."

"Well, no matter now," said the ant looking up at her. "It is past, and doubtless you'll be more considerate in the future. Tell me, who are you, and why are you sitting on my stone?"

"I am Mamugrandae, and I am beautiful. I'm sitting here while I decide which way to go."

"Where are you going?"

"I'm going to look for the purple flax so that I can gather its moon-shadows to bring to Vildachaya, who will make bleeding pillows for us."

"So, do you know where the purple flax grows and how to get there?"

"No," admitted Mamugrandae, "I don't."

"I do," said the ant, "but all I am permitted to tell you is that to find the place, you must follow the setting sun." Then the ant looked down shyly and asked, "Mamugrandae, may I climb onto your knee?"

"Certainly," answered Mamugrandae. The ant climbed onto her knee and looked into her face. Its feet felt warm against her flesh. "You are a strange ant," observed Mamugrandae.

"No doubt," replied the ant. "And your knee is quite lovely," and it stroked Mamugrandae's skin with its feelers.

Mamugrandae felt a quiver start at that spot on her knee and course in ripples up her thighs and across her belly. "That feels very nice, ant," she said.

"May I come up onto the end of your breast so that I can speak with you more intimately?" asked the ant. Mamugrandae nodded, and the ant ran up the rolls of her stomach and onto the end of her breast, bringing a rush of heat to Mamugrandae's body. "I was wondering," the ant said next, "if you would let me kiss you, then lie down with me and hold me and let us make love together."

Mamugrandae shook her head doubtfully. "I just don't know how I could do such a thing with you, ant," she answered.

"Oh, there wouldn't be any problem," said the ant,

174

"because I am a female ant. Then, afterwards, I will come with you and help you to find the place where the purple flax grows."

So Mamugrandae lay down with the ant, and they kissed each other, and she held her; and they were big and small with one another, they were hard and soft with one another, and they made love together. Then the ant kissed Mamugrandae one last time and crawled into her ear, and Mamugrandae fell asleep.

When Mamugrandae awakened, the sun was setting. Remembering what the ant had told her, she got up and began to follow the setting sun in search of the purple flax. She followed the setting sun over the plains and into the hills. She trotted, and then she ran, trying to keep up with it, but the sun continued to gain distance on her; and at last it tipped over the horizon, and she lost it. But for a while, its light still echoed in colors from the edge, and Mamugrandae continued on, until the sun was quite gone, and only starlight was left. Mamugrandae knew she had better stop then, and she sat down to wait for daybreak.

At last the darkness began to grey, and the first light of morning creased the sky. Mamugrandae stood up and stretched her massive body, feeling the ripples of her flesh, feeling the fullness of her strength and her fatness. The sun sprang forth, showering her with its heat, and Mamugrandae flung her arms out and whirled in a circle with exhilaration. When she stopped, a small black fly was sitting on her thumb. Mamugrandae brought her hand close to her face and stared. "What are you doing, bug?"

"I am riding on your thumb, of course. What are you doing yourself, and who are you, anyhow?"

"I am Mamugrandae, and I am beautiful. I am preparing to continue following the sun so that I can find the place where the purple flax grows and gather its moon-shadows to bring to Vildachaya so that she can make bleeding pillows for us."

"And do you know *how* to gather the moon-shadows once you have found the purple flax?" asked the fly.

"No," Mamugrandae frowned, "but I have encountered a discouraging bug like you once before, and it turned out to be only my own shadow. Perhaps you are nothing more than that yourself."

"Well," huffed the fly, "to begin with, I am not a bug, I am a fly; and I am real enough. Of course your notice of me is necessary for you to know that I am, but I do have an existence of my very own. I am not at all dependent on your attention for my being. But you are Mamugrandae, and, in truth, you are beautiful. Love me for a little while, and then I will go with you and show you how to gather the moonshadows of the purple flax."

"You have a flaw, fly," said Mamugrandae. "You are ugly. You have bristles. How can I love you? Your bristles will stick me."

"You have a mote in your eye, then," said the fly, "if you feel I have a flaw; and you must be comparing me with something else if you think that I am ugly. As a fly, I actually am quite lovely. Notice me again, Mamugrandae, and perceive me as I really am."

So Mamugrandae took the tip of her pinky finger and wiped away the mote, and she perceived the fly in all its flyness. "Why you are a female fly," said Mamugrandae in amazement, "and you are beautiful!" Then Mamugrandae took the fly against her massive bosom and loved her, and the fly loved Mamugrandae in turn; and the bristles on the fly did not stick Mamugrandae, nor were they abrasive.

When they were done with their loving and had been still for a while, holding each other in contentment, Mamugrandae fell into a doze, and the fly crawled into her other ear. After a while, Mamugrandae awakened, rose from where she lay, and again followed the sun as it moved in setting toward the far horizon.

Now Mamugrandae was hungry, but there were no roots or berries or nuts to be found. She chewed on some bark, but it only made her light-headed. Then she saw a large bee sitting on a stalk fanning its wings. Mamugrandae walked over to it. "Bee," she said, "I am hungry. Would you please give me some of your honey?"

"I cannot do that," replied the bee. "I am not a honeybee."

"Not a honeybee? Whoever heard of such a thing? What kind of bee are you then, bee?"

"I am a stinging bee."

"Indeed? A stinging bee? I have never been stung by a stinging bee. Will you sting me then, bee, so I will know what it is like?"

"I would be glad to sting you, Mamugrandae, for you are beautiful, but first you must love me. I cannot sting you until you have loved me."

"Well, I have loved an ant and a fly by now," Mamugrandae mumbled to herself, "so I may as well love a bee, too." Then she said more loudly, "Okay, bee, I will love you, but only if you are a female bee."

"Well, then," replied the bee, "let us get to it, for I am indeed a female bee as you will find out."

When they had finished loving and were resting together, Mamugrandae said, "Don't forget, bee, that you will sting me now. Your loving was quite delightful, and I am sure that your sting will be the same."

The bee flew up and landed on Mamugrandae's shoulder. "I must warn you that it will be painful."

"And why not?" responded Mamugrandae. "We all must experience pain in our lives, and what would be a better time than when one is full from loving?"

So the bee stung Mamugrandae on the shoulder, and then she flew away.

Hum, thought Mamugrandae, *that didn't hurt very much at all*, and she rubbed her shoulder disappointedly. But then the poison started to spread, and Mamugrandae felt pain which intensified, became greater with every passing moment, until Mamugrandae wished to have done with it. *She gave me no warning that the pain would be this terrible*, Mamugrandae thought resentfully. She rubbed her shoulder again and felt a great welt forming. Soon she could not lift her arm, and soon after that the pain became so awful that she was forced to sit down and then to lie down. *This is more than I expected,* Mamugrandae thought in dismay. *I must do something about it.* But there was nothing she could do except lie on the ground and endure it, lie on the ground and suffer, lie on the ground powerless, paralyzed by the intensity of her agony, consumed by it; until finally the poison began to dissipate and lose its potency.

After a while, Mamugrandae found that she was able to move again. She raised herself to her knees, bent over, and vomited. "Well," she said aloud, "now I feel better. That was very intense, and I don't think I would want to do it again. Still, loving the bee was rather nice." And to her surprise, she found that the fact of her suffering was hidden now behind the memory of the pleasure of their loving.

Now Mamugrandae was even hungrier. She hurried on her way, following the setting sun, and her hunger became a source of energy for her. She sprang forward in huge leaps, flinging her legs one after the other, pushing herself onward. She began to gain on the sun; and when she realized this, her strength swelled within her like a river cresting flood, coursing through her until it burst from her, pouring forth until it seemed as though the entire universe was filled with her energy.

Then Mamugrandae's foot struck the ground hard, and an ache lanced through her leg and up into her body; and everything grand and wonderful stopped and fell away; and Mamugrandae realized that she had exhausted her strength and was at the end of her endurance. She threw back her head in despair, and there in front of her, within reach, almost within her grasp, was the setting sun.

Mamugrandae summoned strength with all her power to call. She pulled in energy and strove toward the sun with all her might. She pushed away from the earth with all her force, thrust her arms forward with all her reach, leaped toward the setting sun with her entire massive body, and flung herself upon it.

As soon as she touched it she was burned through to her core. Her huge body scorched to a crisp and fell on the ground; while the sun, taking no notice, continued on its way to setting.

Now the stinging bee came flying along, and following her were several other bees. She looked down at the charred Mamugrandae and said, "Oh, dear, we seem to be a little late. These honeybees have come with honey to feed Mamugrandae, but she seems to have been distracted from her purpose. Ant told her to *follow* the sun, not to *catch* it! Well, perhaps there is something we can do to help anyhow." She motioned to the honeybees, who flew down over what was left of Mamugrandae. They spread their honey over her and about her, covering her completely and filling her with it. Then they flew in a circle around her while they hummed a continuous healing vibration which surrounded her and enclosed her in its energy. Mamugrandae absorbed all of this, soaked it into herself; and she healed and mended until she was exactly the same as she had been before she caught the sun.

Mamugrandae got to her feet. "Thank you very much," she said to the bees, for she remembered all that had happened.

"You're very welcome," the bees responded.

Now the ant crawled out of her ear. "Well," said the ant, "here you are at last."

Mamugrandae looked around. She stood at the bottom of a high wall which seemed to extend indefinitely in all directions. "Exactly *where* am I at last, ant?" she asked.

"You are at the bottom of the plateau where the purple flax grows on top."

"Well, that's very nice, ant. Now how do I get to the *top* of the plateau where the purple flax grows?"

"Unfortunately," said the ant, "there is no way."

"What do you mean," Mamugrandae demanded, "no way?"

"Unfortunately," the ant explained, "you are at the right location, but you are not in the proper position."

"Well, then, ant, how do I get in the proper position?"

"I do not think you can do that," said the ant, "and I am

truly sorry."

Hum, thought Mamugrandae, refusing to give up, *as I recall, fly said that she could help.* "Fly," she said aloud, "come on out of there."

The fly crawled out of Mamugrandae's other ear. "Yes?" she said.

"Fly," said Mamugrandae, "here I am at the place where the purple flax grows, and I cannot get up to it. You said once before that you would show me how to gather the moon-shadows."

"That's true," said the fly, "I did, and I wish I could; but to do this you have to be able to get to them, and you are at the right place but in the wrong position."

"How distressing!" said Mamugrandae.

"However," the fly continued, "I can do this for you—I will fly up to the top of the plateau after the moon rises, and I will gather the moon-shadows and toss them down to you."

So as soon as the moon began to rise, fly flew to the top of the plateau. There she gathered the moon-shadows of the purple flax and tossed them down to Mamugrandae; but when Mamugrandae reached to pick them up, her hand passed through them, and she was unable to grasp them. The moon-shadows lay at her feet in a heap where they had fallen, and she could not get them, she was unable to take hold of them; and such a terrible frustration filled her that she felt she must explode with its shrieks.

The moon rose higher, and Mamugrandae felt the drawing in her womb which meant that her bleeding was beginning. She pressed her hands against her body and called to the Moon Mother to help her, and her bleeding broke loose and flooded onto her thighs. The moon shone from behind her, and she looked down and saw her own moon-shadow upon the earth; and her moon-spirit moved from her and into her shadow; and her shadow bent over and took up in its own hands the shadows of the flax. As the moon approached the horizon, it pulled Mamugrandae's moon-shadow up and against her; and the moon-shadows of the purple flax settled into her waiting arms.

A great and joyous gratitude burst through Mamu-grandae, and she embraced her moon sisters ant, fly, and bee. Then she returned home and gave the moon-shadows to Vildachaya, and Vildachaya gave Mamugrandae back her soul; and Vildachaya made for them the most wonderful bleeding pillows ever.

THE GIRL WHO WENT TO THE RICH NEIGHBORHOOD

Rachel Pollack

There was once a widow who lived with her six daughters in the poorest neighborhood in town. In summer the girls all went barefoot, and even in winter they often had to pass one pair of shoes between them as they ran through the street. Even though the mother got a check every month from the welfare department, it never came to enough, despite their all eating as little as possible. They would not have survived at all if the supermarkets hadn't allowed the children to gather behind the loading gates at the end of the day and collect the crushed or fallen vegetables.

Sometimes, when there was no more money, the mother would leave her left leg as credit with the grocer. When her check came, or one of the children found a little work, she would get back her leg and be able to walk without the crutch her oldest daughter had made from a splintery board. One day, however, after she'd paid her bill, she found herself stumbling. When she examined her leg she discovered that the grocery had kept so many legs and arms jumbled together in their big metal cabinet that her foot had become all twisted. She sat down on their only chair and began to cry, waving her arms over her head.

Seeing her mother so unhappy the youngest girl, whose name was Rose, walked up and announced, "Please don't worry. I'll go to the rich neighborhood." Her mother kept crying. "And I'll speak to the mayor. I'll get him to help us." The widow smiled and stroked her daughter's hair.

She doesn't believe me, Rose thought. Maybe she won't let me go. I'd better sneak away. The next day, when the time came to go to the supermarket Rose took the shoes she shared with her sisters and slipped them in her shopping bag. She hated doing this, but she would need the shoes for the long walk to the rich neighborhood. Besides, maybe the mayor wouldn't see her if she came barefoot. Soon, she told herself, she'd bring back shoes for everyone. At the supermarket she filled her bag with seven radishes that had fallen off the bunch, two sticks of yellowed celery, and four half-blackened bananas. Well, she thought, I guess I'd better get started.

As soon as she left the poor neighborhood Rose saw some boys shoving and poking a weak old lady who was trying to cross the street. What a rotten thing to do, the girl thought, and hoped the children in the rich neighborhood weren't all like that. She found a piece of pipe in the street and chased them away.

"Thank you," wheezed the old woman, who wore a yellow dress and had long blonde hair that hung, uncombed, down to her knees. She sat down in the middle of the road, with cars going by on every side. Rose said, "Shouldn't we get out of the street? We could sit on the pavement."

"I can't," said the old woman, "I must eat something first. Don't you have anything to eat?"

Rose reached in her basket to give the old woman a radish. In a moment the shrivelled red thing had vanished and the woman held out her hand. Rose gave her another radish, and then another, until all the radishes had slid down the old woman's densely veined throat. "Now we can go," she said, and instantly jumped to her feet to drag Rose across the road.

Rose told herself that maybe she wouldn't need them. She looked down at the silver pavement and then up at the buildings that reached so far above her head the people in the windows looked like toys. "Is this the rich neighborhood?" she asked.

"Hardly," the woman said, "you have to go a long way to reach the rich neighborhood." Rose thought how she'd better be extra careful with the rest of her food. The old woman said, "But if you really want to go there I can give you something to help you." She ran her fingers through her tangled gold hair and when she took them out she was holding a lumpy yellow coin. "This token will always get you on or off the subway."

What a strange idea, thought Rose. How could you use a token more than once? And even if you could, everyone knew that you didn't need anything to get off the subway. But she put the coin in the bag and thanked the old woman.

All day she walked and when night came she crawled under a fire escape beside some cardboard cartons. She was very hungry but she thought she had better save her celery and bananas for the next day. Trying not to think of the warm mattress she shared with two of her sisters, she went to sleep.

The next morning the sound of people marching to work woke her up. She stretched herself, thinking how silver streets may look very nice but didn't make much of a bed. Then she rubbed her belly and stared at the celery. I'd better get started first, she told herself. But when she began to walk her feet hurt, for her sisters' shoes, much too big for her, had rubbed the skin raw the day before.

Maybe she could take the subway train. Maybe the old woman's token would work at least once. She went down a subway entrance where a guard with a gun walked back and forth, sometimes clapping his hands or stamping his feet. As casually as she could Rose walked up and put her token in the slot. I hope he doesn't shoot me, she thought. But then the wooden blades of the gate turned and she passed through.

A moment later, she was walking down the stairs when she heard a soft clinking sound. She turned around to see the token bouncing on its rim along the corridor and down the stairs until it bounced right into the shopping bag. Rose looked to see if the guard was taking his gun out but he was busy staring out the entrance.

All day she traveled on the subway train, but whenever she tried to read the signs she couldn't make out what they said beneath the huge black marks drawn all over them. Rose wondered if the marks formed the magic that made the trains go. She'd sometimes heard people say that without magic the subway would break down forever. Finally she decided she must have reached the rich neighborhood. She got off the train, half expecting to have to use her token. But the exit door swung open with no trouble and soon she found herself on a gold pavement, with buildings that reached so high the people looked like birds fluttering around in giant caves.

Rose was about to ask someone for the mayor's office when she saw a policeman with a gold mask covering his face slap an old woman. Rose hid in a doorway and made a sound like a siren, a trick she'd learned in the poor neighborhood. The policeman ran off waving his gold truncheon.

"Thank you, thank you," said the old woman whose tangled red hair reached down to her ankles. "I'm so hungry now, could you give me something to eat?" Trying not to cry Rose gave the woman first one piece of celery and then the other. Then she asked, "Is this the rich neighborhood?"

"No, no, no," the woman laughed, "but if you're planning to go there I can give you something that might help you." She ran her fingers through her hair and took out a red feather. "If you need to reach something and cannot, then wave this feather." Rose couldn't imagine how a feather could help her reach anything but she didn't want to sound rude so she put the feather in her bag.

Since it was evening and Rose knew that gangs sometimes ran through the streets after dark she thought she'd better find a place to sleep. She saw a pile of wooden crates in front of a store and lay down behind them, sadly thinking how she'd better save her four bananas for the next day.

The next morning the sound of opening and closing car doors woke her up, and she stretched painfully. The gold streets had hurt her back even more than the silver ones the night before. With a look at her bananas, now completely black, she got to her feet and walked back to the subway.

All day she rode on the train, past underground store windows showing clothes that would tear in a day, and bright flimsy furniture, and strange machines with rows of black buttons. The air became very sweet, but thick, as if someone had sprayed the tunnels with perfume. Finally Rose decided she couldn't breathe and had to get out.

She came up to a street made all of diamond, and buildings so high she couldn't see anything at all in the windows, only flashes of colors. The people walking glided a few inches above the ground, while the cars moved so gently on their white tires they looked like swimmers floating in a pool.

Rose was about to ask for the mayor's office when she saw an old woman surrounded by manicured dogs and rainbow dyed cats whose rich owners had let them roam the street. Rose whistled so high she herself couldn't hear it, but the animals all ran away, thinking their owners had called them for dinner.

"Thank you *so* much," the woman said, dusting off her black dress. Her black hair trailed the ground behind her. "Do you suppose you could give me something to eat?"

Biting back her tears Rose held out the four bananas. The woman laughed and said, "One is more than enough for me. You eat the others." Rose had to stop herself shoving all three bananas into her mouth at once. She was glad she did, for each one tasted like a different food, from chicken to strawberries. She looked up amazed.

"Now," said the woman, "I suppose you want the mayor's house." Her mouth open, Rose nodded yes. The woman told her to look for a street so bright she had to cover her eyes to walk on it. Then she said, "If you ever find the road too crowded blow on this." She ran her fingers through her hair and took out a black whistle shaped like a pigeon. The girl said, "Thank you," though she didn't think people would get out of the street just for a whistle.

When the woman had gone Rose looked around at the diamond street. I'd break my back sleeping here, she thought, and decided to look for the mayor's house that evening. Up and down the streets she hobbled, now and then running out of the way of dark-windowed cars or lines of children dressed all in money and holding hands as they ran screaming through the street.

At one point she saw a great glow of light and thought she must have found the mayor's house, but when she came close she saw only an empty road where bright balls of light on platinum poles shone on giant fountains spouting liquid gold into the air. Rose shook her head and walked on.

Several times she asked people for the mayor's house but no one seemed to hear or see her. As night came Rose thought that at least the rich neighborhood wouldn't get too cold; they probably heated the streets. But instead of warm air a blast of cold came up from the damned pavement. The people in the rich neighborhood chilled the streets so they could use the personal heaters built into their clothes.

For the first time Rose thought she would give up. It was all so strange, how could she ever think the mayor would even listen to her? About to look for a subway entrance she saw a flash of light a few blocks away and began to walk towards it. When she came close the light became so bright she automatically covered her eyes, only to find she could see just as well as before. Scared now that she'd actually found the mayor she slid forward close to the buildings.

The light came from a small star which the mayor's staff had captured and set in a lead cage high above the street. A party was going on, with people dressed in all sorts of costumes. Some looked like birds with beaks instead of noses, and giant feathered wings growing out of their backs; others had become lizards, their heads covered in green scales. In the middle, on a huge chair of black stone sat the mayor looking very small in a white fur robe. Long curved fingernails hooked over the ends of his chair. All around him advisers floated in the air on glittery cushions.

For a time Rose stayed against the wall, afraid to move. Finally she told herself she could starve just standing there. Trying not to limp, she marched forward and said, "Excuse me."

No one paid any attention. And no wonder. Suspended from a helicopter a band played on peculiar horns and boxes. "Excuse me," Rose said louder, then shouted, the way she'd learned to shout in the poor neighborhood when animals from outside the city attacked the children.

Everything stopped. The music sputtered out, the lizards stopped snatching at the birds who stopped dropping jeweled "eggs" on the lizards' heads. Two policemen ran forward. Masks like smooth mirrors covered their heads so that the rich people would only see themselves if they happened to glance at a policeman. They grabbed Rose's arms, but before they could handcuff her the mayor boomed (his voice came through a microphone grafted onto his tongue), "Who are you? What do you want? Did you come to join the party?"

Everyone laughed. Even in the rich neighborhood, they knew, you had to wait years for an invitation to the mayor's party.

"No sir," said Rose. "I came to ask for help for the poor neighborhood. Nobody has any money to buy food and people have to leave their arms and legs at the grocery just to get anything. Can you help us?"

The laughter became a roar. People shouted ways the mayor could help the poor neighborhood. Someone suggested canning the ragged child and sending her back as charity dinners. The mayor held up his hand and everyone became silent. "We could possibly help you," he said. "But first you will have to prove yourself. Will you do that?"

Confused, Rose said yes. She didn't know what he meant. She wondered if she needed a welfare slip or some other identification. "Good," the mayor said. "We've got a small problem here and maybe you could help us solve it."

He waved a hand and a picture appeared in the air in front of Rose. She saw a narrow metal stick about a foot long with a black knob at one end and a white knob at the other. The mayor told Rose that the stick symbolized the mayor's power, but the witches had stolen it.

"Why don't you send the police to get it back?" Rose asked. Again the mayor had to put up his hand to stop the laughter. He told the girl that the witches had taken the stick to their embassy near the United Nations, where diplomatic immunity kept the police from following them.

"I have to go to the witches' embassy?" Rose asked. "I don't even know where it is. How will I find it?" But the mayor paid no attention to her. The music started and the birds and lizards went back to chasing each other.

Rose was walking away when a bird woman flapped down in front of her. "Shall I tell you the way to the witches' embassy?"

"Yes," Rose said. "Please." The woman bent over laughing. Rose thought she would just fly away again, but no, in between the giggles she told the girl exactly how to find the witches. Then she wobbled away on her wingtips, laughing so hard she bumped into buildings whenever she tried to fly.

With her subway token Rose arrived at the embassy in only a few minutes. The iron door was so tall she couldn't even reach the bell, so she walked around looking for a servants' entrance. Shouts came from an open window. She crept forward.

Wearing nothing but brown oily mud all over their bodies the witches were dancing before a weak fire. The whole embassy house smelled of damp moss. Rose was about to slip away when she noticed a charred wooden table near the window, and on top of it the mayor's stick.

She was about to climb over the sill, grab the stick and run, when she noticed little alarm wires strung across the bottom of the window. Carefully she reached in above the wires towards the table. No use. The stick lay a good six inches out of reach.

An image of the woman in red came to her. "If you need

to reach something and cannot, then wave this feather." Though she still couldn't see how the feather could help her, especially with something so heavy, she fluttered it towards the table.

The red-haired woman appeared behind the witches, who nevertheless seemed not to notice her. "I am the East Wind," she said, and Rose saw that her weakness had vanished and her face shone as bright as her hair waving behind her. "Because you helped me and gave me your food when you had so little I will give you what you want." She blew on the table and a gust of wind carried the stick over the wires into Rose's hands.

The girl ran off with all the speed she'd learned running away from trouble in the poor neighborhood. Before she could go half a block, however, the stick cried out, "Mistresses! This little one is stealing me."

In an instant the witches were after her, shrieking and waving their arms as they ran, leaving drops of mud behind them. Soon, however, Rose reached the subway where her token let her inside while the witches, who hadn't taken any money, let alone tokens, could only stand on the other side of the gate and scream at her.

Rose could hardly sit she was so excited. The train clacked along, and only the silly weeping of the stick in her bag kept her from jumping up and down. She imagined her mother's face when she came home in the mayor's car piled so high with money and food.

At the stop for the mayor's house Rose stepped off the train swinging her bag. There, lined up across the exit, stood the witches. They waved their muddy arms and sang peculiar words in warbly high-pitched voices. The stick called, "Mistresses, you found me."

Rose looked over her shoulder at the subway. She could run back, but suppose they were waiting for her in the tunnel? And she still had to get to the mayor. Suddenly she remembered the old woman saying that the token could get her off the subway as well as on. She grabbed it from her bag and held it up.

The woman in yellow appeared before her. "I am the South Wind," she said, "and because you helped me I will help you." Gently she blew on Rose and a wind as soft as an old bed carried the girl over the heads of the witches and right out of the subway to the street.

As fast as she could she ran to the mayor's house. But as soon as she turned the corner to the street with the captured star she stopped and clutched her bag against her chest. The mayor was waiting for her, wrapped in a head-to-toe cylinder of bullet-proof glass, while behind him, filling the whole street, stood a giant squad of police. Their mirrored heads bounced the starlight back to the sky. "Give me the witches' stick," the mayor said.

"The witches? You said—"

"Idiot child. That stick contains the magic of the witches' grandmothers." He then began to rave about smashing the witches' house and putting them to work in the power stations underneath the rich neighborhood. Rose tried to back away. "Arrest her," the mayor said.

What had the old woman in black said? "If you ever find the road too crowded, blow on this." Rose grabbed the pigeon whistle and blew as hard as she could. The woman appeared, her hair wider than the whole wave of police. "I am the North Wind," she told the girl, and might have said more but the squad was advancing. The North Wind threw out her arms and instead of a gust of air a huge flock of black pigeons flew from her dress to pick up the mayor and all the police. Ferociously beating their wings the pigeons carried them straight over the wall into the Bronx, where they were captured by burglars and never heard from again.

"Thank you," Rose said, but the old woman was gone. With a sigh Rose took out the witches' stick. "I'm sorry," she told it. "I just wanted to help the poor neighborhood."

"May I go home now?" the stick asked sarcastically. Before the girl could answer the stick sprang out of her hands and flew end over end through the air, back to the witches' embassy.

Rose found herself limping along the riverside, wondering what she would tell her mother and her sisters. Why didn't I help the West Wind? she said to herself. Maybe she could've done something for me.

A woman all in silver appeared on the water. Her silver hair tumbled behind her into the river. "I do not need to test you to know your goodness," she said. She blew on the river and a large wave rose up to drench the surprised girl.

But when Rose shook the water off she found that every drop had become a jewel. Red, blue, purple, green, stones of all shapes and colors, sapphires in the shape of butterflies, opals with sleeping faces embedded in the center, they all covered Rose's feet up to her ankles. She didn't stop to look at them. With both hands she scooped them up into her basket, and then her shoes. Hurry, she told herself. She knew that no matter how many police you got rid of there were always more. And wouldn't the rich people insist the jewels belonged to them?

So full of jewels she could hardly run Rose waddled to the subway entrance. Only when she got there did she notice that the streets had lost their diamond paving. All around her the rich people stumbled or fell on the lumpy grey concrete. Some of them had begun to cry or to crawl on all fours, feeling the ground like blind people at the edge of a cliff. One woman had taken off all her clothes, her furs and silks and laces, and was spreading them all about the ground to hide its ugliness.

Fascinated, Rose took a step back towards the street. She wondered if anything had happened to the star imprisoned in its cage above the mayor's house. But then she remembered how her mother had limped when the grocer had gotten her foot all twisted. She ran downstairs to use her magic token for the last time.

Though the train was crowded Rose found a seat in the corner where she could bend over her treasures to hide them from any suspicious eyes. What does a tax collector look like, she wondered.

As the rusty wheels of the train shrieked through the gold neighborhood and then the silver one Rose wondered if

192

she'd ever see the old ladies again. She sighed happily. It didn't matter. She was going home, back to her mother and her sisters and all her friends in the poor neighborhood.

SAHREL SHORT SWORDS

Ginger Simpson Curry

Sahrel had made her decision by the time the old witch Beliaat returned to the keep antechamber with the chalice. She would venture out into the kingdom hidden inside a stranger's body—because she must. The city of Meowood was on the verge of being torn apart with those Deformed Ones outside the walls rebelling against her uncle, the elitist ruler. But his 30-year reign had ended abruptly two days ago. A cryp, hidden behind a curtain in the king's bedchamber, had knifed the ruler in his sleep. Why Sahrel had to go out into the fringes, though, she understood not. Whyfor did a future queen have consultants if she could not with their counsel circumvent her uncle's mistakes?

Seated before a small wood table in the secret room, Sahrel watched the deft movements of the witch as Beliaat mixed liquids while murmuring spells over them. Sahrel's head went up and back in that haughty way she had. *Fools!* All the recent leaders had been dolts. The Outcasts merely wished the amenities enjoyed by the inner court circle. When she became ruler, she would see that their own village was new-fashioned and Meowood's troubles would cease.

Her plain face tightened into a frown. Though it be

194

only for a one-night space, she feared leaving all that was familiar. She told herself it was not merely abhorrence of living in an alien body making her skin quiver, but her suspicions about the court mage. Had not Beliaat warned the king that he must open the inner city to the cryps, even inviting them to take part in the council? She shuddered at the image of seeing those mangled people every day, continuously reminded of their differences.

With her lackluster brown hair and ordinary features, she was considered plain by Meowood standards—but at least there were countless others like her. And after all, since cryps could not work as efficiently as other citizens, why should they dwell inside? No, her way was best for all.

As she reached for the goblet, Sahrel tried to comfort herself with the thoughts that Beliaat had been court guardian for centuries, she, Sahrel, would be crowned in two days, and the worst that could happen was that she would be masked behind the features of another human—perhaps more fashionable ones!

The old sorceress drew back the magic potion as if to tease the young girl. "I pray to the Mother Who Spirits All Living Beings that your decision to undergo the Royal Ritual will infuse this sickly nation with the wisdom and heart to breach its differences."

Sahrel ran a hand over her leather tunic before resting it lightly on the sword worn upon her right hip. Strengthened momentarily, she murmured, "It is only for the space of one eve-time that I must remain in stranger's form?"

The witch intoned, "It is that you must return to this form before day's-break or enjoy forever that shape."

Sahrel flinched at the way Beliaat's lips curved up into a mocking grin. She wished only that she might drink the substance quickly. She would prove that she, of the Royal Line of Zayel, could lead the kingdom to stability. Again her slim hand reached for the tumbler.

Black eyes snaking from nests of wrinkles, Beliaat

further cautioned, "Child, I must be certain you understand the edict."

In a voice sounding far-off to her ears, Sahrel intoned the conditions she had first learned at her uncle's death. "It has long been a court-sorceress's duty to assist the spiritual rebirth of Meowood's rulers through their drinking this Purge. Yet none of the male rulers for a 100-year spell would accept the challenge—for only he certain of his ability to be a great leader will voluntarily inhabit an outer shell from which . . . he may not return."

As the old witch held the goblet against the girl's shaking lips, she muttered so low that Sahrel did not comprehend the words until the elixir trickled down her throat, "If ye be found lacking, ye be found forever after in Moth form!"

Throat muscles spasming, Sahrel flung the goblet from her. *Traitor!* Wise had she been to distrust Beliaat. But as the young girl leaped upon the grinning witch, the change began. She felt as though she were smothering as tissue folded in upon tissue, bone structure shifted, and cells rearranged themselves.

Sahrel fell forward into the witch's skinny arms, her new body bursting forth from swollen pupa stage to damp giant Moth—all within the space of ten breaths.

◆◆◆◆◆◆

Dark descended like a great crepuscular bird swooping down to feed upon the dead. Her wings dried sufficiently, Sahrel fluttered away. Had she been wrong to drink the philter? Was the witch trying to get rid of her or was she truly on a quest for knowledge? She knew not. All she could do was follow this path as it unfolded.

It was many leagues later that the transformed girl contained her anger enough to fly to a tree and survey herself in calm lake waters. The full moon lit up the pond nearly as brightly as day-sun. And indeed, as Beliaat had announced, the creature staring back at her was that of a

Moth—a Hawke Moth. But such a splendid one! Each wing was over a man-hand in length and . . . Spreading out her four wings to admire the golden brown fur of scales and the set of artificial eyes, turquoise blue, on the underwings, Sahrel thought abruptly, *Why, I'm beautiful!*

She would have remained there longer but her antennae began vibrating as her tympana caught a low chirping noise. Before she could fly away, the reflection of another Flutterer in the water stilled her anxiety. A large male half her size drifted to her side; his golden scales shimmered with a similar burnished metallic luster.

For a second compound eyes gazed into compound eyes, then the tug of hunger in Sahrel's stomach imposed a more insistent quest for food. Though their eyes were very efficient at detecting motion and distinguishing color, they saw only blurs at a distance. But soon, borne upon the back of a young breeze, the faint scent of a type of moon-glory wafted to their antennae. In tandem the two moths flew toward the vines.

As he glided close to her, a sensation she could not identify caused Sahrel to emit a tiny amount of pheromone. He responded in kind and the air became rife with their fragrance. As if of one mind, linked by a calling older than any of their kind, the two moths spiraled higher and higher, releasing more and more intoxicating perfume, until they neared the clouds. Here, Sahrel coasted on an air current, new sensations swirling thoughts into meaningless tangles.

From a peaceful glissade, the other Flutterer sailed passionately into a series of rolls, one moment falling until he appeared but a smudge against the meadow below, the next whirling, wings climbing the sky with the swiftness of rotating blades. Finally he became a gentle stream, floating upside down on the wind, his brilliant colors displayed for her. In this keel-up position he maneuvered closer to Sahrel.

The deluge of unaccustomed sensations had overwhelmed Sahrel's thoughts. Erotic signals emanating from his velvet body called to something just awakening in the young girl, called more passionately than the forgotten blooms far beneath them.

Soon he was directly under her, alternately slowing down and speeding up, the silken fur of his underbody brushing hers in long sensuous strokes that undulated hair shafts from her head to her tail. The very sky around them seemed to take on their cadence, throbbing in shades of magenta as they carried the courtship ritual to its natural culmination.

On the ground, a small figure shook her fist at the sky and redoubled the Ceasing Spells—to no avail.

Not until the wind shifted did Sahrel feel the undercurrents of an inner voice increase its message of denial and rejection. With great effort she directed her mind back to the aroma of the tubular flowers, flipping a wing in the male's face when he attempted to accompany her.

Not easily put off, the lighter male swiftly outdistanced her, flying almost directly up before wheeling in mid-flight and chirping loudly. Drained of the strange passion, Sahrel discovered her heavier body would fly only man-high. Soon moonlight was hidden amongst the forest into which she flew. But somebody had positioned torches at four corners of the distant meadow. Sahrel found her eyesight acute in their ultraviolet glow. When tiny splashes of iridescent white up ahead foretold the feast that awaited, she flew faster, tingling with anticipation.

As the two of them neared the field of moon vines surrounded by forest, the male Moth sailed in front of her and hovered, displaying vivid red underwing eyes in a warning glare. Sahrel directed flurries of thought probes at him but received back a confusing pattern of fright.

Oh, if only you could think like me, she mind-spoke. Frustrated by their lack of communing, she sped past him and dropped onto a large open moon-glory, hoping he would follow. Instead he shrilled another warning and twirled in the air above her.

Vaguely Sahrel wondered why the witch had sent her out in insect form. How was she to analyze Meowood's problems while being yanked to and fro by powerful urges, first into a sexual orgy and now by an uncontrollable appetite for sustenance?

Primordial instincts overriding thought, for the next two moments Sahrel darted from petal to petal, unfurling and dipping her proboscis down into each flower to lick up the nectar. Tasting receptors on palpi located adjacent to her "tongue" quivered from the sugar. After landing on a stalk, she picked her way daintily to the heart of each flower, taste-recepting tarsi soles swelling from the unaccustomed richness of this feeding place as she lifted and put down her six feet. Oh, the sense of sating oneself without having to worry about others, the freedom of utter abandonment never before hers.

Once, tottering, she glanced about briefly, slightly drunk but enjoying the feast too much to stop. Through a haze of sweets-induced lethargy, she noted hundreds of Hawke Moths flitting from blossom to blossom in a feeding frenzy. Even in the midst of her stupor, a tickle of uneasiness caused her to hesitate and look up. The male was still there! Why had he not joined them? Another thought superseded that query. The moths all sported iridescent bodies, nearly identical to her, but . . . none were larger than the male hovering above them. She stood out among them as prominently as a cryp among Zayelians.

Still, as she began associating their sounds with their actions, an awareness crept over her that they were using a type of language.

Soon she became giddy with the heavy fragrance and taste of her bounty. So engrossed were they in supping, none noticed the nets affixed to trees enclosing the flower meadow.

In the midst of their gluttony, Sahrel heard a shrill command, "Shoot!" and in a daze saw bands of silk cord catapult into the air, suspend like spider webs for a moment, and then spread out over the feeding Moths. All but a few near the edges of the field were caught fast. In a simultaneous melding of senses, Sahrel watched the hovering male flit up and away, smelled the acrid odor of body fluids as fellow vegetarians fought a horde of hungry, insect-eating humans, and felt the terror of claustrophobia when strands tightened against her body.

A man well past mid-years, his flowing white beard as fine as cornsilk, limped toward her. "Heyo, what have we here? By the gods, you're a monster of a flutterer, aren't you?" Though his right arm ended below his shoulder, the remainder of his body was scarred and muscled from a lifetime of battles. The worn hilt of the polished sword scabbarded below the arm stump told her he had once been an able warrior.

Though she had never seen any, she recognized him at once as a cryp—one of the Outcasts from her kingdom. Ensuing panic caused her to flex wing tendons in one desperate attempt to escape the tightening net, to flee the slaughter taking place all around her. Over the triumphant hoots of the victors, she heard a low click and felt bony protuberances as sharp as knives protrude from the base of her front wings. *Hah! Better than a sword are these natural weapons.* She rubbed the short knives against the knotted material until the net shredded.

When a gnarled hand grabbed for her, she reacted instinctively, reeling into a spin from which she dove at his face. His hands went up and she felt a brief pride as her right wing knife slashed a narrow trail of red over his cheek.

To her surprise, he roared with laughter, feinted to his left, and reached from nowhere to pluck her from the sky. Calloused fingers pinched her wings together in an iron grip as he dangled her before intent emerald eyes. Compound eyes tried to sear green ones. Though he spoke not, he made no attempt to wound her and she thought she detected a flicker of compassion within him.

She reached out toward that emotion, trying to reinforce it with an empathy of her own. Perhaps if his flames could be kindled bright enough, he would loose her. But what had they in common that she could use to bind his feelings to her? Her glance flicked over the dozens of men and women wading in among the carnage, their short swords flashing as they murdered the flock with no regard for pregnant females. Those they intended to eat straight-away they beheaded. The most vociferous fighters they de-winged. Others they thrust whole into leather pouches tied around their waists to stash away for future meals.

Rage against the marauders consumed Sahrel as she took in the completeness of the butchery. The winged ones aimed back leg nettles, attempting to sting the aggressors. Sliding their sharpened blades downward, the cryps sheared off the poisonous hairs as easily as shaving a beard. And the wing-blades of the smaller Moth-kindred were too small to be effective against the Outcasts' swords.

Suddenly Sahrel realized that she could hear the squeaks of injured Moths, but their cries were beyond human range of hearing. Unaware of the suffering they imparted, the cryps continued havesting.

Feeling helpless, she fought down the rush of hatred and focused on a communality, using terror to hone a mind-controlling ability she hadn't known was hers. Aha! None of the victors were whole. The hands of one ended in stubs, the foot of another faced sideways, and yet another wore such a hump on her back that she was bent double.

With utter horror, Sahrel realized the only way to project concern for the offenders was to fuse with them in her thoughts. Telling herself she had no time to be squeamish, she homed in on their infirmities, gathering streams of pity that she focused into a river of empathy. Then, using an inner voice much like bird-song, she sang this to her captor.

The furrow between deep-set eyes smoothed and his hand flung Sahrel an arm's distance away, fingers loosening slightly.

Before she could squirm out, she saw his lips curl in contempt and she read his thoughts as clearly as if he mind-spoke.

Hmph! A freak flutterer has pity for me, Hundrel, the Hunter! It's out-of-my-senses I must be. Into the sup bag with you, you of the strange-colored eyes and short swords.

During the brief journey to the storage place, Sahrel dredged up bits of buried memories about the Outsiders. They were human-kind who could not or would not fit into the Meowood life and were exiled. From jubilant boasting going on all around her, she gleaned that over the years these scavengers had banded together and devised a simple method of gathering staples—lure and net. Their victims were imprisoned in an ice cave located in a vast volcano tube—stored as matter-of-factly as grain for journey bread.

Twisting and turning in the snugness of the mildewed pouch, she tried to no avail to find a corner that she might saw with her wing-knives. Soon realizing the futility of expending energy, it was a quiescent flutterer whose wings Hundrel pinned to the wooden wall of the storage cave. "A pity, it is, Missy, that we'uns cannot loose such a strange one as you be."

He hesitated a moment, studying her with eyes that became lusterless, then shook his head in regret. "Twon't take long 'til the cold will suck the feeling from you. Many's the soldier that yearns for such a death when his entrails be trailin' out over a battlefield."

Since the Outcasts must harvest at sun-end when Moth-folk eat, they had positioned lanterns throughout the tunnels.

Sahrel turned her body and impaled the old warrior with her eyes, shaping the flames of her angst into a sword-form that she slung at him.

He recoiled slightly and she saw the stump of his right arm lift before his left hand absent-mindedly stroked the beard. A hump-backed woman hobbled past them.

Spinning around, he grasped one shoulder. "By the gods, Varta, this bugger seems to be tryin' to talk to me. It's a female—don't suppose she's got the Silent Voice, do ye?"

Sahrel tried to impart a message to the ugly woman who only snorted. "Must o' sprinkled ye with some of her flapper perfumie, Hundrel. Ever'body knows only human females has the Way—and nary a one o' them since th' Zayel Family took rule over 100 years ago."

Hundrel stiffened and his left hand rubbed at the useless stump of arm. "Woman, do not poison the air of the Preserving Place with that rotter's name."

He took Varta's hand and they hurried from the cave.

Sahrel realized she was already drowsy from the cold. If she meant to escape, it must be soon. Hundrel had fastened her to the wall in such a way that she faced out and she scanned the cave. A thick slab of green ice covered one wall. No wonder the frigid air crinkled the edges of her wings.

Their smaller wings first moistened with spittle then slapped fast against this ice, hand-sized Moths hung like golden ghosts in the reflection.

Suddenly Sahrel remembered the male Flutterer. Was he close enough to receive? Not pausing to wonder from whence came her newfound gift, she formed an image of him in her mind, coloring it with hues of brown and scenting it with his bouquet. Lastly she etched the quivering bodies of pegged kindred onto his eyes. This she catapulted again and again from the cave high into the outside air.

Eventually exhaustion told her that she must discover a means of escaping—no one had heeded her message. Now so cold it took great effort to move, she had little time left. She began throwing herself away from the pegs in the wall. She paid no attention to ripping sounds made by soft tissue of wings splitting.

In the midst of imminent death, she felt a twitch in her heart for winged ones who would never soar free again, never feel the shock of luscious nectar bubbling over nerve tips, never feel goddess-like in the heat of overwhelming passion.

Just as she felt herself fall free, the echo of thudding boots and the babble of an excited voice reached her. Hundrel rushed up and pinioned her wings together with one gnarled hand.

She screamed at him in a silent tirade. *Old fool, loose me that I might save my kindred!*

Recognition lit up the old man's features softening his mouth into a smile that transformed the brutal face into one more pleasurable to behold.

"Missy, ye *do* have the Silent Voice! Aye, will I loose you—to help fight the Zayel soldiers. They've searched out our village and plan to massacre us to the last girl-child!"

What care I for your kind, old hunter? My moth-clan be peaceful, gentle folk. Why would I help their killers?

A look of growing comprehension caused his features to sag as he nodded, unable to meet her eyes. "Your Voice be not only silent but true, Winged Missy."

Relaxing his grip on her, Hundrel pivoted and stomped away, muttering over his shoulder, "Save those of your kind that you can, Flutterer, and I to mine."

Wings tattered too badly to fly, Sahrel's searching gaze spotted netting heaped before the ice-wall. The duress of the moment heightened her newly gained sense. Concentrating an image of fire onto the rotted fabric, she caused sparks to dance hither and fro until a ragged line of red tongued the green ice. As the ice melted, Sahrel used her mind to revive and help those Moths still living to free themselves.

Instead of fleeing their prison, the loosed Moths did a curious thing. Huddling together they began chattering, a noise unintelligible to Sahrel. Then, as if of one consciousness, the survivors wriggled beneath Sahrel, supporting her on a winged stretcher.

With day swiftly approaching, the dark funnel of beating wings careened through the maze of tunnels and into the outside. Torn and wracked, the clan zigzagged over the walled-in small town. Looking down Sahrel was amazed at the quiet beauty the Deformed Ones had produced, natural-stone homes blending into wide flagged paths, some terminating at courtyards containing hand-chiseled statues and gurgling fountains.

Her gaze lifted to the west and a widening breach in the stone wall through which tumbled Zayel soldiers, shields clasped against chests, swords flashing. A strong current tugged at the minds of the Moths, drawing them like a great migrating bird toward the thin figure of the witch standing just outside the northernmost wall. As the birthing sun began to paint color into the gray figures of the battlers, tiny alarm feelers crawled from Sahrel's geas-enshrouded mind.

She was suddenly suffused with the full import of *what* the dawning light meant. "Ye must return before daybreak or remain imprisoned in that body forever."

Even though the Moth Flock flapped their wings more and more forcefully, the weight of their burden bore them closer and closer to the ground.

Then like a shroud being lifted, golden slivers of light stung the earth into wakefulness. Sahrel knew she would not reach the witch in time. She would die in this alien form.

Exhausted, the smaller Moths lowered Sahrel onto a bed of moss. Her gaze roamed the walls, seeking aid. It was then that she saw a soldier leap upon the prostrate body of Hundrel the Hunter and raise back his arm to thrust his knife into the old man's heart. A golden sun dart struck the blade, causing it to gleam like silver.

By the Mother of us all, you are Zayel, too, she thought, *as much as my soldiers.* Without knowing why she must, Sahrel stripped from each battling one the heat of his rancor. She gathered this swelling tide of emotion to her. She felt a sense of power come over her, the force of her great feeling enabling her to transmute their wrath into sharp blue arrows. These she slung at each participant. Lapis blue streaks splintered the foreheads of the warring ones. Stung by pain too deep to endure, they lurched about, hands tugging futilely at the missiles.

Aware that the blue shafts would soon disintegrate, Sahrel thrust her first order into each arrow. *Halt! I, Sahrel of the family of Zayel, command you! In the name of the Mother Who Spirits All Living Beings, I adjure you to never again open the veins of those who walk on legs, neither shall you slay the winged ones—from this day hence may this geas be upon you.*

She saw Hundrel, disbelief warring elation on his face, kneel before her and stroke her torn wings. A feeling of defeat shook her, more bitter than the abyss of death. For she knew if she could save her life by trading places with a Moth-kindred or such a noble cryp as Hundrel, she would not. No great leader would she make. Indeed no leader at all.

As she awaited death, through Sahrel's closed eyes seeped an aureole of light that increased in brightness, circumgyrating the witch emitting it until she flared brighter than a village of tapers.

"Come back to us, Sahrel," the luminary sang, glowing with an intensity that made Sahrel turn her head away.

"I am not worthy. I wish only for the restful calm of never-ending dark. Take your light from me."

The Luminary placed an incandescent finger against Sahrel's heart. "For the space of 100 years have I sought a leader who would give her life for that Being Who Is *Unlike*. Not now will I have you slip away."

Slowly, almost against her will, Sahrel's mind twined with that of the Mother-Creator. With the gripping motion of a newly cured leather scabbard resisting the homeward thrust of a sword into its pocket, she felt her human shape reassert itself.

It was not many days after Sahrel took rule that she felt the first flutter in her womb. Then she knew that her quest to accept and to help her people accept those who are different had barely begun. Even now a child was forming within her, into what strange being she knew not. Neither did she know if she could love it. But try she would.

MY LADY TONGUE

Lucy Sussex

Honeycomb, my honey, sweet Honey Coombe. I love her so much I daubed her name on the biggest white wall in the ghetto and round it a six-foot heart. The paint was shocking pink, and it dribbled, when I so wanted my ideogram to be perfect! She passed by that wall every day, but unfortunately so did others, and that was how the trouble started.

"Vandalism!" That was the Neighborhood Watch, our ghetto guards. I was minding my own business, thinking of Honey, but cat curious I followed the groups of womyn drifting towards the clamor. It was only when I was in the main square that I realized the offense was mine. Ah well, I'd brazen it out—I'm nothing if not brazen.

There was a crowd in the square, which included the off-duty Watch and most of the powers-that-be in Womyn Only. One of the most dignified of these Elders was actually atop a stepladder inspecting my splash.

"Honeycomb," she announced to the groundlings as if every womyn Jill of them couldn't already read. "Possibly male reference to our genitals?"

"Ishtar!" cried the Watch Chief. "They got in this far?" There was a horrified mumble from the masses.

"Tsk tsk. Sleeping on the job," I said, just loudly

208

enough for the Watch to hear and not pinpoint me. Zoska, who'd reared me, came forward trailing her youngest.

"Not quite down to their usual standard, is it?" she said. "Bar the color."

It was strident, but that's my style.

"They go in for dribbling cocks usually, not dribbling hearts."

Some of the hearers drew in their breaths hard, and she snapped: "Don't be silly, this isn't the Hive."

"You think it's a Sister?" asked the Watch Chief, catching on at last.

Zoska nodded her coif of plaits and I cursed silently: if she got much warmer things would be hot for me.

"Our vandal," said Zoska, "loves Honeycomb."

"There aren't any Sisters of that name," said the Ladder-climber. "Unless you mean Marthe's daughter Honey . . ."

Their heads followed one direction and I thought I saw my sweeting, so I waved my floppy hat at her. But it was only her grim mamma and I knew I was for it.

"I own up! I did it, I did it!" I shouted, jumping up and down.

"Thought so," said Zoska.

Marthe was looking black and I was beginning to realize why.

"Sister Raffy," said the Chief, "Womyn Only supports artistic expression but isn't this over the top?"

"Shucks Officer, I'm in love."

"Honeycomb," said Marthe as though that sweet name was wormwood in her mouth. "Is that your name for her?"

I nodded, thinking oh oh! My darling's name was Honey Marthe, the mother's name affixed to the daughter's, as is ghetto custom. Me, I'm Raphael Grania, but I only answer to Raffy. Coombe had been Honey's father, a sperm donor anonymous except in the genetic profile of his daughter. Hardcore dykes like Marthe (who never ventured from the ghetto nor indeed much from the

Hive, our inner sanctum) detested the profiles—but kept them in case of genetic disorders. Honey had found the document, and discovered her humorless mother had made an accidental pun. I had laughed at that, at Marthe, but now I had made a laughingstock of her, and worse. It was bad taste to remind Womyn Only that its girl children were not spontaneously generated.

Me and my big paintbrush. There was a long, really nasty silence during which I mentally gave myself a hundred lashes, and crossed miles of paving on my knee-bones.

"You'll never call her that again," said Marthe and strode off followed by a curious knot of Elders. The crowd was staring and Zoska had piggybacked her child and was pushing towards me. I didn't need comfort now, just action! So I pretended not to see her and nipped around the corner and over a couple of back gardens, shortcutting to Honey's home. It was empty; and I stood outside and thought of the hydroponic flowers I had thrown through her window. Then I embarked on a long and increasingly desperate tour of our trysting places. I found nobody waiting, alas! and at the last the Watch Chief found me. She was embarrassed but stern.

"Marthe and Honey are in the Hive, from which the Elders have banned you until further notice."

I lay down by *our* fountain and imitated it for a while. Then I recovered and went to see Zoska.

"Ninny," she said.

We sat in the sunny brick courtyard behind her little house, she at her embroidery frame and Basienka, who had accompanied her to the meeting, wandering around the confined space in her enigmatic two-year-old's way.

"Oh, I agree absolutely. Now what do I do?"

"Go to Bozena at Haven, until the fuss dies down."

Haven was the refuge we dykes were building in the country. I had scouted the site and normally would go there gladly.

"Can't leave Honey." Puck puck puck went the

needle into the stiff linen cloth. "I get soppy just thinking about her."

"Creamy you mean," said Zoska. "I know you."

"No, this is the real thing. I'm so sentimental I could die."

Zoska sighed.

"You're old enough to be her mother."

"Not quite. Honey may be sixteen, but I—as you ought to remember—had a late menarche."

She did the sums with her lips.

"So you did. I was confusing you with Boz."

"Quite a party we had for it," I said, hopping over a wall in my mind into memory lane.

"Was it ever! You tore up the poem Grania had written for the occasion and when she created lit out with Boz. The pair of you didn't come back until six the next morning, when you burst into my bedroom shouting you were in love with each other. I haven't had intoxicants at a menarche party since. Won't have it at hers either."

She grinned at Basienka.

"Look at her. Aren't I clever? Forty-eight years and three months I was when I bore her. Broke the ghetto record."

I recollected that Zoska had begun the career of mothering with Bozena and had had thirty-two years at it since. Some daughters were hers; others came from Sisters who like Grania preferred not to have the rearing of their young.

She looked at me, reading my face.

"You and Boz may have had your adventures with Haven, but I've reared seven fine womyn. Mind you, it's early days with Basienka and with Urszula I'm not sure."

I stirred, perceiving how my least favorite sister might help my purpose.

"You could use Urszula as an example to Marthe. She's not much older than Honey, she's taken up with Bea, who's my age . . ."

"I've got enough chickens to take chances with them.

211

Marthe's only got one."

"Let me finish. And Urszula's leaving the ghetto!"

"Oh Ishtar, don't even think of saying that to Marthe!"

"Why not? Honey wants to."

"After she's been reared hardcore? To go among *men*? Raffy, she really must love you."

"I want to swear committal."

She reached into the basket between us for a new skein of wool, the colors jewel bright against her fingers.

"Wow, Raffy settling down at last. Okay, I'll talk to Marthe."

She snipped off a length of wool viciously.

"It won't be easy."

Her gaze was like a mirror, in which my scarecrow image—in old camouflage duds from Haven (worn to annoy the hardcores, who never went Outside), lurid pink shirt, embroidered scarf and old hat—was reflected with censure.

"Raffy, you're disreputable. You'll have to smarten up if I'm to get anywhere with Marthe and while I'm at it also stop teasing the Elders and getting into fights with the Watch. You're the last match Marthe wants for Honey."

"I'm the daughter of a famous poet."

"Yes, and Grania denounces you in verse for being undutiful."

"We never ever got on."

"So I got the rearing of you, half my luck. Raffy, I can't win Marthe without Grania's help. You'll have to make up with her."

"I'll put a girdle round about the earth in forty minutes!"

"What's that? What do you mean?"

"It's poetry. Shakespeare, a man. I mean, I'll do it."

She was looking puzzled and I got up to stretch my skinny legs in the courtyard, puzzled myself. I keep my Shakespeare well hid in Womyn Only, because of what it means to me: lost time with Benedict, a man. Swashbuckling Raffy might have had a child, a son even, and not by donor but by the old way, which Shakespeare writes about a lot.

There was no telling what a hardcore dyke would do if she knew her daughter was marrying tainted flesh. But Marthe would never hear of it, would she?

In my perambulations I nearly tripped over Basienka, who looked up from trying to unpick a wool flower on the skirt of the little peasant dress all Zoska's daughters, even tatty Raffy, wore. On her face was the same knowing smile as the Cumaean Sibyl, whose painting adorns a wall in the Hive, and I was suddenly afraid. Marthe could discover Raffy's little secret, from Grania, who might tell her if we two were unreconciled.

I looked away from Basienka, to Zoska.

"Can you talk to Marthe? I'll do Grania."

She nodded her silver-brown head, and I took leave of her. Grania lived outside Womyn Only, in a small brick house with a studied bohemian air. There was a hammock on the front verandah with a huge hole in it; the garden was a careful mixture of weeds and color-clashing flowers; the brass nameplate said "Poet's Corner." Before I could knock the door was opened by Bea, lover of my foster-sister Urszula. She carried a carton of books for her shop, my mother's literary children, new branded with her squiggly signature.

"Hi Raffy, surprise to see you . . ."

"Here?" I asked dangerously.

She looked embarrassed.

"I'll get out of your way. Raffy . . . do you really want Marthe for a mum-in-law?"

"Anything for Honey."

She walked down the pathway with my brothers and sisters. I waved, then went noisily inside. Grania was in her visitor's chair, a monster of carved mahogany chosen to diminish the bulk of the womyn within it. From my mother I had my height, but I blessed her donor for a lithe

213

figure, for his genes dominated over those which would have made me resemble a hippo. She batted not an eyelid as I sauntered in.

"Come to your mummikins, lambie-pie," she said icily. It was the standard greeting and as usual I kept my distance, leaning against a wall of this book-lined grotto, with its troll-queen enthroned.

"What, no fond greeting?"

Go cautiously, I thought.

"Did you ask Bea about me?"

"Of course. She said you were in trouble, big trouble if you come and visit me. There was mention of a sweet young thing locked away from your wickedness. Then she spied your approach and bolted, leaving me in a state of gossipus interruptus."

"I shall bring you to climax."

"This sounds like the tale of your lost month. The one time you confided in me."

I stared at her.

"Mother, we are of one mind. I want you to recall the incident."

She grinned evilly.

"How could I forget Raphael's *True Confessions?*"

My lost time had been thirteen years back, before Haven even, but it was vivid to me. When I dipped into the past with Zoska I had half seen the brickwork and moss beneath my feet strewn with colored streamers and crushed paper cups. Now, instead of books I could see pollution-bleached grass, weird trees and eroded hills with knob rocks sticking out. She's very visual, Honey's Raffy.

I had been Outside both ghetto and City, sussing out a site for Haven in the countryside. When I remember, the mind's eye comes through first, then later the body with what my past self was feeling. I had been happy, despite the desolation, which was coldly beautiful, and the dan-

214

gers. The country had unmarked pollution dumps, which had already claimed one scout, wild dogs, and of course the bogey of man.

Ah, who cared! I was wearing camouflage clothes that were weatherproof; I had survival rations, weapons, mini-communicator, compass, heat detector, Auntie Cobley and all. The paraphernalia fitted neatly into a five-kilo pack on my shoulders that left me unencumbered, feeling free. There was a wild wind blowing, early spring sunlight and Raffy who had lived behind walls was madly in love with wide open spaces.

This was my first solo voyage. Previously I had gone with senior members of the Watch, who were supposed to restrain young hotheads like Boz and me, and then with Boz. That trip had been a mistake, for in the excitement we had revived our first love, only to quarrel so bitterly we resolved: never again. We were too alike, and I crave opposites, Honey.

I was walking through a narrow valley peaceful even though bisected by a service road, when I heard a droning roar, steadily increasing in volume. Diving into the nearest cover, a ditch curtained with green weed, I checked the heat sensor, which registered zero. My fears of a behemoth mutant vanished and I peered through the green to see a robotruck on the road, making its slow thunder from a macrofarm somewhere. False alarm; but nonetheless I left the road and went cross-country, moving swiftly until I came to a patch of burnt-out ground.

I started to weep then, and my future self, standing in Grania's study, sought for a reason. There was a memory within the memory and it was red, the color of the fire that had engulfed a house on the edge of the ghetto. Five womyn had been inside and there were more dead, Watch members who had surprised the arsonists. "Men did it," Zoska had explained to little Urszula, who had only stared at her uncomprehendingly.

After the fire had been doused there had been more red, with a torchlit meeting in the main square I was later to defile with my "honeycomb." The Elders had argued and argued what to do and slowly a consensus was reached. We were easily attacked within our enclosure, we needed to go beyond the city, found a city of our own. And so the Haven movement began, and changed the lives of Boz and me. We had been feckless ghetto girls, too wild for the Watch and too hardcore to find work in the straight world. Now we had a goal in life.

Standing amongst charcoal and singed trees, I wept for the dead, until it occurred to me that were it not for them I would still be cooped up in Zoska's living room. There was a site for me to look at; I went on.

Our Haven was defined by a list of desiderata, a majority of which had to be ticked before the Elders would approve the site. My destination had already accrued some ticks, if we were to believe the intermediary feminists who had investigated the site in the guise of a macrofarm consortium. They had liked it. Yet the site needed to be seen with a dyke's eyes, and secretly. The memory of the incinerated house still burnt.

I spent a day at the prospective site, being thorough. Womyn Only looked at many locations, finding some too marshy, too polluted, too grim et cetera. I was writing the report in my head as I trudged: "Eminently suitable for our *queendom*, our *newfoundland*"—words Grania had used when she heard of my vocation, laughing all the while—"except . . ." It was insufficiently secluded, being too close to the farm I had seen the truck trundling towards earlier. And this farm, as the intermediaries had discovered, was not staffed entirely by robots.

I inked in the last mental full stop of my report and turned to go, when the late afternoon light caught a spot of color on a distant hillside. When I pulled out my viewfinder I saw a scrawny blossom tree in its spring best. The flowers were chalky pink, beautiful.

I glanced at the sun and again at the tree, estimating it was a kilometer away. Why not? I could take a pressed flower home for Zoska to copy and maybe another for a young lady of the Watch I had my eye on. What I had not expected, though, was the macrofarm's fence between me and tree, impenetrable even for a Scout equipped to the eyeballs. I followed it hopefully and came at last to a spot where an animal had burrowed beneath it. There was just room for Raffy, but not if she were humpbacked: I had to discard the pack in order to squeeze through.

The detour had eaten at the daylight and the hill was dusked over by the time I arrived at the tree. Feeling uneasy, I decided not to stay long and reached for a blossom. There was a growl and automatically I jumped into the branches as a low shaggy shape came up the slope towards me. It was a feral dog and it was followed by its brethren.

They clustered snarling around the base of the tree and I climbed higher. Hormones from the macrofarm had affected this tree's growth: it was some seven meters high, with sturdy branches. I sat in the highest of these, watching the dogs leap upward, snapping teeth on air and scrabbling their paws on the bark before falling to earth again. I was well out of reach, but I cursed, the dogs replying in their language. Any idiot would have checked the heat sensor for these pests, or considered that they might have dug under the fence. Any idiot, but not Raffy.

Packless I was not quite defenseless, wearing under my camo shirt a weapon as unphallic as a dyke could make it. I took out the gun and shot experimentally at the dog chieftain, remembering my target practice with the Scouts. It was close: there was a smell of singed hair and the pack ran off a little, yelping. I gloated until I registered another smell, that of singed tree. The shot had nicked a lower bough, had almost cut it through.

Rather than whittle my sanctuary away I stopped, and the dogs settled under the tree for a long wait. I considered my options: the gun had a limited number of charges and the waning light would not improve my aim. Better to wait until the morning. I ate a couple of blossoms and found them tasteless, then had the joy of a half-eaten lolly Urszula had dropped in my pocket during the farewell. Lest I fall in sleep, I buckled my belt around flesh and tree trunk. The sun set and like the dogs I waited.

In the darkness maybe I slept, for when I awoke suddenly it was moonrise and all the landscape silvery. There was a pawing and moaning at the foot of the tree, as the dogs milled around something strange—a metal canister. As I watched it emitted white mist; the dogs sniffed at it and whined. I could smell chemicals now, stupefying, and below the dogs were staggering like drunks. I pulled my scarf over my face for a filter, feeling weak and glad of the belt that bound me.

Walking among the fallen, twitching forms was a figure oddly distorted around the face. It stopped and stared upwards at my form outlined against branches and sky.

"Here, catch!" and it threw a package to me expertly. The gift was a mask like the mask, I saw now, of the giver. I pulled it over my head and breathed freely again.

"You can come down now."

For the first time I noticed the lower timbre: a man's voice. Was I going from frying pan to firing squad? I began to pick at my self-made bonds watching *him* all the while. The canister had disgorged its drug and he was walking from dog to dog, pressing a rod against each head. There was a faint click, then death.

A deep-voiced thank you, I decided, then scram! I rebuckled my belt and clambered down, too fast, for in the haste I put foot to the half-severed branch. It cracked beneath me and I fell in a shower of pink flowers made silver. With a splintering crash, bough, Raffy and all hit earth, just missing the hillock of a dead dog.

"Are you all right?"

He was bending over me now, and I heard him draw his breath in deep. I looked and noticed my leg caught between wood and ground. Funny, it never used to bend that way.

218

"If you don't mind me saying so, that's a godawful break. I'll have to take you back to the farm."

He was fumbling in a pocket of his coat.

"Can't have you screaming blue murder all the way there . . . sorry about this, mate."

His hand emerged from the pocket with another canister, and simultaneously he reached forward and snapped my mask off.

"Sorry," he repeated and cracked the canister under my nose.

Much later I awoke in yellow artificial light and found myself lying on a table, head propped up on foam. There was a machine covering one leg.

"Robo doctor," he said, from where he sat watching. "They gave me one 'cos I'm all alone here."

I stared at him; a smallish man with a lined, weary face, not young, not particularly muscled, and not threatening at the moment, although you never could trust them.

"Well, say something! Think you'll give yourself away? I can tell you're a woman."

"Womyn."

"And that you're one of those."

"I'm Raph-ael."

"That's a man's name, an archangel's."

"My mother says angels don't have gender, so there."

"Your mum knows her theology, Raphael. I'm Benedict. That means blessings, and I don't mean you harm. I even left your toy with you."

Sure enough, my right hand had been folded around the gun. I lifted both cautiously.

"Don't burn me," he said, and I lowered my hand.

"We aren't all beasts," he said seriously, and at that moment the machine on my leg thrummed. He got up to inspect it, and satisfied, lifted it off. Revealed were my camo pants cut off at mid-thigh and the rest encased in pale, stiff plastic.

"Like I said, bad break, and you'll find bruises and

cuts too. To get you down to my transport I had to hook your belt onto the branch and drag it behind me like a peacock's tail."

Our gaze met.

"You're bigger than me, in case you hadn't noticed."

Perhaps he expected me to smirk. I merely changed the subject: "Can I have some water? That mist dehydrates."

"I'll make some coffee, grow it myself. Ambrosia!"

I looked puzzled, and he added: "Food of the gods."

"Goddesses."

He disappeared from my view, and I got up on one elbow to see where I was. From the curving plastic walls I guessed I was inside a housing module, but the high-tech was offset by an incredible mess. There was furniture, mainly in disrepair, plants in pots, odd bits of machinery, some half dismantled, tools, rusty wire, music tapes, collections of colored stones—clutter everywhere. Vaguely I wondered how Benedict had managed to bring me in here, then realized with a grimace that he must have carried me.

When he returned from the small cook-unit set against one wall he handed me a cup, taking care our flesh never touched in the transaction.

"How did you find me?"

"I'm the caretaker, I know what goes on down the farm. The dogs showed up on the heat sensor when they broke in and so did you. When all the blips were grouped round the old cherry I could kill two jobs at once: get the pack and see who you were. From the wavelength I knew it was human."

"Homo sapiens."

He put his cup down on the table hard. "Raphael, I've been talking to you fifteen minutes and this is the third time you've corrected me!"

"It offends my sensibilities."

"And being corrected offends mine!"

We glared at each other and he sighed.

"Sorry, I'm not used to *people* much. Maybe I'll leave you and your leg alone for now."

He went over to a packing case and dragged out a blanket, which he draped carefully on the table beside me.

"I sleep in the next module. If you want something, scream."

He shuffled away, following some invisible path that led him to the door without falling over anything. Pausing at the threshold, he put his hand to a knob in the plastic and the yellow glare dimmed down to nightlight.

"Thanks for the rescue," I said, and threw the blanket over my head before he could respond.

Daylight shining through the translucent plastic woke me, that and a pain in my groin.

"Benedict!"

He appeared in the doorway, in a change of clothes, but unshaven.

"I wanna piss!"

"Oh gawd," he said, looking from door to table and at the mess in between. I flung off the blanket and slid to a one-legged stop on the floor, forcing the issue.

He bent down and rose with a large broom, which he used to clear a haphazard path from me to the exit. Experimentally I hopped, and nearly went face first into a robot of some kind, its sharp guts exposed for maintenance. As I wobbled, he restored my balance with a hand to my sleeve.

"Can you lean on me, perhaps?"

Once Boz and I had gone out of the ghetto to visit Bea, now Urszula's Bea, and a man had grabbed at me. After we had rubbed his face in a mud puddle it had vaguely registered that his flesh felt no different from a womyn's. Then, as now.

Benedict lived in three small modules, living, sleeping and bathroom, all detached from each other and set in a circle. Although the day was overcast and chill it felt good to be outside, so afterwards I let go of him and sat on the little grass courtyard between the ovals of plastic. He brought coffee and insta-bread from the module and we breakfasted.

"Raphael . . ."

Only Grania called me that, and now Benedict. After his outburst I did not want to correct him again, to say: *Just Raffy.*

"What's to be done with you?"

"I'll contact the Sisters. There's a communicator in my pack."

"Pack, where?" and I said: "By the hole under the fence."

He groaned.

"Knew I'd have to fix it sometime. Okay, I'll kill two jobs again: get your handbag and seal the fence."

It was starting to drizzle, so he helped me inside again, then left. I very soon got bored silly in the crowded room and gazing around spotted a fat old book. After one glance I dropped it—full of strange words. Then I thought to clean my gun and found that Benedict had removed the charges when I was unconscious.

When he came back I threw it at him, shouting: "Pig!"

The impact left a white mark on his face, but he stood still as the gun clattered to the floor.

"How was I to know you wouldn't fry me for laying hands on you?"

"I don't care! Pig!"

His gaze flitted about the room.

"You've been at my Shakespeare."

I recalled the name on the old book.

"I'd have ripped it to shreds if I'd known you valued it."

He lunged forward and grabbed the volume. "For that I'd have killed you."

I had never cared for poetry, thanks to Grania, and so was struck mum by his feeling.

"You've never heard of Bill," he said sadly and opened the book. Seeing him distracted, I snatched at the pack, but he deftly kicked my good leg from under me. I fell heavily, breath and pride knocked out of me. While I lay, he began quietly to read:

"O! She doth teach the torches to burn bright.
It seems she hangs upon the cheek of night
Like a rich jewel in an Ethiop's ear;
Beauty too rich for use, for earth too dear!
So shows a snowy dove trooping with crows,
As yonder lady o'er her fellows shows.
The measure done, I'll watch her place of stand,
And, touching hers, make blessed my rude hand.
Did my heart love till now? forswear it, sight!
For I ne'er saw true beauty till this night."

I was a captive audience, but it was words rather than a shackle of plastic that held me. Word that summoned memories: in front of me was the beautiful face of a dark girl who had come just once into the ghetto. I had made inquiries about her and found her irrevocably straight, so I kicked a wall and went on living.

(Never would a face have the same effect on me until, years later, I came back from Haven to find little Honey had grown up. But by then I knew Romeo's speech by rote.)

Benedict stopped, and spoke his own words:

"See, it's not all rapes."

I was sitting up by then; he dropped the pack into my lap and went out. I opened it, found the communicator and began to cry.

"What is it?" he asked from the doorway.

"I—can't. I've blown it, I'm better off dead."

He sat down on the arm of a laden armchair.

"Have you noticed, Raphael, that I've never asked you what you're doing out here? You lot haven't been careful enough. For months now there's been rumors on the computer of walkers in the waste, consortiums nobody's heard of waving big money, a girl dressed like you found dead in a dioxin dump . . ."

223

I scowled, remembering how the Scouts had ascribed the death to inexperience: "Poor thing, let her go alone too soon." Now they would say the same about Raffy.

"Stop crying. I don't care what you're up to so long as I'm left alone. And I never dob in anyone. Call the ladies!"

Maybe I trusted him, but the Sisters never would. Besides:

"I'd be a laughingstock, skiving off after flowers and having to be rescued—by an andro! They'd never let me scout again."

"So," he said. "I'm not going to tell my bosses and you're not going to tell your bossesses. What then?"

"How long before I walk?"

"Coupla months. The robo gave you a calcium accelerator, but you can't hurry *Mother* Nature."

He was looking glum and the emotion was infectious; the consequences of our silence were an unwanted guest for him and dependence on a man for me.

"I can modify a robo into transport for you," he said. "But it'll take time."

"Gimme materials and I'll make crutches."

He fished in the litter behind the chair, emerging with an all-purpose kit, its plastic grimy and dented.

"You can make one crutch from the broom—never use it anyway. I'll see what's handy for the other."

He was half out the door when I yelled at him: "Benedict! I want something else."

He turned and I tapped the gun meaningfully.

"Promise you won't burn me?"

"I promise only if you promise not to . . ."

I stopped, for an extraordinary expression of grief had taken hold of his face.

"Lord, what we've done to deserve this, and rightly too!"

He took the charges from his coat pocket and rolled them across the floor to me, where they were stopped by my leg in its plastic chitin. I picked them up, counted them, slotted them into their pods—and looked up to see that Benedict had gone.

Good, because I needed to consider the strange situation we had fallen into. An analogy came to mind: Edge City, when two wildly differing ghetto factions united against the middle ground. Just because their interests coincided did not mean opportunities were lost for mischief to each other; I should remember that. He had several Edges on me: mobility and his computer, wherever it was, with which he could summon his bosses if the guest proved irksome. On the other hand I had the Edges of a gun and my communicator, for a last-resort SOS.

Thinking of a Mayday caused me to remember that I had not given my daily position report to the ghetto. I glanced at my watch, noting I was several hours late. If I didn't send the Scouts off on a wild-gorse chase they would go straight to my last location, just south of the site, and from there track me to the macrofarm. Loss of face for me: but of life for Benedict, who despite his hospitality would be killed out of hand.

I unfolded my map, looking for a labyrinth or tanglewood, and found a marsh, probably once a sewage farm. It was off-course; perfect. I fed its coordinates into the flute, a coding device that unravelled information into its component yarns and sent it across space, to be knit up only at the other end. "Chased by wild dogs," I added for explanation, and flicked the communicator to receiving mode.

A jumble of symbols appeared on the little screen, resolving first into letters, then words. "OK. Come on home." Whoever was on the other end was in a laconic mood. I had a moment of conscience, as I remembered Zoska, Boz and my other foster sisters, even despised Grania—then I turned the communicator off.

"The rest is silence," I said, as I returned the communicator to my pack.

Benedict spoke from the doorway, and I jumped:

"Do you know where that comes from?"

"How long have you been there?"

"Only long enough to hear you quote Bill."

He came in lugging a collection of staves.

"Any of these do?"

"Yeah, the longest," and we set to woodwork. Our hands dipped in and out of the kitbox, never coinciding.

After a while he returned to the quotation:

"Where'd you hear that?"

"Probably my mother."

"The authority on angels?"

"Yeah, I've got two mothers." He blinked. "One gave birth to me, the other reared me."

"So which knows Bill?"

"My blood mother, Grania Erato."

"Poetry woman, eh?"

Now I blinked, then I remembered that he read.

"You know her?"

He shook his head.

"I only read one book. See Raphael, I decided long ago that a man, begging your pardon, didn't have time to read everything. There's too many people writing and nearly all of them are mediocre. There ought to be a pogrom—they hide the really good writers with their verbiage. So I just stuck with the very best."

He gestured at the book.

"Before you flare up at me again, I'm not saying your mum's no good. I never read her . . . I'm restricted in my reading."

"But how do you know she writes verse?"

"Erato's the muse of love poetry."

"How pretentious," I said without thinking, and bit my lip, too late.

He looked at me, reading more than I wished him to, so I bent over the crutch and worked like a machine. After a pause, he followed suit. Even when we broke briefly for more bread and coffee, we did not speak—until the crutches were finished.

"Yeay!"

I pulled myself up to standing and fitted the pads under my arms. Suddenly Raffy metamorphosed from crawling caterpillar to a mummy-long-legs, with limbs of wood, plastic and flesh. It was fleet, in a lurching fashion, for with three long steps I was down Benedict's pathway and outside, being buffeted by the late afternoon wind.

"Whee!"

He had followed me outside protectively.

"Don't overdo it. Years ago I was on those things and took days getting used to them. Don't think because you're muscled like a racehorse that you won't be sore."

Just for that, I left the courtyard, hopping through the gaps between the modules to the farm proper. It consisted of more modules, but giant, in row after row with tidy concrete paths in between. I lolloped to the nearest and stared through the plastic opaqued by my breath, like a child at a shop window. There were many green plants, and the glint of steel as a robot gardener rolled up and down.

I glanced behind me and saw Benedict watching like a guardian angel. Irritated by his solicitude I swung away from the wall and went for a long walk along concrete, walled in always by plastic. He did not follow, perhaps expecting a clout over the head with a crutch.

When I returned, doused in sweat and radiating heat like a boiler, I found the courtyard littered with Benedict's junk. Dust blew like a mist from the door of the living module.

I sat down with a thump on the packing case and at the noise he came out, wearing a faded red scarf over his grizzled hair.

"You want your broom back for the spring-cleaning?"

He scowled. "I'm making space. If you're living here you'll need territory of your own. For *my* sanity I'm making a moiety of the living room."

"Need help?"

He stared at me. "Move furniture when you've buggered yourself with the most strenuous walk you could manage? Braggadocia!"

He disappeared inside again and I, feeling parched, went to the bathroom to get a drink without disturbing him. There was a mirror there, overlooked previously, and it reflected the new face like a stranger. I saw a girl weary and strained, with twigs in her brown hair and smears from bark on her face. The man's glass told me what I had not noticed in his gaze: this girl was attractive.

The water splashed into my hands and I longed for a bath, but only cleaned my face. To strip, and to have him sneak up behind me . . .

When I went out it was sunset and I shivered at the memory of dogs and flowers. I sat on the crate again and watched lights come on inside the living module. It resembled a giant phosphorescent slug.

"You can come in now, Raphael."

Within, a low wall had been built of odds and ends; on one side was Benedict's clutter, on the other was an area cleared of all save a mattress with my pack and blanket set neatly upon it.

"I'll make the wall higher, give you privacy, promise. I'm just out of energy now."

"It's not urgent," I lied politely.

He grunted and dodged effortlessly to the cook-unit, where a saucepan bubbled. I looked for the table and found it pushed against the wall, at the end of the path. There were two chairs by it; I sat down and noticed the Shakespeare on the table, like a second guest for dinner.

Benedict brought stewpot, butlery and crockery to the table.

"Let good digestion wait on appetite!"

"I suppose that's in your book too," I said.

"Bill says something about everything."

Chit-chat was forgotten then, as we ate like a pair of wild beasts. When the meal was over I reached for the book.

"What are you doing?" he asked suspiciously.

"Seeing what he says about the likes of me . . . *them*,

as you put it. What's this, *The Taming of the* . . ."

"I doubt you'll find it there," he said and pulled the book from me. "How 'bout this: 'Would it not grieve a woman to be overmastered with a piece of valiant dust? to make account of her life to a clod of wayward marl?' That's feminist at least."

"Nice. Who is she?"

"Lass called Beatrice. A bit like you: fierce."

I twitched the book into my grasp again, accidentally losing the place. In front of me was a list of names followed by their speeches and I looked for Beatrice.

"Phooey. Here she's saying: 'I love you with so much of my heart that none is left to protest' to a clod named . . ."

"Benedict," he finished. Picking up the book he walked to the door.

"Goodnight," he said without turning.

"Goodnight."

I fidgeted for a while then shoved the robot against the door and went to sleep. In the morning I was awakened by the sound of an electric motor. Moving, I found my muscles sore (prophetic Benedict!), but pushed the robot aside and swung out. The courtyard was empty but through the gap I could see Benedict atop a squat vehicle with fat rubber wheels. He zoomed it down a pathway and out of sight.

Tied to the largest bit of the courtyard junk was a note:

"Off to check fences. Back late today. Place yours."

I stood there like a tripod, listening to the motor fade out of earshot. How lovely to be alone again! Then my solitude was interrupted by the tock of rain—within moments my hair was soaked and drops trickled down my neck. I laughed, throwing my head back to drink rain, and went to the bathroom module to finish what the cloudburst had begun. Only the mirror marred my mood; its big round eye seemed prurient so I made it stare at the wall.

Showered, I went searching for Benedict's computer

and found the console behind a filing cabinet that looked as if the robot had kicked it in a pet. Raffy was never a hacker, except for a romantic summer with the ghetto's computer whiz, yet the sight revived memories. Benedict was no hacker either, for log-on instructions were taped to the keyboard. There was no password, but I guessed "Shakespeare" and guessed right.

The screen lit up with a list of options and I chose "Security" and after that "Heat Sensor." An infra-red picture of the farm covered the screen, with the small blips of wildlife and one big blip moving slowly around the perimeter. It would appear Benedict was truthful. I returned to the original list and took the option "Maintenance." This killed the curious kitten for diagram after confusing diagram of the giant modules appeared. The care involved indicated that the green crop I had glimpsed so briefly was highly lucrative. What was it? Best not ask. The seclusion of the farm and the fact that the intermediaries had not been able to discover the names of its owners argued a need for secrecy.

Benedict returned after dark, to the lukewarm half of a meal I had concocted from various odd edibles found around the cook-unit. He devoured it, then looked closely at me.

"Good, you had a bath. Thought if I went away you would—you were starting to pong."

I was silent, and he gazed around the module. After my hacking I had got sick of having to weave through his mess like a drunkard, so had added the more maneuverable furniture to the wall.

"And you made space! I can work in here."

"What on?"

"Robo-digger. To modify for *your* transport."

"I've got the wood legs."

He shook his head.

"Very soon you'll find them restricting."

He spread a plastic groundsheet on the floor and wheeled in the digger, which—shovel apart—was the baby of his transport. I opened my mouth and he said, raising his voice an octave:

"Need help?" Then, in his normal pitch, "No thanks Raphael, unless you're an expert on robotics."

I shook my head, reluctantly. He grinned, then saw my expression and pulled the corners of his mouth down.

"Why don't you talk to me while I work?"

"About what?"

"The ghetto. See, I'm curious—it's natural with something that excludes you. Years ago, before your wall went up, I walked through the ghetto fringes. Dirty looks galore, but nobody beat me up. I suppose being a little tich saved me."

I agreed silently.

"What did you see, Benedict?"

"Nothing much, just no men."

I snorted and he blushed rosy pink.

"I was only there five minutes, girl."

I gazed at him, gauging what information to give and what to withhold. At Bea's house I had met straight women who would politely, deviously, direct the conversation to my lifestyle. All I need do was think of the most unsound of them, add a dash of caution, and I would have a recipe for Benedict.

"Why are you staring at me?" he asked.

Just for the moment, the image of a woman had flickered on his face.

"It's just a place where womyn live. We have the wall, and beyond that are 'suburbs' where feminists and dykes who don't mind mixing"—like Bea and Grania—"live. The Watch, that's our Police, call them the first line of defense. Softcores live just inside the wall, hardcores further in."

"What's them?"

"Degrees of ideological rigidity."

"And what are you?"

"Guess," I said coldly.

"In between, I'd say."

Correct, but he needn't know that. He waited, then

ventured: "What of your economy?"

"The suburbans pay tithes from their work in the andro's world." Grania had been bankrolling the ghetto for decades, to name one prominent instance. "There's also workshops, factories, where goods are made to sell Outside."

"Like what?"

"I'm not going to tell you."

"Knitting," he fished, half-seriously. I smiled at his little joke and also at the thought of the systems that my old hacker love marketed to a lot of blissful ignoramuses.

"The ideal is self-sufficiency," I said, imagining the walled Haven in the country, our City of Womyn.

"In more ways than one," he muttered. "I've heard talk of a Hive."

Loose lips! I thought, but continued, trying not to let the exchange become an Edge Game.

"It's the center, for us. To stay there long is to forget that your kind exist. Call it an editing device."

Any mention of andros was forbidden in our temple to the Gyn principle, which caused some bizarre conversations. Once Urszula, being a brat, had asked Zoska in front of hardcores where babies come from. ("Yes Mama, but what makes the baby grow in your belly? Why aren't I growing one now?") She had got a flustered answer about cabbages and my accompanying raucous laughter got me thrown out of the Hive for the very first time. It had been "unseemly," in this quiet place decorated with murals of Ishtar, Athena and Joan of Arc sans Ur-Nammu, Zeus and the English clerics. I could feel uplifted, even refreshed in the Hive but ultimately it was claustrophobic. All restrictions annoy Raffy.

Benedict should not hear criticisms, but neither could I voice vague platitudes. I clammed up. The cessation obviously irritated him, for he began to quote his Bill, half to himself, a quarter to the digger and a quarter to me. I listened until we parted for the night.

In the morning it rained again, and Benedict's robotics were interrupted by the visit of a truck. He dealt with it, returned, and worked with a mixture of care and haste. By a happy coincidence the sun poked out moments after the contraption was finished. He pushed it out into the courtyard and through a gap to the start of a sloping path.

"Hop on."

He took the crutches, slotting them into a niche at the back of the transport.

"Oh, so that's what it's for."

"That, by your hand, is direction and this is speed. This starts the motor."

I forestalled him and switched it on myself. As the machine purred he grinned at his handiwork. Seeing him off guard I put my hand hard on the speed button.

"Hey, wait! Whoa!"

"Wowee!"

The machine shot down the path straight for one of the giant modules, and I grabbed the steering just in time to execute a two-wheeled turn. To show Benedict I had mistressed the vehicle I did a circuit of the module and risked glancing behind for his reaction. He was open-mouthed like a yokel, so with a wave I disappeared around the module again.

When I had explored on crutches I had found the farm monotonous; riding, it was the same, although I passed a processing plant and the road for the trucks, which relieved the uniformity. There was more fun in being Raffy the speed maniac, careening like a pinball. Pride cometh before a crash, of course, and I was sobered by a near-collision with a robot gardener.

"Roadhog!" I shouted at its featureless metal carapace, largely to cover the pain from my leg, which had been jarred. Then I continued down the path and found I was free of modules, in open, tussocked country. Still adventurous, I rode to the fence and back, but at an invalid's pace.

It was late when I puttered nervously up to

Benedict's home, and to my relief he was not waiting outside. I parked the transport and became a stick insect again.

He was sitting at the console.

"Have a nice time?"

"Yes, thank you."

"I watched your blip until it slowed down. Then I did some hacking."

I poled to where I could see the screen, which resembled the old samplers displayed in the Hive: across the screen was verse, Grania's verse:

"Battersea blues couldn't keep me apart
I got to play songs in a grimy gutter
With you along—your clutter.

There's leaves in your hair, have you
been dancing with your old man again?
Walk on the wind of September evening
Don't come down until I've finished playing.

Lend me a mood, oh no
I'm not wistful, not jealous.
I have the music and you have the heart
Battersea blues couldn't keep me apart."

"She was very young when she wrote that," I said. "She still had her father's name."

"So I saw."

"You didn't get far with her verse."

"On the contrary. I accessed the biography first, which was mainly a list of prizes, then the contents page of the *Collected Works.* There were lots of poems about R. and Raphael, but I thought you'd thump me if I read them. So I accessed the cheapest poem about anything else."

"Thanks."

"Amazing! She's said thank you to me twice in one conversation."

234

There was a round scrap of plastic temptingly near; I leaned on one crutch and savagely batted it across the module with the other. It hit the wall with a satisfying clunk.

"I live in glass. Anything she hears about me goes into her verse! Vampire!"

"The parent feeds the child and then feeds off him . . . her."

I stared at him.

"You're not unique," he said. "With me it was my father."

"My father was 10cc of sticky fluid," I said viciously. He ignored the goad.

"Lucky you."

He switched off the console.

"Dad was a drunk. Only good thing he did was desert the family. Trouble was he kept coming back."

I too had been incompletely deserted.

"Mum was all right," he said. "Earth mother type."

"Like my foster mother."

"That's right," he recalled. "You said you had two."

"She says the world's oldest profession isn't whoring, it's motherhood. That's what she does."

"She good at it?"

I laughed. "You think so, on the evidence of me?"

"I meant, is she respected for it?"

"It's high status in the ghetto."

Zoska had been nominated as an Elder, but had dodged the election by beginning Basienka.

"That's how it should be," he said.

Both of us had become embarrassed by the confessions, and so gravitated to the table, where there was a bowl of fresh greens.

"Grow it myself," he said proudly. "One of the perks of the job."

"That and being alone," I said, and he nodded, a little too emphatically. We sat and ate, crushing crisp leaves between our teeth. The crunching made me aggressive, revived my daredevil high with the transport. Foolhardy as ever, I decided on an Edge Game. If Benedict was in a confessing mood, he might give information valuable to the ghetto and my curiosity.

I waved a strip of bok choy: "You grow other greens in the modules."

"You noticed?"

This was not a good sign, but I persisted: "I don't know botany, but they're like no plants I've seen."

"They're intoxicants. The only other perk of the job."

I had not expected him to fold so easily. Careful, a biochemical sensor warned.

"They come from what used to be the Amazon rainforest. Got saved from extinction when a scientist et one and had a nice time. They're still only quasi-legal, like the other substances that relax society's rules a little. That's why this farm is far from awkward questions."

He paused. "Except when asked by Raphaels. You want to try some?"

We were both on the razor's edge now. His suggestion had caught me off-guard, but to signal that might be dangerous. I had to answer quickly.

"Sure."

He went out and I grinned like a wedge of cheese. Free intoxicant!

Benedict was gone a long time and returned, not with the expected green sheaf, but carrying a small box.

"Could have got raw stuff, just pull it off the vine, but it's rough. This is processed, ready for the truck."

He opened the box, to reveal grey crystals, more intoxicant than I had ever seen before. I nodded warily, thinking about dosages—in the ghetto only Boz had had a stronger head than Raffy for the drug. He set the box on the table and to my surprise ignited the crystals. A soft grey smoke, reminiscent of Zoska's old homespun shawl, drifted upwards.

"This is freebasing. Extravagant, but the best."

I attempted the worldly-wise expression of a drug

236

savant, and obviously failed, for he continued:

"This extract's euphoric. Other types make people concentrate, make 'em sexy, send 'em to sleep . . . the many words that describe emotions, they're all covered by the drug. It's a universal, like Bill."

The smoke swirled round me, like the three witches on a panel in the Hive.

"Weird sisters," he said, and I goggled: did the drug cause telepathy?

"From the book," he explained. "Want to hear it?"

"Yes."

He read from his memory, speech after fantastical speech, and I savored them. All, except for the initial extract from *Macbeth*, were descants on the theme of heterosexual love, which might have been oppressive had not the language transcended gender. I heard the love-talk of men and women, and interpreted it as that of womyn.

He stopped, dried out, and an eerie silence descended. The room was a ball of smoke and we were silhouettes to each other. Feeling nervous, I moved closer to him, and he turned his head.

"Did that upset you?"

"No."

"Very sexist. I'm sorry. I forgot with you it was girl and girl."

"It's much like the other," I said, recalling the language.

"Really? You've tried?"

I was feeling pleasantly confused.

"No, although Grania said I'd try anything except incest and folk dancing."

He had never seemed threatening; that was his advantage, or Edge. Perhaps to convince myself he was still there, in this witches' brew, or perhaps for Raffy's damned curiosity, I reached out and touched him. His chest was as hard as that of a prepubescent girl.

"Is this an advance?" he said, cautiously flattered.

It was now. Raffy is also tactile.

He put his hand reverently over mine—they were almost the same size.

"Who'd have thought it? An old man like me."

Actually he was younger than Grania. Our other hands were grappled now.

"I'm out of practice," he said, and glanced around. The smoke had cleared a little.

"Not on that hard little mattress," I said.

We stood up, and I teetered as I tried to fit the crutches.

"Are we ever stoned!" he said. "You'll never make it out the door."

He tried to lift me but got hopelessly tangled with a crutch, and nearly fell over himself.

"Any suggestions?"

"Pig-back," I said muzzily.

He laughed: "Yeah, appropriate for a pig."

He knelt in front of me and I stood on my good leg, tucking the crutches under one arm.

"Hupsy-daisy," he said, and I rode him out the door to the sleeping module.

I awoke, again to daylight diffused through module plastic, and looked into the face of Benedict. Asleep, he looked like something the cat had dragged in: a little beat-up mouse.

As if on cue he opened his eyes.

"Raphael, that was sweet."

I rolled over on my back, to get the weight off my cast and also to escape his sooky expression. There, above me, was flesh, holos of naked women, all breasts, buttocks, thighs, taped to the module ceiling. They had a look of vacuous unreality suggesting the counterfeit; if not, they were like no womyn I had ever seen.

It had been dark in here last night. Intentionally? He saw my expression and groaned like a creaky door. I shot up and began to extract my clothes from the mess around his bed, swearing under my breath. Pulling on a garment

I overbalanced and fell on top of him; he lay still beneath me. I scrambled up again and finished dressing. Then I found my crutches at the foot of the bed and poled furiously for the living module. There was a box of grey ash on the table and I knocked it to the floor, before grabbing my pack and heading for my transport.

He was standing in the courtyard, wrapped in a blanket.

"Raphael!" he shouted. "I'm only human and I mean a man!"

"That's no excuse!"

I started the motor and sped away, making a grand exit. Moments later I remembered my gun: should I return and use it? No. I never wanted to see him again.

My intent had been to follow the roboroad to the gate, the weak spot in most defenses. However in my haste I had made a wrong turning and was as lost among identical paths and modules as an ant on a draughtsboard. The sun was out; I estimated east and headed that way. The maze of modules ended and I continued towards the fence, thinking to circumnavigate to the farm entrance. Idly I noticed the tracks of a larger transport on the grass before me. Then there was a cherry bough, its flowers withered and dry, and beyond it, up a steep slope, the rock-a-bye-Raffy tree.

I pulled out the communicator and held it in my hand like a shell. It was no use, for the same restrictions still applied. If I returned to the ghetto on a stolen transport questions would still be asked about my leg. For expediency's sake I would have to return and make peace with Benedict.

I drove along the fence to the gate, as planned, and found it open. Was this an invitation to leave? If so, I refused it and took the road back to Benedict.

He was waiting outside this time, looking worried.

"Why didn't you go?"

Dismounting, I tapped the cast with a crutch, in answer: it made a dull sound, like a prison door slamming.

"Yes, but after what we did? I did?"

His tone was guilty and something occurred to me: he had mentioned that the drug could make people "sexy."

"Benedict, was there aphrodisiac in that blend?"

"A little," he said sheepishly, a repentant ram. "Didn't think it'd work."

I struck him with a crutch, not hard, but sufficient to send him reeling back against the nearest piece of junk. He hit it at an angle, gashing his scalp. Blood dribbled down like water into his eyes.

"I can't see! Raphael, help!"

He was crouched on the ground, both hands over the wound. There was no way I could lift him.

"Stand up!" I said like the Watch Chief and he obeyed.

"Easy. I'm here."

He reached one blood-sticky hand out to the voice. I anchored the crutches and took hold of it.

"Inside," he said. "Doctor!"

Now I had the problem of getting him to the living module, for while he clasped me as though drowning I could not use the crutches. They required both hands. A sudden gust of wind flapped my scarf, left untied in the hasty dressing, and I had an idea.

"Benedict, let go!"

Very slowly, he complied.

"Now take this," I said, and brushed one fringed end of the scarf against his fingers. He took it, and I wrapped the other end around one crutch handgrip. Carefully I swung into the module, leading him by an embroidered tether.

"The lame leading the blind," he said.

Inside I sat him down at the table and found the doctor unit. When I activated it, the optical sensors swivelled and it made a clicking noise, tsk, tsk, tsk. Metal hands shot out of the body and began to minister. Within minutes the blood had been cleaned from him and the hair shaved from around the gash, which was staunched with a dab of sealant. The robot went into inert mode and I switched it off.

He opened his eyes and stared down at an anthill of spilt ash. Absently he smoothed it with the side of his hand.

"Raphael . . ."

"Yes?"

He doodled in the ash with a forefinger, then erased the design.

"Don't hit me again, but I'm not protected against fertility. Are you?"

I sat down too, feeling sick to my boots.

"Of course not. And I'm at full moon."

He sighed, and as if his head was suddenly too heavy, rested his cheek on the ashy hand. Realizing too late, he withdrew the hand and stared at it glumly.

"Next it'll be sackcloth."

I made no reply.

"Say something. Laugh at slapstick old me."

'The doctor," I said incoherently.

"They programmed it for a man on his own, no gynecology. I've heard that jumping with your legs in splints . . ."

"Very funny."

"Well, surely the ghetto has herbal remedies."

"No need."

"No, I suppose not."

"I'm *not* speaking to you," and with that I retired behind the wall of China, or rather of junk, and huddled under the blanket. After a pause he went out, and I heard the noise of his transport, moving away.

He did not come into the living module the rest of that day, nor did I go out—thus we avoided each other. The following day the pattern was reversed: I took the little transport out around the farm while he was a stay-at-home. In this way we had the necessary illusion of being alone. If our paths crossed the junctions were marked by a chilling silence.

The routine was finally aborted one rainy morning, as we breakfasted—he on fresh-brewed coffee and I on food-concentrate from the pack. An electronic whine crossed the wall.

"The heat sensor!" he said, and dashed to the console. I followed in seven-league strides.

"What is it?"

He jabbed a stubby finger at the screen.

"Figures, just north. Your mates?"

I leaned closer to stare at the sexless blobs. The marsh had been north of the farm.

"Relax, this isn't the dyke cavalry. They're just being curious."

(Taking a look at the farm and also the site, but I couldn't say that.)

He frowned.

"Don't think much of their tracking. You and the tree were on the other side."

"I gave them a position reading for the marsh center."

"Gulper? They could have been killed looking for you there."

After all that had happened since I had crawled under the fence, I should have been immune to shock. Yet that jarred me. With my luck it would probably be Boz.

"Well, I didn't know it was dangerous. If I hadn't they'd have burst in here thinking I'd been kidnapped for a sex slave—which is partly true."

He winced.

"Take the cart and catch up with them."

They would come back and kill you, I thought, but only said: "I'd be pitied for the rest of my life."

"A fate worse than death," he said drily.

"And what if I were carrying?"

We had agonized silently about that question for three days now, but to voice it hurt not at all. He took the cue quickly.

"Any reason you might not?"

242

"I never tried. And you?"

"The ladies all took precautions. I never got close to one so she'd stop using them and have my baby . . . have a child with me."

I rocked on the crutches and considered.

"What are our options?"

"One—nothing's cooking. Two, there is, but you want to stop it."

That option was tricky: the knowledge lay outside the ghetto and I would have to consult with feminists, who might blab.

"Three, you don't."

"It might be a boy!" I cried. How unpleasant, to have the enemy growing inside me.

"Can't see him being reared by manhaters," he said.

"I suppose you'd want to keep him."

"I just remember," he said reasonably, "the one nice thing my dad did with me, which was fishing. Sitting by a stream, if I can find one unpolluted, teaching a small me . . ."

"Small you!"

He looked at me.

"He might take after his tearaway mum."

There was a pause while I tried to imagine a male Raffy.

"You'd not let me keep a girl?" he said.

I shrugged, recalling Grania's poems about father-daughter incest. On the other hand, the idea of returning to the ghetto with a female infant, claiming to have found her in bulrushes—the idea was preposterous.

"Look Benedict, aren't we counting chickens before they're hatched? There might be nothing in the eggshell."

"True," he said dubiously, and we left it at that. At least we were talking again, but the cautious camaraderie was gone. In the days that followed we ate together, did odd jobs around the farm together, but were emotionally apart. The book remained a common ground but we read it to ourselves separately.

Time passed in this waiting game. One day he put in hours at the terminal, while I hogged the book, enjoying the three witches and disagreeing with their images in the Hive (not evil enough). Sensing from his absorption that this was no farm matter, I sneaked up behind him, as quietly as a Woodeny could.

He was searching scientific literature, combining the terms "calcium accelerator" and "embryology."

"Raphael, quit reading over my shoulder," he said mildly.

"Tell me what you found first."

"See for yourself," and he dodged past me. I sat down at the terminal and saw that he had accessed several articles, full-text. One dealt with white mice, the other with monotremes.

"What about people?"

"I tried that," he said from the other side of the room. "No research reports."

The door of the module slammed and I began to read the articles. The monotreme one was inconclusive and the white mice had eaten their young—not an encouraging prognosis.

I glanced back and saw that Benedict had snaffled the Shakespeare. Ah, well, it was his turn for it. To complete the reversal I began hacking myself, first checking the account to which the searches were credited. It worried me that Benedict's bosses might smell a lady rat if their employee ticked up searches unconnected with their product. However, the account was private, its searches—until recently—solely of the database Shaklit.

I returned to the original inquiry and discarded "embryology" to concentrate on the drug that was healing my leg. After an hour I knew that in the young and healthy the period of accelerated cure could be as short as one month. I patted the cast thoughtfully; it would be rushing things, but if Option One occurred I could be away much sooner than Benedict expected. A quick getaway was desirable—he was starting to look sooky again.

He made one more attempt to discuss our possible parenthood:

"Have you decided yet?"

"On what?"

"Options Two or Three?"

"Oh Ishtar, it might well be neither!"

I stormed off, more bluster, for I was late and I think he knew it. Of course, the upsets I had experienced this month would have disturbed the cycle of a she-elephant . . .

One pale spring dawn I woke up very early and found it was Remembrance day, as in Grania's famous poem. Her words had never bobbed up in my mind much before, but now I was thinking in a mixture of Grania and Bill. I activated the Doctor and addressed it to my leg. It whirred, clicked again, shone lights, prodded me here and there—and then it extruded a nozzle which sprayed the cast with pink mist. The plastic melted away as I watched, leaving not even a discarded cocoon to mark my change. The leg underneath was scaly and looked strange; I cautiously tried exercises, then shuffled up and down. It was whole.

Much of my silence had been put to the devising of contingency plans, and I knew what to do. I laid the crutches aside and *walked* to the console, where I instructed the gates to open. Then I shouldered my pack and left, pausing only to streak blood on the door of the sleeping module: my explanation.

He must have slept late that morning, for I had escaped the farm and was following the road through thickets of yellow gorse before he came after me. Hearing the motor, I moved to the roadside. Prickly leaves brushed my bare new leg—if I hid there I would be scratched raw. Instead I pulled out the gun, hating to use it.

Benedict was astride the little transport and for the first time I noticed, as he must have before, that riders of the converted digger looked absurd. He brought it to a stop on the other side of the road, several meters from me. Now I was in sight he seemed unable to speak.

"You got the message," I finally said.

He nodded. "Raphael! Not a word goodbye."

A buzzing insect shot past my head, going from gorse bush to gorse bush and incidentally from Raffy to Benedict. He continued:

"Oh I know that you couldn't predict what I'd do. Suspicious minds! I'm not here to compel you."

"What then?"

"I'm worried. What if you meet another pack of dogs? I know you accessed CA data, and that you think the leg's sound. But you could refracture if you run on it, and this time nobody might help you."

He was right: although I had paced myself carefully over the distance, I had developed a limp.

"Do you want to guard me back to the ghetto?"

"And ruin your reputation? No girl, just take the transport."

I started to demur, but he kept speaking:

"You can ditch it near the city. There's a homing circuit and it'll make its way back down the road."

"I can't."

He looked astounded.

"How do I repay you? I've taken and given nothing in return."

"But you have."

He clambered off the transport.

"Raphael, you've not been easy to live with. 'I cannot endure my Lady Tongue,' not lately. But I've fallen in love with her."

He stopped.

"My first love! A lesbian who won't be tamed, won't play Beatrice with Benedict."

Slowly he moved away from the vehicle.

"It's a gift to me if you take it, stops me imagining you et by dogs."

There was no real answer to this speech, not one which would satisfy him. I took one step, then two, towards the transport.

"Thank you," he said, when I got onto it.

"Thank you! Goodbye."

"Goodbye," he replied, his expression bleak. I started the motor and coasted away, glancing back now and then to see him standing there against the yellow like a spoon in mustard. A bend of the road hid him, and I never saw him again.

Now I knew how he had felt. Oh Honey! The emotional ache had become physical—I stared at Grania, and suffered.

"How could I forget?" she said. "You limped in here like a wounded bellatrice, expecting me to shred the—quite good—elegy I'd written for you. When I didn't, you told me what you thought of me. It was a strange speech, first ghetto-gutter, then becoming arcane and archaic. 'Cacodemon' was one word used—I had not heard it outside *Richard III*. How strange to hear it from my Raphael's foul mouth. When you finished, your womynly chest panting up and down like a bellows, I remarked, quoting as is my way . . ."

"'She was wont to speak plain and to the purpose . . . and now is she turned orthography, her words are a very fantastical banquet—just so many strange dishes.'"

"And you turned to the bookshelf, and following the alpha-beta round, you discovered Shakes-rags and opened it."

"I said, '*Much Ado About Nothing*, Act 2, Scene 3, nyaagh!'"

"Whereupon I remarked that while missing, presumed dead, you had attended classes on Shakespeare."

"And I told you the whole story."

"Which made me wonder why you, so secretive—"

"Because you write about me!"

". . . should spiel the most profound experience of your life. Raphael, I know a dare when I see one. You were daring me to write that Raphael Grania had fornicated with an andro. Being contrary, a trait you have inherited,

I didn't."

"Would you, now?"

"It's stale bread news. Haven's half-completed and I doubt anyone would murder that poor man for slipping you a mickey thirteen years ago. The hardcores wouldn't like it, but you dislike them."

"I intend to marry into them."

This time she did blink.

"Oh, the sweet young thing. What's her name?"

"Honey Marthe."

"Is she pretty?"

"Very. And with a mother like a meataxe."

She put her pink hands to her mouth. "So that's why you want my silence!"

"I want a vow of it."

"On one condition."

"What?"

"Raphael, on that night you withheld information from your dear mamma. You never said what you thought of the heterosexual act."

I considered.

"Very well, but you must swear first."

"On something sacred. I know, you."

Feeling foolish, as she no doubt intended, I knelt down by the chair and she put her heavy hand on my head. An opportunity for caress, I realized.

"I swear, on Raphael, not to tattle."

I stood up.

"That promise covers what I shall tell you."

She nodded.

"Spit it out, this byte, this titbit."

I was silent, thinking of words.

"Mumchance! I see I must interrogate you. Was it pleasurable?"

"Of course. But not the real thing. Hence Honey."

She stored the information away.

"Well, my heretic, we both lose by this transaction, you some privacy, I for not being able to put this grain through the art mill."

"Crushing me," I said, continuing the conceit.

"You exaggerate, nothing could do that. I know being muse-food, muesli, was irksome, but it cracked your indifference wonderfully. Naughty of me, but fun—you always bit."

"No more."

"No, if we are to be at peace. Allow me at least an epithalamium."

"You do that. Make it good."

Interview concluded, I strolled down the hall and out. The garden summoned memories of other flowers, but I brushed them away. Benedict, my apologies . . .

I returned to the ghetto, encountering the on-duty Watch at the gate. Considering my scuffles with that body, they were friendly, which made me suspect some support. This inkling and the news of Grania I wanted to share with Zoska, but when I returned to her little house, she was out. From Basienka's room came a voice singing lullabies, probably Urszula bullied into babysitting. Not wanting questions, I raided the larder, mouse-quiet, and went to bed. Sated physically but not emotionally, I slept.

In the morning Basienka awakened me by crawling into my bed with a huge rag doll.

"You want breakfast, kid?"

She considered it like a duchess.

"Yes."

"Well, we'll make some for everyone."

We brewed coffee, chopped fruit and toasted bread rolls, then I carried the tray into the bedroom. Zoska was weeping.

"What is it? Row with your lover again?"

In answer she waved her hand at the little radio beside the bed, which received only the ghetto's weak FM signal. I listened, to an Elder talking excitedly about—

"Parthenogenesis! They've done it at last!"

Zoska blew her nose loudly.

"And it's too late for me. Curse the biological clock!"

With exquisite timing, Basienka plonked herself in her mother's lap. Zoska hugged her.

"Still, you two will benefit. No more seed and egg, just egg and egg."

"Omelette."

"Don't be facetious, you dreadful child. Other dreadful child, don't spill my coffee!"

Complete independence, I thought, as she fussed over Basienka. It had been the inevitable consequence of the Sisters' path, an ideal from the beginnings of the ghetto. Just because I had once been friendly with a man did not mean I regretted this innovation, that cast my kind adrift from his. Benedict, I was a Sister first, and there was no changing it.

"How did it go last night?" asked Zoska, munching fruit.

"All fixed."

"Good girl."

"How about you?"

"I talked my head off, first to Marthe, then I had tea with the Scouts and dropped in on the softcore leaders. On the way home I was met by the faction of hardcores at odds with Marthe. We're getting an Edge City."

"There's still the Elders."

"A Scout talked on the flute with Boz, and she sent the Elders a rocket, saying Marthe was behaving like a heavy father. I thought that too, but it takes the Head of Haven to say it and remain unscathed."

She gestured at the radio.

"But this news has done it."

I finished my coffee and lounged back.

"Sure it's wonderful, but how does it affect Raffy 'n' Honey?"

"Well it's like I'm fighting with the baby and the sky rains honey apples. Instant end to hostilities as we gorge."

"Honey apple," said Basienka.

"Silly," I said. "Now you'll have to get her one."

"Honey apple."

"Later, sweet tooth," said Zoska. "Talking of H-O-N-E-Y, I saw her."

I sat up straight, rocking the bed.

"What she say, what she say?"

"She loves you."

I jumped off the bed and capered around it, followed by the imitative Basienka.

"She got Marthe out of the room to tell me that. Not as submissive as I thought."

"My bad influence."

"No doubt. But I still think you'll be doing the fighting when that girl leaves the ghetto."

"What if I take her to Haven?"

"A good compromise."

She paused.

"Is it as utopic as Boz claims?"

"We're working on it," I said.

"You do that. I'll stay at home, old imperfect ghetto, in case Haven goes . . ."

"Dystopic?"

"Dystopic. Forget I said that. I just realized I'm being thrown out with the bathwater. Still, it's the best way to get Marthe out of your hair, which now I think of it—"

She put her head on one side.

"—needs a cut."

She hopped out of bed.

"Let me bully you for the last time."

First she made me wash in the little bathroom cluttered with water-toys, then combed down my damp mop and trimmed it. With an air of relish, she next produced respectable clothes, bought in between the visits of the day before. There were grey pants, grey shirt, smart black boots and a stiff, sobersides hat. As I admired my well-behaved self in the bedroom mirror, I noticed her sidling out the door with my old gaudy rags.

"What are you doing?"

"Throwing these out."

"Including the scarf, your handiwork?"

She pulled it out and inspected it.

"No! But it's filthy, I'll get you another."

She rummaged in her workbasket and withdrew a strip of linen embroidered with pink cherry blossoms. I wondered vaguely if there was a cosmic conspiracy to remind me of Benedict—Zoska had never seen the flowers, the dogs had prevented me plucking one for her. Smiling wryly, I put the scarf on.

"You look very eligible," she said and kissed me.

"Honey apple," said the repeating machine.

"Come on," I said. "Let's buy one for her."

Outside the little street was bustling with womyn, some carrying flowers and all smiling.

"What's this?" I said to nobody in particular and a passing softcore replied:

"Party in the main square. To celebrate!"

We strolled towards square and Hive, infected by the festive mood. A junior Scout dashed by, came to a dead stop, twirled round and gaped at me. Recovering, she ran off in the opposite direction and returned with two giggling girlfriends, and the Watch Chief.

"Lay off," I said, embarrassed.

"Well," said the Chief, "you are nicely turned out."

"For the books," I muttered.

"Doesn't she look fine?" said Zoska.

"My word yes. Almost unrecognizable."

I clenched my fists behind my back, momentarily regretting that all my rowdiness must be past. To my annoyance, the Watch Chief fell into step with us, chatting to Zoska about weddings:

"I cried and cried when my eldest . . ."

"Honey apple," said the tireless Basienka.

"Soon, when we reach the square," I said. The Watch Chief bent close to me:

"We whitewashed your graffiti."

"Censorship."

"It benefits you. Marthe was turning cartwheels every time she passed it."

"What a sight. Well, thank you."

But she was not finished yet. "One of my lasses let in Bea this morning with a message for Marthe. From Grania."

She eyed me, awaiting the reaction.

"How nice," I said blithely. Maybe it was the festival ambience, but I felt as if I was riding the crest of a wave, which would not suddenly dump me in a welter of foam and sand. We were nearly at the square now, its proximity marked by music, the whiff of intoxicant, and thankfully for the little girl clasping my hand, a sticky-sweet smell.

"There you are, persistent child," said Zoska. "Raffy, do you want one?"

"Not in these clothes."

The Watch Chief had already, incongruously, been tempted by the confection.

In a procession of four, and attracting more womyn in our wake, hardcores, softcores, stray lovers, friends and the curious, we crossed the square to the Hive, our sunken fortress. The girl on guard was unexpectedly confronted by her superior, sticky.

"Tell Marthe she has visitors," said the Chief.

We waited, the crowd jostling and muttering around us. After a suitable delay, the door at the foot of the ramp opened and Marthe, flanked by the two hardcore Elders, ascended.

"Greetings, Raphael Grania," she said formally.

"Greetings, Marthe Maria," I replied, tit for tat.

I saw her gaze roll down my attire, but being as good an actor as Grania, she made no verbal or physical comment.

"I have received a verse letter from Grania Erato. It commends our alliance."

Behind me, I heard Zoska intake breath in gleeful surprise and then let it out slowly, as if she would have liked to whoop. Several of the rowdier Scouts actually cheered, and this was picked up by the young, the noisy and the disaffected. It was in the end an impressive sound, threatening even. Marthe suddenly looked, and I think felt, vulnerable.

"I am, of course, honored to communicate with the great poet."

And mediocre parent, I thought.

"Having long admired her verse, I am pleased—my words can't express how much—to be given a holograph sample of it."

And to be the subject of it, I thought. Vanity! I could tell her it was no pleasure.

"For some reason," she added, her tone changing, "it's called *'To a Fellow Widow Twankey.'*"

She looked flustered; the crowd, equally puzzled, was silent.

"I never understand all her allusions," I said quickly, well-knowing Grania's dangerous humor. "Marthe Maria! Has my mother's intervention changed your mind?"

She regained a little of her dark composure.

"The Elders have informed me that in a day of such celebration, Hive cannot be off-limits. In view of that, the letter, and other factors . . ."

She looked pointedly at someone behind me, from the opposite faction of hardcores, I presumed.

"I have no choice but to withdraw the prohibition."

Zoska hugged me, releasing Basienka, who for some time had been tugging at her mother's hand. Seizing the opportunity, she ran down the ramp and through the slit of door held open by the Watchgirl. There were stairs behind that door—Zoska looked over my shoulder and screamed. The guard started and let the door clang shut.

There was a moment of agony and then the door opened slowly again. My Honey came out cradling my foster-sister.

Beautiful Honeycomb! I wanted to shout it, but that would have ruined everything. Instead I stood silent as a doll, watching Basienka offer Honey some of her apple. Honey, smiling, took a bite and the crowd went "Ooh!"

"Little scene-stealer," muttered Zoska. She walked

halfway down the ramp and collected the baby. Marthe took *her* baby by the hand for a moment: goodbye. Then we faced each other, with no womyn between us.

"Get a move on," yelled somebody.

So, shyly, we met at the top of the ramp and kissed. The ghetto cheered and we parted, half-embarrassed by the noise. Her lips had tasted sweet from the candied fruit.

"Honeymouth," I said.

"Yes, that is her name," said her mother. "Honey Marthe."

And I laughed, and Honey laughed, and it was all right.

HILLS OF BLUE, AN ORANGE MOON

Ruth Shigezawa

She remembered walking quickly to her car, late, after a Philharmonic performance at the Theatre Arts Center. She was humming snatches of a melody from the Mozart Concerto they had played that evening. She had been the soloist, she and the orchestra performing the concerto in D. It was after eleven when she finally left—that's what people told her later—what with an eight P.M. concert, congratulations, chatting with two violinists afterward. Rather than go out for celebration drinks afterward, she left the performing arts complex and crossed the street to the outdoor parking lot on the corner; litter glutted the storm drain and only one or two cars passed. This memory was the clearest: the blinding flash of light, which disappeared a moment, and then reappeared glowing brightly. She thought at first that it must have been headlights—and then she also searched the sky for a police helicopter hovering, although she had not noticed engines chumming above. The glare lasted far too long and was far too silent. She heard nothing above her and she could see nothing beyond the light. She froze, the terror in her growing as she felt the urge to crouch like a frightened animal paralyzed by sudden light.

Her head drooped. "I can never remember beyond that point," Serena confessed to the doctor.

"Oh, don't worry about it," the doctor replied with a heartiness that somehow seemed ominous. After scribbling briefly on the patient chart, the doctor left the hospital room with a little nod. "Things will get clearer, don't you worry," he said before the door drifted shut.

The patient in 511, Serena Jackson, dozed off.

Dr. Kirkland patted her hand and then leaned back from the bed. "You're in better shape now, enough to go home," he said. He was in his early fifties, his face creased, a bald spot a halo at the top of his head, shining when he leaned over her. "How are you feeling today?"

"I can't remember. It's as simple as that," Serena replied, anticipating his question. "At least I remember my name from day to day after you told me what it was." She tried to laugh. "I hope I remember how to drive."

"If you can find a friend or family member to drive you home, you may feel more comfortable," Dr. Kirkland said. He left soon after.

She could not remember anything, simple as that. She would not have minded so much if she were living elsewhere, but she upset people she used to know and was constantly embarrassed by her lack of history. Or rather her lack of memory about her history. Everyone expected her to be someone she was not, to know things she no longer knew. People were offended when they called her or arrived at her house to wish her well and she could not recognize them or recall their names. From what she gathered, she was twenty-seven years old, principal flutist in a major orchestra, and yet when she picked up the instrument case in her closet and opened it, she did not even know how to assemble the flute.

She spent her time learning to get around the city again (fortunately she remembered how to drive) and spent most of her time hiding in the county art museum.

Why she was attracted to the paintings there, she did not know, but she was happy for the first time since she had regained consciousness in the hospital, feeling in the museum as though she were surrounded by close friends.

One of the first paintings Serena examined was one of a gangly man on his rooftop, struggling to install a television antenna. Norman Rockwell, she read. She chuckled and moved closer to study the pale colors, the dots of pastels. She blinked. The painting exploded into a mosaic: she could not read the whole, only dots, splashes, and lumps of color. She could not find the man nor the rooftop, the toppling antenna. She backed away and stared at another wall, a tapestry, then anything else in the gallery. She breathed again when she gazed at a bench across the room where an older woman spoke quietly to a small boy. She looked back. The painting had fallen back into place: the man again grappling with television wires.

But she spent much of her time looking at two paintings, one of a wooded area, a girl on a swing, a man pushing her into the air from behind. It was a pastoral scene, one of innocence and frivolity. Her other preoccupation was exactly the opposite in tone. A painting of a face and torso, elongated, stretched, warbling out of shape, the mouth a screaming "O." The painting had caught her eye on her first day in the museum and she had gone back to it ever since.

The man on the bridge, the normal people like shadows behind him, he facing the unknown terror. Hands on cheeks, everything wavering, shimmering, out of control. She felt more relieved somehow, looking at it.

Serena bought two prints, the Edvard Munch with the man on the bridge and a Van Gogh, "The Starry Night." The clerk smiled at her as she paid her, looking at her as though she recognized her. Serena ducked her head and hurried out with her purchases, not wanting to be recognized again, not wanting to go through the awkward conversations about memory. She drove home and hung the prints on her bedroom wall above her bed so that they were reflected back at her in the dressing table mirror. She stared at the mirror while leaning back on pillows on the bed, slouching down as much as possible so that only the paintings were reflected in the mirror. Sometimes she could see the top part of her head in the mirror, halfway down her forehead, and somehow she liked that, being able to see her head smooth like a stone in a mirror lake, set below a starry sky and an eerie bridge.

"I don't think I caught your name." Serena hovered near the open door, still grasping the flute she was attempting to practice. The man, who had walked right in, pulled at his beard, then slumped onto the sofa, setting his instrument case on the floor beside him. "God, Serena," he said, staring at her. "If you didn't know me, why in the world did you let me in? I naturally assumed—"

"I'm terribly sorry," Serena said, although she wondered why she was apologizing to a man who barged into her living room. "I'm still recuperating," she offered as a consolation, although Dr. Kirkland had told her that her physical recovery was practically complete.

"Yes, of course." The man stood and quickly approached her, hand outstretched. "Let me introduce myself. James Bonner here. Oboe player extraordinaire." She took his hand.

"The formality isn't really necessary," she said, smiling. "I do know I'm supposed to know you. I felt I knew you well." She hesitated. "May I call you James or Jim?"

"Oh, Jim, by all means," James said in a voice that reverberated throughout the room. "You didn't know me and yet you let me in—"

"Perhaps I did sense that I knew you before." She laid the flute down on the coffee table and sat in the armchair across from this man on the sofa. "I'm remembering more every day."

That did it: brought a smile to Jim's face. "You're not yourself, I know that." James got up and walked across the room, standing before the fireplace, the back of his head reflected in the ornate mirror above the mantelpiece. James turned. "You're young, you'll bounce back. Mason is doing right by you, I'm seeing to that. He feels himself mighty generous to be holding your position."

"Mason? Jerome Mason? He's the music director, isn't he?"

"Good for you." James looked as if he were a teacher and Serena had recited a lesson, letter perfect.

"Actually," she said, "I wasn't sure until a nurse at the hospital showed me pictures in the newspaper."

James glanced at his watch. "I'm going to be late for rehearsal. I only stopped by to say hello." He walked to the door and Serena followed. "Clare sends her love. When will we see you again? We both miss having you over for our Friday midnight suppers."

Serena murmured something purposefully indistinct. She opened the door, but James paused.

"Listen, it might do you good to sit in on the rehearsal today. Don't play, just listen. Maybe that would bring back some more of that old memory."

Serena glanced at the flute lying like a knotty branch snapped from an ash tree. "I'm still not able to play," she said uneasily. But James ushered her to the flute case and stood over her while she put the instrument away. He grinned at her when she closed the case, as though she had performed a miraculous task.

"As I said, no need to play yet," James said heartily. "The pieces we're playing for this next concert are pretty much tacet for flutes anyway."

"Tacet?" Serena asked.

James looked away and then walked to the door again and opened it. He frowned, but sadly. "You used to have a joke. About how you and the rest of the flute section would take up crocheting because so much of the music Mason chose was skimpy on the flute parts." He walked outside without looking at her.

"Yes, yes. Now I remember." Serena rushed through the front door, flute case in hand, and wondered while locking up the place if her face would soon start wavering like the man on the bridge.

In rehearsal, the music swirled about her but failed to lift her, soothe her, as it obviously did the others. She stared at the sheets of music in front of her and several times felt the glance of the young brunette woman next to her. At last the young woman whispered, "Shall I take your parts today, Serena?" The flute lay in Serena's lap and she looked down at it and nodded, wondering why she let herself be convinced to take it out in the first place. The young woman played beautifully, not that Serena could comprehend her sounds, only judging from the reaction of Jerome Mason, his surprise and then his approving glance at the second flutist. When the orchestra finished rehearsing that piece, Serena quietly packed up the flute and left.

Soon after that rehearsal, Serena applied for a job as a waitress at a bowling alley coffeeshop. "I got the job," she told James when he called her. "A coffeeshop. That and savings will do me for a year or so while I decide what to do. By that time I'm hoping there will be a breakthrough one way or another."

"You're coming along splendidly," James said in a tone that told her he did not believe it for a minute. "Giving yourself time. Exactly what you need."

"Working in a coffeeshop isn't exactly stimulating," Serena admitted. "But I don't know what else to do right now."

"Exactly right."

She blurted just because James was trying so hard to be comforting. "I hope no one sees me behind the counter."

"Oh?"

She stared at the swirling starry night and the bridge with the terror-stricken man, both reversed in the mirror. "They'll feel embarrassed for me." She closed her eyes against the mirror images. "A renowned flutist who is now a short-order waitress."

"With your new interest in art, maybe you can find a painting class," said James. "Fill up your spare time now that you won't be practicing or teaching flute."

"Is it a new interest?" Serena asked, mostly to fill the discomfort of her confrontation with the past again.

"How should I know?" said James.

She settled into her new routine as though it were a bodystocking. She was assigned the busy shifts at the coffeeshop, breakfast and businessmen's lunch, Monday through Friday. She finished work at three, napped, cooked an egg for herself in the early evening and then, after she had bought art supplies in West Los Angeles, began to paint until late at night, not so much because James suggested it, but because she suddenly wanted to paint. She used her living room as a studio, selling her sofas and spreading canvas over the carpet. She sometimes did not sleep all night but reported to work again at six A.M., with scarcely a glance in the mirror to check her appearance beforehand. She would watch the short-order cooks flip eggs and dollop pancake batter on their griddles before she swept the plates of breakfast out to the booths that lined the windows facing the boulevard. After she was trained in the first few weeks, she was entertaining the customers with witty remarks, anticipated their requests for coffee and cream, knew exactly how to cajole slightly larger servings from the cooks for certain regulars, and treated the bus boy well so that he cleared the tables with alacrity.

Her painting progressed, and she was immersed in images. Her hand moved wherever it pleased. That was what amazed her most when she painted. She scarcely knew what stroke, what color, what shape would appear next. Her brush tickled the canvas (she painted with her left hand although she was normally right-handed). She was an invisible audience for her hand, observing landscapes appearing in sketch, on napkins, discarded receipts, then blocked out on the canvas. Every version until the final painting was unexpected, new and stark details emerging each time. She felt this landscape pulled from deep within her until she sometimes glanced at the mirror in her bedroom and saw from the corner of her eye the same landscape she was painting rather than merely the starry sky and the bridge.

It was always the same: blue hills, the shade of a Siamese cat's eyes, an orange moon in ascendance. There were several moons in this landscape, but the orange one appeared in the violet sky most frequently, a slice of grinning orange, a grimace in the sky. This is the romantic moon for them, she thought once. Immediately she forced herself to ask: for whom? After several moments of silence, her hand still, she could only shrug and resume painting.

Each day she painted, she remembered further past the point of the glaring flash that night. The nurse had mentioned that she had wandered into the County Medical Center, flute case in hand, babbling. She remembered now, stumbling toward the concrete edifice, toward the light, searching for the light again. The nurse had asked about her flute but she remembered the blank in her mind and had handed it over meekly, as though she had been caught stealing it. The doctors kept asking her time and again to retell her last known memory until she felt she had memorized it and began to question whether it was an actual memory or something she created to fill the void. The glare. Then as she painted their museum, a brilliant pink underneath their romantic orange moon, she remembered falling. She was in something and she fell. Or was it that the woman pushed her out, urged her out the way one might urge a reluctant parachutist?

What woman? She asked herself. Nothing. She shook her head and continued painting.

When her mentor's image unfolded in her mind a few weeks later, she had not spoken much to anyone except calling out the orders to the cooks: "Sausage-pan-san, up. No. 3, bacon, scrambled." Although she was quiet and her regulars certainly noticed, she listened to them all most attentively and her tips did not decrease because she was not talking. Her series of landscapes—always from different angles of that other plane of existence (for she was not certain whether it was another planet or another existence that coexisted in the same space as the earth plane, the way the television antenna and the dots and dashes of paint coexisted in the museum painting)—was rapidly being completed. There were twelve canvases—the township with its motley colors and geometrically shaped buildings from pyramid to orb, the wooded areas outside the cities with their vegetation as colorful as a child's drawing, the sky with its odd star configurations and its endless parade of moons in their various phases.

Her mentor's image appeared one morning while she was serving scrambled eggs to a customer who then asked for a piece of pie. She was drawing out the pie tin to cut a wedge and glanced into the mirrored shelf in back of the pies to see lime green eyes and tufted hair above a smooth red forehead. As soon as she closed the pie shelf the pie images reappeared as though sticking like flies to the perpendicular wall and the face disappeared.

Serena could scarcely wait to reach home that day. When she did, she selected a tall, narrow canvas she had primed only days before and without a preliminary drawing, dashed her brush across its surface and, absorbed, watched her mentor appear.

Her pose was languid, standing near a marble-like column, her cheek resting against it, her eyes alert and gracious. Her coloring and clothing were garish, the same lime green eyes, her skin tinged with red, her robes purple against the dark violet evening sky. She seemed human in appearance, at first. Then Serena painted two tufts at the top of the woman's head, like doe's ears, one turned slightly toward her. Her mentor's hands each had an extra little finger, withered, projecting from her palms. The woman seemed to be searching the horizon, her gaze tilted upward, although she also seemed to pretend not to be looking for anything in particular. Serena's brush moved deftly, assuredly, painting across the canvas as though she had sketched this portrait for months.

The portrait occupied her for weeks although she worked steadily on it each night. When she tired of painting and did not care to stay in her house to breathe paint fumes any longer, she would walk up her neighborhood, up the hill until she could see the city lights to the east and blank darkness where the ocean lay to the west. She remembered doing this walking at night before the blinding light and she remembered the same safety she felt, an assurance, because no one was out at night, that she could walk anywhere. She walked along cul-de-sacs and into quiet alleys until more colors and shapes exploded in her mind and she hurried back to the portrait again.

The day she finished the portrait, she felt a sharpening, a sudden focusing of her mind. She laid the brush down and rummaged about her closet. She pulled out the flute from its case, put it together, and without hesitation whipped out a flurry of scales, chromatic and then a major and minor scale sequence, along with part of the Mozart cadenza she had performed before the incident. She sat down on the bed and stared into the mirror at the bridge and the man with his mouth shaped into a large "O," her own head blocking part of the image, the flute lying discarded in her lap.

James could scarcely believe it when she told him on her break at the coffeeshop. "You insist on retirement?" he asked in disbelief. "You've remembered everything. You play as well as ever. What's going on?"

"This isn't hallucination," Serena insisted. "They'll be back for me and I must be ready. They took me to their home."

"Who did?" James looked around at the street as though to find the "they" she was referring to.

"I don't know who they are. All I know is that they aren't from here."

James did not even raise an eyebrow. His voice was as level as though he were commenting on a passage in a concerto. "Is that so?"

"They taught me to paint. Particularly one woman who was my dearest friend. I played earth music for them at first. But our music is primitive. Like the random trilling of a nightingale: inherently pretty but hardly complex in their world. But my paintings, even my simple sketches. My mentor taught me to paint. They raved over them. The paintings hung in the most famous museums in their world."

James glanced at his watch. "I must get to rehearsal soon. I suppose I thought you had dabbled in painting somewhere along the line and it surfaced when you lost your music."

"They can't visualize color, at least not in our perception of color. Their vision translated only into khaki or brown. Then once they saw my colors on the canvas, the wilder the better, the reds, oranges, purples, deep deep blues, they saw them as we do. Until then, nothing. And they could not get enough of the paintings."

"It didn't take them long to teach you. Will you walk me to the car? I have to get going."

Serena sighed and accompanied James to the parking lot. "Their time is different. I was there decades."

"I see." James unlocked the car door and got inside. He hesitated a moment and then rolled down his window. "Why did they ever allow you to return to earth?"

"I didn't want to come back," Serena confessed. "I had to. I was killing them. They had to return me."

"They returned you?"

Serena touched James' elbow and leaned toward him. "I wasn't well that night. Not all of them were immune to earthly diseases. I had a cold. They traced the plague to me. It took them years. I killed thousands of children, like sailors carrying measles to the South Seas. They had to send me away."

James stared into the windshield. "Surely your paintings were contaminated also?"

"They are kept in glassed exhibits now."

James tapped the steering wheel and started the car engine. "Who was the woman you painted?"

"My mentor. One of those who died." Serena whispered this, her head bowed slightly. James leaned forward to hear her answer, but when he heard her reply, he leaned back and put the car into gear.

"Serena, what now?"

"I'm back to normal as far as my memory is concerned."

"Yes?" James leaned toward her as though she had a valuable fragment of wisdom to offer him in her next words, something he was eager to hear.

Serena touched his arm and then stepped back. "I'll continue to paint and work in this coffeeshop. That's why the retirement. My painting is more important to them than my music." James nodded quickly and then backed the car out of the parking spot without saying good-bye. Serena stared after his car and then lifted her hand to wave after him. She could see the lime green eyes of her mentor most vividly.

She walked back toward the coffeeshop entrance. "When they invent a vaccination . . ." she said to her reflection in the glass doors as she pushed them open, speaking aloud as though James were still there to hear her explanation. "When they invent a vaccination, they'll be back for me."

CONTRIBUTOR'S NOTES

Carol Severance is a Hawaii-based writer with a special interest in Pacific Island customs and mythology. She lived for several years in the remote atolls of Truk, Micronesia, first as a Peace Corps volunteer and later doing anthropological fieldwork. Since 1977, she has made her home in Hilo, under the shadow of erupting volcanoes and just minutes from shark-filled Hilo Bay. "Shark-Killer" was inspired by various aspects of both Trukese and Hawaiian lifestyle and folklore.

A former journalist, Carol attended Clarion West 1984 and has since published fiction in anthologies and magazines. She is also a novelist and prize-winning playwright. Currently, she is working on a novel based on the further adventures of Shark-Killer and her eager young companion Tarawe.

Cathy Hinga Haustein is a chemistry professor at Central College in Pella, Iowa, where she also teaches science and literature and technology and literature. She has an MFA from the Iowa Writers Workshop and her most recent stories have appeared in *The Albany Review, Iowa Woman,* and *Fiction 86.* She has written articles for scientific journals and has also written for the ACT and MCAT admissions tests. She is married and is expecting her third child this summer (1990). She has also recently received a grant from the William and Flora Hewlett Foundation of Research Corporation for a new spectrophotofluorimeter with a solid sample holder. She is fascinated by things that glow in the dark.

Cleo Kocol's writing started as an avocation and became an addiction. First she wrote and published humor, went on to write and occasionally publish short stories and articles before she discovered theater. Then, in a flurry of creation, she wrote four plays, and for five years she gave her one-woman, many-character shows throughout the United States at colleges and universities, before women's groups, and for governmental organizations. She also went to China, lectured at Guangxi University, and gave an excerpt from one of her plays there. Then, sticking closer to home, her short story "Julio's Revenge" was judged best of the year at Shoreline College.

For the next four years she also wrote a column, "Feminist Update," for *The Humanist* magazine, and in 1989 she had one of her essays published in the college composition textbook *Model Voices*.

She teaches creative writing to adults at Nathan Hale High School and at Lake Washington Vocational Technical Institute in the Seattle area, where she lives. She has just completed a novel, and except for an occasional foray into the short-story field, she believes she's found the ultimate mind-bending writing trip.

Deborah H. Fruin's short stories have appeared in the *Womansleuth* anthology of mystery stories and *If I Had a Hammer*, a collection of stories on women and work published by Papier-Mâché Press. She lives in the San Francisco Bay area with her husband and two-year-old son.

Elaine Bergstrom: "'Net Songs' is an angry story. I wrote it at the time AIDS was being spotlighted in the mainstream news media. As I listened to the first hysterical suggestions for containing the disease, I began to wonder what the Jimmy Swaggarts and Jerry Falwells lurking in the halls of the conservative White House would do if they had control of a sexually transmitted disease—one so deadly that society would demand government enforced morality whatever the cost in individual liberties.

"Today there is so much more to be angry about. The media spotlight has moved from AIDS to the war on drugs and, from killer caterpillars to international search and seizure, government pronouncements are becoming increasingly surreal and all too often tragic.

"If this is a political statement, so be it. Susanna said I could write anything.

"As a final biographical note, I am the author of two horror novels concerning the Austra vampire family. *Shattered Glass* and *Blood Alone* are available in paperback from Jove. I live in Wisconsin with my husband, two daughters, four cats, and a pair of uneasy 'keets, and am working on a sequel to *Shattered Glass* and a historical Austra novel set in the time of Elizabeth Bethoray.

Eleanor Arnason is 47 years old and lives in Minneapolis in a high-rise apartment with a view of downtown. She has published three novels, the most recent being *Daughter of the Bear King* in 1987. Her stories have appeared in *Orbit, New Worlds, Amazons II,* and *New Women of Wonder.* She has a poem in *Women in Search of Utopia* and a biographical essay in *Women of Vision.* Her fourth novel— *A Woman of the Iron People*—has been turned in to the publisher and ought to come out in 1991. She is vice-president for the central region of the National Writers Union and treasurer for the union's Twin Cities local. As Joe Hill said, "Don't mourn . . . Organize."

G. K. Sprinkle: "Unlike other authors, not even one English teacher encouraged me to write. In fact, a college instructor once scribbled on an essay exam that I wrote exactly as I spoke. As the words accompanied a grade of C minus, I did not take that as a compliment. Now I spend at least 40 percent of my work life writing.

"Besides four other short stories, I have numerous nonfiction pieces in regional magazines and newspapers. Most are political opinion pieces with a feminist slant. I work in political campaigns. Someone decides what a Yard sign will *say* and the exact wording of 'quotes' in support of a candidate. I also craft résumés, specializing in ones for women returning to the workforce.

"The rest of my time, I lobby the Texas legislature for public interest groups and trade and professional association. I'm uniquely qualified to do so as I have a master's degree in Vertebrate Paleontology from Harvard University, where I learned how to research the issues and how to work with 'old fossils.' My clients include NOW, the Older Women's League, battered women, school and licensed counselors, rehabilitation counselors, the National Audubon Society, Travis Audubon, lay midwives, and farmers."

Transplanted from Ohio to West Palm Beach at the age of three, by age five **Ginger Simpson Curry** learned from her father not only to love the Atlantic Ocean but also to swim its rough waters. She is the mother of two big sons—Tom and Mike—one tiny parakeet, and a marine tank of denizens of the deep. When her fingers are not scampering over a keyboard, she is rambling through a Florida scrub or slogging along the Atlantic Ocean with her husband Jim.

Writing about the native South Florida she loves, Ginger Curry has been published in numerous national magazines, won dozens of prizes, and been awarded the Florida State Fellowship for Literature by the Florida Arts Council. She is president of ANRALD (Absolutely No Resemblance to Anyone Living or Dead), an NWC chapter; fiction chair for the Florida Freelance Writers Association; and an active member of Science Fiction Writers of America (SFWA). She was awarded a two-week camp scholarship by the National Audubon Society for her nature fiction.

Her short story sales reflect her interests: literary, romance, fantasy, suspense, and science fiction. She has stories in two Andre Norton anthologies, *Tales of the Witch World 2* and *Magic in Ithkar 3*.

J. L. Comeau is a native of the Washington metropolitan area and full-time writer who shares her Falls Church, Virginia, home with a variety of exotic birds. She attended George Mason University and is presently enrolled in a course of women's literature and mythology studies. Her dark fantasies have appeared in most of the popular small press magazines, including *Grue*, *Dark Regions*, *Haunts*, and others. She will also make an appearance in Doubleday's upcoming *Women of the West*. Judy is presently at work on her first novel.

L. Timmel Duchamp lives in Seattle. She would like to dedicate "The Forbidden Words of Margaret A." to the memory of Febe Elizabeth Valásquez, a Salvadoran union leader and activist who courageously defied death threats, rape, and torture to speak the truth. Murder by a death squad on October 31, 1989, silenced Febe at the age of thirty-five, but her words and the power of her voice live on in the memory of all who heard and were inspired by her.

Timmi's "O's Story" appears in *Memories and Visions*.

Lucy Sussex was born in Christchurch, New Zealand, in 1957. After periods in France and England, she moved to Australia in 1971. She has a BA (Honors) in English and an MA in Librarianship from Monash University and is now a research assistant at Melbourne University.

Her works include critical writing and reviews, as well as a children's book, *The Peace Garden* (Oxford University Press, 1989). In 1987 she solved the literary mystery of one of the first woman crime writers, revealing the writer behind the pseudonym Waif Wander to be Mary Helena Fortune. As a result, she edited *The Fortunes of Mary Fortune* (Penguin, 1989).

"My Lady Tongue" won a Ditmar Award for the best Australian short sf of 1989.

Merril Mushroom lives in Tennessee and is a little bit strange, although *she* doesn't think so. The first Mamu-grandae tale was serialized in *Maize* magazine, the second in this anthology, the third tale in *Lesbian Bedtime Stories*, the fourth tale is in the notebook, and the fifth tale is in the works.

Phyllis Ann Karr: "I was born July 25, 1944—that's historical fact. I died Dec. 25, 2029, visiting southern California at the time of the Great Christmas Quake—that's speculative fiction. Grew up in the northwestern-most county of Indiana, with frequent trips to my mother's people downstate. College undergraduate work in Fort Collins, Colorado—called an unusual choice to study modern languages (French & Russian). Worked about eight years as a librarian before going full-time into freelance writing. Married Clifton Hoyt on June 2, 1990.

"I met Thorn and Frostflower at a summer writing workshop led by George R. R. Martin in Dubuque, Iowa. Not that they are based on anyone I ever met in 'real life.' Since long before I knew any theory about the Astral Plane, I have believed that characters are real entities who allow writers to use them. Thus, my fiction is a cooperative effort between the characters and myself; but Frostflower and Thorn answered a call for Sword and Sorcery figures in particular. Because people have so often come up to me at conventions and such with remarks that lead me to believe they expect to find Thorn, I'd like to state here that, while making every effort to balance them evenly, it is Frostflower with whom I have always more personally identified.

"Frostflower and Thorn have appeared, among other places, in two novels: *Frostflower and Thorn* and *Frostflower and Windbourne*."

Rachel Pollack: Born in 1945 in Brooklyn, N.Y., grew up in Poughkeepsie, the site of her novel *Unquenchable Fire*. In 1971 Rachel went to live in Europe "for a year or two" and has lived there ever since, first in England, then in Amsterdam, the Netherlands. Her first short story was published in 1972, her first novel, *Golden Vanity*, in 1980. *Alqua Dreams* followed, and then *Unquenchable Fire*, which won the Arthur C. Clarke Award in Britain and was described by *The New York Review of Science Fiction* as "possibly the best fantasy of the decade."

She has also written seven books on Tarot cards and edited a collection of short stories, *Tarot Tales*, with Caitlin Matthews. Currently she is creating her own Tarot deck, traveling Europe for research for a book on the body of the Goddess, and writing a novel based on *Grimm's Fairy Tales*.

Rosalind A. Warren: "I'm a feminist, a mom, a bankruptcy attorney, and a writer. I'm (happily) married to Richard C. Smith, also an attorney, a writer, and a feminist. My fiction has appeared in *Seventeen*, *The Magazine of Fantasy & Science Fiction*, *Fiction Network*, *Iowa Woman*, and others. I am the (grateful) recipient of a 1990 Pennsylvania Council on the Arts Literature Fellowship to enable me to complete a collection of my stories. My reviews and short essays have appeared in *The Women's Review of Books*, *New Directions for Women*, *The Utne Reader*, and others.

"I'm currently editing an anthology of feminist humor for The Crossing Press. I collect funny cards, postcards, and cartoons. Send me one at Box 259, Bala Cynwyd, PA 19004."

Ruth Shigezawa has completed two novels set in turn-of-the-century Hawaii and is writing her third, a novel about a first-grade teacher who moonlights as a classical musician. Ms. Shigezawa has published in various literary journals and newspapers, including *Amelia*, *Hawaii Pacific Review*, *Los Angeles Times*, *Outerbridge*, and *Pulpsmith*. Her short story, "A Photo Marriage," won the third annual American Japanese National Literary Award ($1,000 prize and publication), a short fiction contest established by author James Clavell.

She has also earned a master of fine arts degree in writing from the University of California, Irvine, and an undergraduate degree in English from the University of

Southern California (where she also played in the Trojan Marching Band).

She lives with her husband, Gordon, in southern California, leads a study group in *A Course in Miracles*, and plays flute in a community concert band and a flute choir.

ADDITIONAL SCIENCE FICTION/FANTASY TITLES FROM THE CROSSING PRESS—